Colter didn't know been staring at Willa.

Ten minutes? Twenty? No one around them commented, so it probably wasn't a full lunar cycle, but it sure felt that way.

She'd been pretty at nineteen, but now she was stunning. Her hair barely brushed her shoulders. The little scar on her chin she'd gotten from flipping over her bicycle handlebars was still there. She was still Willa, but with a new determination in her eyes and wisdom etched in faint lines on her forehead.

Willa swallowed. Colter was struck with the familiarity of the movement of her throat.

She searched his face, as though she couldn't possibly be seeing him. He knew the feeling.

"Colter?"

He breathed in deeply, ready to spew every apology he'd ever failed to make. But she held up a hand. The wonder on her face turned to disappointment, then anger and was finally masked with bland disinterest. Any connection that might have been building between them snapped as she dropped her gaze.

Dear Reader,

Welcome to Pronghorn, Oregon! I'm excited to introduce you to five energetic young teachers as they start their careers in this tiny anything-but-idyllic town. The Teacher Project is a romance series (of course!), but these stories are also about the bond between teachers. Education is a demanding, rewarding, ever-changing field, and I'm grateful for the friendships that help me to thrive in this profession.

In *Lessons from the Rancher*, former rodeo champion Colter Wayne will do anything to support the high school in Pronghorn. But when one of the new teachers turns out to be Willa Marshall, his first love and biggest regret, Colter needs to cowboy up and show Willa that there's more to his town than meets the eye.

I'd love to hear what you think of Willa and Colter's story! You can find me on social media and at my website, anna-grace-author.com.

Happy reading!

Anna

HEARTWARMING

Lessons from the Rancher

——

Anna Grace

HARLEQUIN
HEARTWARMING

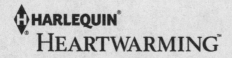

ISBN-13: 978-1-335-47574-9

Lessons from the Rancher

Recycling programs for this product may not exist in your area.

Harlequin Enterprises ULC
22 Adelaide St. West, 41st Floor
Toronto, Ontario M5H 4E3, Canada
www.Harlequin.com

Printed in U.S.A.

Anna Grace justifies her espresso addiction by writing fun modern romance novels in the early-morning hours. Once the sun comes up, you can find her teaching high school history or outside with her adventure-loving husband. Anna is a mediocre rock climber, award-winning author, mom of two fun kids and snack enthusiast. She lives rurally in Oregon and travels to big cities whenever she gets the chance. Anna loves connecting with readers, and you can find her on social media and at her website, anna-grace-author.com.

Twitter: @AnnaEmilyGrace
IG: @AnnaGraceAuthor
Facebook: Anna Grace Author

Books by Anna Grace

Harlequin Heartwarming

Love, Oregon

A Rancher Worth Remembering
The Firefighter's Rescue
The Cowboy and the Coach
Her Hometown Christmas
Reunited with the Rancher

Visit the Author Profile page
at Harlequin.com for more titles.

To my wonderful editor Dana Grimaldi

CHAPTER ONE

THIS CAN'T BE PRONGHORN.

Willa Marshall gazed down the empty stretch of highway to her right, then turned to the left as the bus pulled away from the five young teachers. The air was warm and still, like the atmosphere was holding its breath, too. The only movement was a one-eyed cat darting out from behind a brick building. The animal trotted to the middle of the road, then sat on the faded yellow pavement markings and stared at them.

Willa blinked, then redirected her gaze to their surroundings.

Seven buildings, no people.

"I thought Pronghorn had a downtown," one of the other teachers said.

"I thought Pronghorn had a *school*," another quipped, gesturing to the building across the street. *Pronghorn Public Day School* had been painted in bright yellow over the main door of a small, two-story, redbrick structure. It leaned slightly to one side, its better days a good half century behind it. The letters on the sign were as off-kilter as the building, like someone had climbed up on a shaky ladder and painted it freehand. Underneath the name was painted, Proud Home Of The Pronghorn "Pronghorns."

As an English teacher, Willa involuntarily shuddered at the misuse of quotation marks. As a human, she shuddered for a whole host of other reasons.

Three months ago, she'd been sitting across a table at a job fair, laughing with the principal of Pronghorn Public. Loretta Lazarus had big ideas for the little school, and she told Willa she was recruiting five top-notch teachers to revive education in Pronghorn. The institution had shut down three years ago due to budget cuts, and the district had offered families online school. That hadn't gone over well with the community, so Pronghorn had raised the funds and laid out a plan: new teachers, new ideas, new life for their town. The educators all agreed to a relatively low salary in exchange for free lodging, vehicles to drive, and the opportunity to get in on the ground floor of building an exceptional educational experience for rural students. Willa had felt in her bones that she was meant to take the position.

Now she was feeling other, less positive things in her bones. Like panic.

Stay optimistic.

"Okay, Pronghorn isn't exactly as Loretta Lazarus described it," she acknowledged. "I think she said something about it being a bustling, charming little town—"

"—bouncing back after a few tough years," several others finished the sentence with her.

"You all got the same story?"

Her colleagues nodded grimly, eyes roving the desolate Main Street.

Yeah, this *really* did not look like the vibrant community Lazarus had described. Safe to say she'd oversold it.

Pronghorn was as far away from Willa's hometown of Junction City as she could get and still live in the great state of Oregon. And she felt for the desolate little map dot. She, too, needed to bounce back after a few tough years. Or more accurately, fourteen tough years.

A gust of wind stirred up a dust devil that spun past the cat. Willa half expected a lone cowboy to come sauntering out of a saloon, an ominous, three-note whistle alerting onlookers to trouble.

"They have a restaurant," one guy said, pointing to a bend in the road where another small building was making unnecessary use of quotation marks. "The Restaurant."

"Do you suppose they serve 'food' there?" a woman asked, using air quotes.

Willa glanced at her, then the other teachers, reminding herself of their names again. She'd be working closely with this team for the next ten months and wanted to get off on the best foot possible.

Vander Tourn, from Portland, was the only one smiling right now. "I kinda like it here," he said. He was a quiet, enigmatic science teacher whose comments on the bus had been sparse but had shown a keen interest in the ever-changing ecosystems as they crossed the state. His handsome features were intriguing, all the more so because he drew almost no attention to himself. Vander traveled with one small bag and a guitar.

Luci Walker, on the other hand, traveled with six large bags and a designer tote. Her shiny blond hair was pulled back in a ponytail, and her stylish outfit of a pink collared shirt and white jeans still looked perfect, even after she'd traveled six hours on a bus to the middle of nowhere. She was so beautiful and perfectly put together Willa could imagine someone misjudging her as superficial, but her knowledge of history and geography was fierce. "I don't dislike it," Luci said. "But I'm a social studies teacher. This doesn't seem all that…social."

Tate Ryman laughed. He was tall with pale skin, bright blue eyes and a thatch of black hair. Gregarious and funny, he'd kept the bus entertained with stories of his athletic achievements and mishaps. He would teach health and PE. "I think we're gonna have to bring the party."

"I'm down for that," Mateo Lander's dark eyes crinkled at the corners as he smiled. He seemed like the most easygoing math teacher on the planet. During the bus ride he'd moved from seat to seat, chatting with everyone. Well, everyone except Luci, for some reason. He had an open, carefree personality that would make him a favorite among the high school students.

And then there's me. Thirty-three-year-old Willa Marshall, finally taking control of her life.

Willa had wasted her twenties bobbing along, attending to the problems of others, letting the ebb and flow of everyday take her further adrift from her plans. For years she'd blamed Colter Wayne, and the torpedo he'd launched at her heart, for demolishing her dreams. Truth was she'd used her heartache as an excuse to let her life stall out. Getting her teaching degree and taking this job were Willa's positive, proactive steps toward creating her own life.

And here she was in Pronghorn. New town, new life, new colleagues. They were an eclectic bunch, to be sure. The only thing they had in common was they were all straight out of ed school and had never taught before.

It was going to be fine, right?

"Dang! Is that literally a tumbleweed?" Mateo asked.

Willa turned back to the vacant street before them. A feathery, brown mass of dried sticks came rolling down the road. The cat took no notice but continued to eye them with disinterested appraisal.

"Cool." Vander trotted into the street to grab the tumbleweed. He turned it in his hands as he walked back to the group.

"What are you planning on doing with it?" Luci asked.

"Keep it in my classroom." The volume of Vander's personal belongings had now doubled with the acquisition of the windblown weed.

"So, what do we—" Tate put his hands in his pockets and twisted his torso as he looked around at the town "—do?"

Willa pulled in a deep breath. She was the oldest of the bunch, and since no one else was stepping up, she took the lead. "The email said we'd arrive at our lodgings around twelve."

Luci checked the thin gold watch on her wrist, then held it out for the others. High noon.

"Great." Willa smiled, hoping to make everyone feel at ease. "Loretta Lazarus said we should leave our bags in front of the old hotel and meet the greeting committee at the school."

"Is it safe to leave our bags out?" Tate asked.

"I think we're okay." Mateo scanned the empty sidewalks. "It doesn't look like this place gets a lot of foot traffic."

"Or any traffic," Tate muttered.

Vander tossed and caught his tumbleweed, watching as the seeds shook out. "This area is so flat we could watch a thief run away for a week."

"I think it's fine," Willa said. "It feels weird to leave our stuff, but I can't imagine Loretta would have made the suggestion if there was any chance our bags would get stolen. She doesn't want to scare off the new teachers."

"Too late," Mateo quipped.

Willa *had* to keep this group optimistic. Because

if their thoughts turned south, hers would hop right on that bandwagon and seize the reins. She summoned a grin for Mateo, then batted his arm. "This is going to be great. Let's find the hotel, leave our bags, and get this school year rolling."

Mateo gave her a long look, then nodded as though he understood. They were walking into this situation with no control over anything but their own attitudes. "Yeah. Let's do this."

Tate gave her a mock salute. "Loud and clear, Captain."

Willa rolled her eyes. But yeah, *Captain*. She kinda liked it.

The guys scanned the street, most likely assuming they'd find yellow lettering proclaiming something to be a *"Hotel."* But Luci just turned around and gestured to the structure directly behind them.

"Oh, whoa." Tate leaned back as he gazed up at the hotel. "It's actually—"

"Nice," Vander finished for him.

Willa's heart picked up as she examined their new home. It was a large, brick building with art deco details. A bronze plaque by the door proclaimed it to be The City Hotel, and on the national registry of historic buildings. Luci took a few steps down the sidewalk to an open archway, then nodded as though she was expecting what she saw.

"It's got a nice courtyard," Luci called, with her first smile since the bus rolled away.

Willa joined her at the archway. Inside, the landscaping needed some love, and a few of the decorative details were hanging on for dear life, but it was charming. Willa grinned at Luci, then at the other teachers.

"Okay, this town is a little smaller than we expected. But it looks like we've got a cool place to stay, and we have important work ahead of us. We signed on for a challenge. You guys ready?"

Vander nodded.

Mateo's eyes crinkled up at the corners as he said, "One hundred percent."

Tate held out his hand and gestured for the others to circle around. They piled their hands together.

"Pronghorns, on three," Tate commanded like a coach.

"One, two, three," Luci counted and together they all shouted, "Pronghorns!"

Laughing, they broke out of the huddle and headed across the street toward the school. Tate slapped Vander on the back as he jogged past him. The tumbleweed bobbed as Vander took the bait and ran. Mateo and Luci picked up speed and joined the race.

The cat remained unimpressed.

Willa drew in a deep breath. This was her time. She was here to change her life and help improve the lives of others. The tailspin she'd fallen into all those years ago when Colter broke her heart had finally come to a stop. She was in charge now.

Her fellow teachers waited for her in front of the school. Willa smiled encouragingly and led the charge up the steps. She was no longer adrift and lonely, watching life pass her by, but a leader, doing something important for the first time. Her twenties weren't her best decade, but she was older, more confident now. She and her colleagues were going to create an exceptional learning environment for the kids in Pronghorn. This was the work she was born to do.

COLTER WAYNE GRABBED a hammer and pounded a second nail into the detached floorboard. The teachers would be here any minute and he didn't want them tripping over the threshold as they entered the building. The stakes were way too high to risk scaring off even one of the five new teachers.

And since Loretta Lazarus, local real estate agent and self-proclaimed school principal, was part of the greeting committee, some level of concern was to be expected.

"It's going to be fine." Mrs. Moran's cool, shriveled hand came to rest on his shoulder.

Colter raised his brow. "You sure about that?"

The octogenarian nodded. "It will either work out, or it will make a great story."

He chuckled. "I don't need another story." His years on the rodeo circuit had provided enough stories and hard lessons for a lifetime. "I need a school for my daughter."

"Sylvie would do well if all we had was one teacher and a broken piece of chalk. She has a good dad. That's half the battle."

Colter grunted in acknowledgement. The other

half of the battle, he had to assume, would be a good mom. Sadly, that wasn't in the cards.

The floorboard firmly in its place, Colter stood, then nearly folded himself in half again as he reached down to hug Mrs. Moran. She'd taught in Pronghorn for five decades and had been the last teacher standing when they switched to online school three years ago. While Loretta was taking the lion's share of the credit for reviving in-person school, Colter suspected Mrs. Moran was the rainmaker in this, and many other situations.

He couldn't be more grateful to her for rekindling the school. As his dreams had been stripped away one by one due to his own rash decisions and impulsive nature, Sylvie had been his saving grace. His daughter was the only thing that mattered. By agreeing to be school board president, and offering to fix up the school and the old hotel, he could finally get her the education she deserved.

Colter glanced around at the supposedly fixed-up school.

About that...

The hotel was looking decidedly better than the school right now. Loretta didn't interfere with his work on the residence for the teachers. The school building, on the other hand, had been remodeled by committee. As a result, some of the work was sloppy, some top-notch, some simply unfinished. And the aggressive yellow paint Loretta had found on extreme sale? It was everywhere.

A knock sounded on the front door. No time to fix anything else now. The teachers had arrived.

"Here we go!" Loretta squealed.

He chuckled at her enthusiasm. Mrs. Moran was right: this *was* going to be fine. Better than fine, it was going to be awesome. Five young, energetic teachers committed to new ideas were exactly what his daughter, and this town, needed.

Colter pulled back the door with a huge smile and so much hope it nearly lifted him off the uneven treads of the threshold.

A breeze dipped in, so the scent and image of his first love hit him in tandem.

Willa Marshall.

Beautiful, smart, winsome Willa Marshall smiled brightly, stepping forward with her hand extended.

Then she froze.

Memories rushed through his mind, like soldiers storming a coastline. Willa trying to keep him from stealing bites of her popcorn during a movie. Climbing up to where she sat on the gabled roof of her house on a hot summer night. Willa laughing as she turned the hose on him while watering her father's garden.

Memory after memory marched on, flattening him with their persistence.

Colter didn't know how long he'd been staring at Willa. Ten minutes? Twenty? No one around them commented, so it probably wasn't a full lunar cycle, but it sure felt that way.

She'd been pretty at nineteen, but now she was

stunning. Her brown hair barely brushed her shoulders, with long bangs framing her face. The little scar on her chin she'd gotten from flipping over her bicycle handlebars was still there, as kissable as it had ever been. She was still Willa, but with a new determination in her eyes, and wisdom etched in faint lines on her forehead.

Willa swallowed. Colter was struck with the familiarity of the movement of her throat.

She searched his face, as though she couldn't possibly be seeing him. He knew the feeling.

"Colter?"

He breathed in deeply, ready to spew every apology he'd ever failed to make. But she held up a hand. The wonder on her face turned to disappointment, then anger, and was finally masked with bland disinterest. Any connection that might have been building between them snapped as she dropped her gaze.

"Great to meet you," she coughed out. Colter tried to respond but she shook her head and stepped around him, faking a smile as she held out a hand to Loretta.

The other teachers passed by him in a blur, as though no one noticed the ocean of unspoken pain they moved through. Colter remained at the door, staring out into the sun-washed street. Connie trotted through the door and swished her crooked tail in annoyance. But she gave his leg a thoughtful brush as she passed. The cat was the only one who'd picked up on any tension at all. But was the feline even on his side?

"Here. We. Go!" Loretta, overdressed in a plaid pantsuit, gave both fists a shake in the air, like a contestant on a game show. "Look at them!" She grabbed Mrs. Moran's arm. "They're so good-looking. Did I do good, or what?"

Mrs. Moran kept smiling as she greeted the new teachers. Colter shook his head and forced his gaze off Willa. The other teachers looked *young*. With the exception of Willa, they looked more like students.

"We are so glad you're here. I'm Mrs. Moran, your one and only old timer at the school."

Willa engaged her in conversation, but Colter couldn't track it. She was introducing the others, smiling like he, and their lost love, were nothing but a momentary inconvenience.

Maybe it had been nothing to her. Just a young, misguided crush on her brother's best friend.

"Tour time!" Loretta clapped her hands and hustled the teachers into something like a conga line. She started humming.

Definitely a conga line.

Colter didn't know much about education, but it was a safe assumption that teachers didn't conga on the first day.

He cleared his throat. "Loretta, let's, uh, let's allow the teachers to direct this tour. I'm sure they have questions, and things they'd like to see."

"But I have a plan!"

Colter blocked the principal to stave off the conga. "You often do. But let's let the teachers take the lead here."

"O-kay." Loretta gave an exaggerated pout. "Well, kids, the cowboy has spoken. And in Pronghorn, when the cowboy speaks, you gotta listen."

Colter shook his head, trying to convey to the teachers that most people in this town were pretty low-key. "Just a thought, Loretta."

"What kind of cowboy are you?" a guy holding a tumbleweed asked.

"The ranching kind. I have eleven hundred acres outside of town." The tall one whistled, but Colter shook his head. "Around here eleven hundred acres is barely a ranch, but it's a living."

"You're a ranching cowboy?" Willa asked, eyebrows raised. "Not a rodeo cowboy?"

He tried to hold her gaze, but it slipped away. "Not anymore."

A young woman who looked like she should be rushing a sorority at Dartmouth said, "Is there a library? I'd love to see what we have in terms of books and research materials."

"Do we have a library!" Loretta slipped an arm around the young woman. "We have a fantastic library, almost entirely stocked with books I got for free, including *two* sets of Funk & Wagnalls encyclopedias."

Loretta whisked the blonde down the hall, but not so quickly that the latter couldn't turn around and give Willa a panicked glance as she mouthed, *"Encyclopedias?"*

The others followed along. Colter seized the moment and impulsively reached out to grab Willa's arm. His hand curled around her elbow like his fingers were meant to be there.

"Willa," he said quietly.

She glared down at his fingers, then back at him. Colter dropped his hand.

He opened his mouth to say the right thing, but all that came out was, "You're here."

"And you...live in Pronghorn." She glanced around the room, keeping her eyes averted. "That's unexpected."

"Yeah. I've been here for thirteen years."

"Is this where you settled with your wife?"

Colter wasn't sure if he heard anger or disappointment in her voice, or if it was only wishful thinking on his part.

"This is where I settled with my daughter."

She glanced up. He knew that look, interested and almost ready to listen. Then her face closed off. "Well, thanks for letting my family know."

The sarcasm in her voice felt like an undeserved lash across his back. He'd only been twenty-one at the time, heartbroken and a new father. Did she think he could call up Holden and say, *"Dude, sorry I broke your sister's heart. You were right, I should have stayed away from her. But hey, I'm a dad now and going through a vicious child custody battle in Pronghorn. Stop by if you get the chance."*

He folded his arms over his chest. "It didn't seem appropriate at the time."

"Yeah. But what *is* appropriate when you ask someone to spend her life with you, then haul off and marry someone else without telling anyone?"

"There was a lot more to the situation—"

"I'm sure there was," she said, cutting him off. "Look, I have important work to do here, and I won't let anything get in the way. This matters." She gestured to the space around them that would soon be filled with students, the gleaming oak floor, the high ceilings, the mostly functioning lockers. Her eye caught on the parade of mismatched, inspirational wooden signs Loretta had found at a Goodwill in Pendleton.

These Are Your Good Old Days.

Follow Your Dream.

In a World Where You Can Choose to Be Anything, Be Kind.

And somewhat randomly,

World's Most Okayest Mom.

"Loretta loves a bargain," he explained.

Her lips twisted, like they wanted to smile but were afraid of the consequences. A spark of connection passed between them, filling him with a lightness he hadn't felt in years. Then her eyes clouded again, like the hint of humor made her even angrier.

"I won't let this—" she gestured between them "—throw me off-balance. Let's just stay out of each other's way."

Colter nodded. He'd love to stay out of her way,

but Pronghorn was a small, small town. "We can try, but I should let you know, I'm the school board president."

She gave an incredulous laugh and flung her hands out before her. "Of course you're the school board president. Who else could possibly be the school board president?" She turned away, muttering to herself, "Great to have my life back on track."

"Willa, I'm sorry—"

She held out a hand to stop him from speaking. "Just don't. Don't."

Colter froze. What was it he wasn't supposed to do? He knew he was in the wrong here; he'd beaten himself up for hurting Willa every day for the last fourteen years. But a direct order of *"don't"* was gonna be a little hard to follow.

He straightened his spine. He'd survived five years on the rodeo circuit, a nasty divorce, a newly teenage daughter. He could work with Willa.

Colter softened his voice, shifting his posture as he put his hands on his hips. He gazed at her and asked, "What do you need to make this okay?"

"You're about thirteen years, eleven months late with that one, Colter."

"I don't want there to be bad blood between us."

"I don't want there to be anything between us, but apparently you're the school board president in the smallest, most random town I could find to run away to."

Colter turned his head. Had something happened that inspired Willa to move here?

"What are you running away from?"

She met his gaze. "Nothing. I don't run away."

"You just said you were running away."

"It's a figure of speech."

"Well, obviously. You took a bus here."

Her laugh sputtered out, a brief moment of joy crossing her face. Then she closed her eyes and blew out a breath.

"Stop it," she commanded.

"Stop what?"

"Just stop."

Stop? Don't?

"I need a little more direction here, Willa."

She threw her arms out, inadvertently hitting an open locker door. "Stop being funny."

The locker slammed, setting the wooden signs swaying overhead. Choose Joy fell off the wall. Colter pressed his lips together, sensing that if it wasn't okay to be funny, laughing was definitely off the list.

"Colter, you are literally the last person I expected to see here. And I'm sorry, but I can't forgive what you did to our family. What you did to me. I came here to get my life on track, and I really don't want you derailing my attempts at happiness again."

He closed his eyes against the hurtful words. He had been so young, so utterly naive, and one mistake had destroyed his relationship with the people he loved most in the world.

But over the years he'd rebuilt his life. He had new responsibilities, and he was going to meet every one of them. Colter straightened and reminded himself of what mattered here.

"My daughter is a ninth grader this year."

Willa let out a dry laugh. "Right. Naturally, you have a daughter in my class."

Colter held out a hand and spoke over her, "Don't make this about Sylvie. You can think whatever you want about me, but my daughter deserves an education."

Willa blanched. "O-of course, I won't bring your daughter into this—"

"Sylvie has been wilting in front of a computer for the last three years." Colter worked his jaw against the emotion. He would not let his mistakes hurt his daughter, and Willa had better understand that. "I will do *whatever* it takes to get this school running."

She looked up sharply and met his eye. Then she softened some, and nodded. "Me, too."

The army of memories took up position, then launched another assault. Trying to distract Willa as she did her homework. Stealing wildflowers out of the neighbor's yard because he wanted her to have them. Winning his first buckle at the Sister's Rodeo and looking up in the stands to see her watching. His gaze connecting with hers, feeling the rightness of Willa roll through his body, washing away the pain sustained by the bronco ride.

Willa took three determined steps to follow the others, then stopped.

"To answer your earlier question, what I need

is for our past never to have happened." She was cool and composed. "Short of that, I think we can both do baseline professional courtesy. But I *don't* want to work things out, or to reconnect, or hear you say you're sorry. I don't want a single reminder that I was ever in love with you." Her voice twisted on the words, and he had to wonder if the pain in the back of her throat was anything like his. "I just want to do my job."

CHAPTER TWO

KEEPING HER TEARS at bay for four hours felt like trying to cover up the holes on a backyard sprinkler with her bare hands. Doing so while being led on a carnival madhouse tour by the world's most unfit principal was even trickier. When they were finally released to the hotel, Willa practically sprinted to her room.

The door closed with a satisfying click, and she flopped back on her bed.

Colter Wayne.

How? How on earth had she wound up in the one whistle stop in America that was home to her first love and biggest heartache?

Okay, only heartache.

Fat tears rolled down her cheeks and onto the hotel linens.

Colter Wayne? Seriously?

It would be funny if it weren't so totally pathetic.

Five years ago, Willa had gone to see a therapist about the cowboy she couldn't forget. The therapist had given her a series of mindfulness practices and trained Willa to reframe her thinking whenever the gorgeous, sweet man of her youth came moseying across her mind. It had helped her get over the hurt, or at least not spend so much time dwelling on it. The mindfulness practices came in handy in other areas, too, like visualizing what she wanted out of life. They'd helped her settle on a career path, make it through her master's degree and choose *this* job.

But right now, mindfulness could take a hike. She was giving herself a half hour to wallow in self-pity.

Tears, regrets, chocolate, the works.

Tap, tap, tap.

"Willa?" a voice at the door called.

Willa sat up and pulled the back of her hand across her wet cheeks.

"It's Vander. Can I ask you a question?"

"Uh…yeah." Willa grabbed the crisp white bed-spread and wiped her face. "Gimme a sec."

If it had been anyone but Vander, there was no way she'd let them in. But there was something about the quiet science teacher that made her think he wouldn't come knocking unless he really needed help.

No, that was a lie. She had no boundaries when it came to helping others. She'd probably let Geng-his Khan in if he needed to talk.

"Hey, thanks," Vander said as she opened the door. He walked into her room, his eyes taking in the pale pink walls, the well-kept antiques, and the thin white curtains moving with the breeze. The teachers were housed in fourth-floor suites over-looking the courtyard. *Suite* was a generous label:

the rooms were simply large rectangles with a sitting area set up at one end and a bed at the other. Still, they'd been freshly painted, and crisp new linens made up the beds. A bouquet of wildflowers had been waiting on the windowsill. Someone had gone to a lot of trouble to make their rooms comfortable.

It was an excellent reminder that they mattered to this town. She might have landed right in the middle of her own personal hell, but this hell really wanted her here.

Willa gestured to the sitting area, but Vander wandered over to the window to examine her wildflowers.

"So, I don't know what you're thinking, but this whole thing seems a little—"

"Sketchy? Half-baked? Hackneyed?"

He laughed. "Yeah. The vibe was really off today."

Willa pressed her lips together, knowing a big part of the vibe was her weirdness with Colter.

But she and Colter could have been as weird as a pair of hairless sphynx cats and Loretta Lazarus still would've taken best in show. Willa dropped into one of the wingback chairs and pulled a knee up to her chest.

"I agree. We didn't know what to expect, but it wasn't this."

"Principal Lazarus has a lot of big ideas." Vander pulled a small daisy from the bunch and studied it. "But her ideas don't seem to fit with the day-to-day, you know? Like, how are we going to run the school?"

That was the question. Loretta had yammered on about potential murals, exchange programs, musical performances, but didn't have any information regarding minor details like what classes they would be offering, how many students were in each grade, or where they would eat lunch.

Vander swallowed. Keeping his focus on the petals of the flower, he said, "Since none of us has taught before, outside of our practicum work, I'm a little nervous."

Willa's heart went out to him. As much as she wanted to break her habit of solving other people's problems, she knew she could help here. He needed some reassurance and a reminder of their mission. She could give him that. They'd talk it out, then she could return to her pity party.

"I'm nervous, too. But we've got important work ahead of us, and we're all determined. Let's brainstorm a few—"

"Willa?" There was another knock at the door.

"Come on in," Vander called.

Tate came striding in, face red and agitated. "The principal lady?" He gestured in the direction of the school. "She's out of control." He sat down across from Willa and laced his fingers together over his knees. "What are we going to do?"

Willa glanced longingly toward her bed. This was the first time she'd let herself have a good mope in years, and these guys wanted to problem-solve? *Typical.*

"Well, Vander and I were just discussing—"

"Hey." Mateo materialized in the doorway. "I was hoping to talk to Willa, get your take on the—" he, too, gestured out the open window toward the school "—situation."

"It's not a situation, it's a disaster." Tate ran both hands through his hair, the thick black strands standing on end. "There's no way we can run a school with that lady in charge."

"Yeah." Mateo looked at Vander, then Tate. "What do you guys think about putting Willa in charge?"

Vander looked up from the flowers. "That's what I was thinking."

"No," Willa stood. She did not move 350 miles away from home to mop up after someone else's bad decision. And she definitely wasn't going to put herself in a position where she had anything to do with the school board, or its president.

She made eye contact with each of the guys. They weren't much younger than she was, but that didn't mean she wasn't able or willing to pull out the mom energy. "The school already has a principal, albeit a quirky one. I'm not doing her job *and* my job."

"I didn't mean to suggest that." Mateo looked sheepish.

"I did," Vander admitted.

Tate nodded. "Me, too. That's exactly what I had in mind."

She gave a dry laugh. "I appreciate the vote of confidence, but no. It's going to be fine. One week into the school year we'll be so busy we'll hardly notice her."

She drifted toward the door, with the intention of waving them out so she could indulge in her previously scheduled mope.

"Willa!" Luci's voice came ringing through the wall separating their rooms, uncharacteristically concerned. Willa counted down from three, and right on schedule Luci appeared in the doorway. "Hey, sorry to break up the party. There's a hedgehog in my room."

All four heads swung toward Luci.

"A hedgehog?" Willa asked.

"Pretty sure."

A minute later they were all gathered in Luci's room, staring into her closet, where there was not one but four hedgehogs, asleep on a cushion in the corner.

"Why?" Tate asked. "Why are there hedgehogs?"

"Why did I take this job?" Mateo asked.

"What are we going to do about any of this?" Tate tugged at his hair.

Willa leaned in to get a closer look. Four little prickly pears were all snuggled up, breathing together in their slumber. There were worse things to find in a closet.

Luci flopped down in a chair. "We should call the guy."

Willa turned abruptly. "What guy?"

"The cowboy. Colter. He said to call if anything

came up." She gestured to the closet. "We have hedgehogs. And the Mad Hatter for a principal."

"Nobody's calling anybody," Willa snapped, before realizing how foolish she sounded. The other teachers could call whoever they wanted. If they could get cell service. She tried again, more softly this time, "We're professionals. We can handle a family of hedgehogs."

"Can we?" Tate asked. "Because if Hedgehog 501 was offered at the U of O, great. But we didn't cover them in my education program."

"Is there a lot of handling involved in hedgehogs?" Vander asked. "They're nocturnal foragers, existing on insects and vegetation."

Mateo pointed at Luci. "She's the one who was freaking out."

"I wasn't freaking out."

"You screamed."

"I *exclaimed*. And to be clear, I didn't say I had a problem with the hedgehogs. It's more that these ones exist in my closet. I felt it was worth a mention."

Despite everything, their bickering struck Willa as funny. She started to laugh. It was all so inconceivable, yet par for the course of her last few years. She'd come here to get control of her life, but if this first day was any indication, she had about as much control as Vander's tumbleweed in a tornado.

Luci let out a giggle, then Tate laughed, and the others joined in. Willa wiped at another tear, this one from laughing so hard.

Vander lay down on the floor in front of the

closet and reached out a hand toward the hedge-hogs. "They're waking up." A roly-poly ball of soft spines sniffed at his fingers, then waddled back to the family pile. "I think they like people."

"Then they're living in the wrong town," Tate quipped.

"*We're* living in the wrong town," Mateo said.

"Nope," Willa cut him off. "We are exactly where we're meant to be. There are kids in this town who need us." An image of Colter, distress crossing his face as he said, *"Sylvie has been wilting in front of a computer for the last three years,"* passed through her mind. "We're here to give these kids the education they deserve. We may have no experience, and a self-proclaimed principal who doesn't seem to know what the job entails, but we can do this."

The others murmured assent. They'd all heard the same call and were here for the same reason: to build an exceptional educational experience for rural students.

"So, let's do it. We've all got our strengths. Let's play to them and work together." As the other teachers nodded, she realized what that meant for her. She was the oldest, the de facto leader, the first person anyone called when they found a hedgehog. "Okay, we know there's a school board meeting tomorrow. You guys want me to be the teacher rep?"

"Yes," they all said in unison.

Willa squared her shoulders. That meant more time with Colter, but she wasn't going to let their past weigh down her future. She was tough. She'd taken this job to shape and direct her own life, and she wasn't going to let one minor, incredibly gorgeous hiccup get in her way.

"Great. Let's make a list of concerns, and I'll present them. Tomorrow morning, we can check out our classrooms and see what materials we have to work with, then hopefully get some answers in the afternoon."

"Thank you, Willa," Mateo said, his eyes crinkling around the corners.

"Really." Luci wrapped an arm around her. "You're our rock."

"Your rock?"

"Like a cool rock," Tate clarified.

"A really nice, smart rock," Vander said.

Willa warmed at their gratitude. They would all have a piece to play in the complicated game of getting a school up and running. Hers appeared to be teacher-leader. She could do that for her colleagues, and for their prospective students. She didn't need to throw herself a pity party for Colter. If nothing else, this was a chance to show him, and herself, that she was fine without him. She was going to move ahead and plant herself in Pronghorn.

"You know, I'm actually a really hungry rock. Anyone want to go check out *'The Restaurant'*?"

"Sure!" Mateo said.

"You think they have *'beverages'*?" Tate asked with a grin.

"I could totally go for a *'beverage.'*" Luci grabbed a light jacket that coordinated with her outfit.

"Let's pick up some greens to feed the closet dwellers while we're out," Vander suggested.

"Great idea." Willa grinned. "It'll be a night on the town."

COLTER CLIMBED OUT of his truck and slammed the door. It had been one miserable afternoon, and if today was any indication, he was in for a miserable school year.

He strode across the yard, jamming his hands in his pockets. Seeing Willa had knocked the wind out of him, and every time he thought he could catch a breath, Loretta came in with a sucker punch. He'd been concerned about Loretta's habit of wild scheming but hadn't realized just how little time she'd put into actually planning the school year. Mrs. Moran, bless her heart, seemed to take it all in stride. He knew the elderly woman could teach anything to anyone, with nothing more than a chipped slate and half a stick of chalk, but he suspected the new teachers might not come with the same set of skills.

Except for one of them—the one who didn't want to have anything to do with him. And by proxy, she might not want to have anything to do with his daughter.

Colter gazed across the land. The sun was heading west, not setting yet but washing the prairie grass with gold. Soon it would dip lower. Pink, then deep red would spread across the land. How many times had he watched the sun set and wished he could share it with Willa?

Well, she wasn't interested in sharing anything with him now.

Dirt crunched under his boots as he headed toward the house. She'd better treat his daughter fairly. He didn't deserve her consideration, but Sylvie should not be made to suffer for his mistakes. If he heard one peep from his daughter that Willa wasn't treating her like the other students...

"Dad?"

Colter looked up from under his Stetson. Sylvie was on the front porch in another one of her wild outfits. She wore a pair of his old work pants that she'd cut off above the ankle, cinched tight with a belt at her waist. Over that she had a tank top and an oversize plaid jacket. It looked like something she'd seen online and tried to recreate with meager resources.

He didn't know how it was going to go over at school, but he thought she looked great.

"How's my girl?"

"Did you meet the new teachers?" she asked, ignoring his question.

"I did."

"And?"

"And," he glanced up at the sky, then said steadily, "you're gonna have a great year."

It wasn't a lie. The school was in disarray, Loretta was out of control, and one of the teachers hated him with all her being. But as school board president, he would do whatever it took to make sure his daughter had the best school year of her life.

Sylvie pressed her lips together and studied the wooden plank flooring of the front porch.

"What's wrong?" he asked.

"Nothing."

Nothing was ever wrong. For the last three years Sylvie had been slipping further into her shell. He'd thought about moving to a bigger town with more social opportunities, but the only time Sylvie was ever really happy was when she was with the horses. This ranch was their livelihood and their life. He and other parents arranged get-togethers for their kids, but the kids always seemed uncomfortable in these adult-planned social gatherings.

School was the answer. She'd get back into regular contact with her peers, start having fun again.

Sylvie sat down on the front steps. Colter dropped down next to her.

"You do any sewing today?"

"A little."

"Whatcha making?"

She pressed her lips together, this time in a smile. "It's like a skirt."

"It's *like* a skirt?"

"Yeah."

"Can I see it?"

She shrugged. "It's not done yet."

Colter nodded as he gazed out at the land. He tried to think of something else to say, something else to ask, but his mind came up blank. The frustration of not knowing how to talk to his daughter anymore crashed over him again. When he was thirteen, he barely spent any time with his parents. They didn't need to know how to talk to him beyond calling him into dinner and making him brush his teeth. Life with Sylvie was a whole new ball game, one for which there didn't appear to be a playbook.

And after being confronted with his failure with Willa this afternoon, he really couldn't stand to hang around and fail all evening.

Colter pulled his hat off and ran his fingers through his hair. "I'll tell you what. Let's head into town for dinner."

She squished up her face.

"I'm not suggesting we're going to *like* what we have to eat—The Restaurant is what it is. But it would be fun to head into town, hear what everyone is saying about the new teachers."

Her eyes lit up. That interested her. She was dying to get a peek at the teachers. "Can we ride?"

"Of course we can ride." He scoffed. "I don't want to show up at a fine establishment like The Restaurant in a truck."

Sylvie jumped up. "I'll get my boots."

It was a half an hour before Sylvie had changed her outfit three times and was ready to go. She emerged from the house in her slightly-too-large riding boots, wearing an oversize sweatshirt and leggings, topped with the same plaid jacket from earlier. Again, the outfit seemed a little out there, but Colter was not going to argue fashion with a thirteen-year-old.

He knew some folks in Pronghorn were critical of how he raised his daughter. Word got around—people knew Sylvie's mom was in prison for fraud. Colter did the best he could as a single dad with full custody. Picking his battles was a foundation of his parenting style. If Sylvie wanted to wear a sweatshirt three sizes too large, he wasn't going to make a fuss over it.

It was a short horseback ride into town, and Sylvie started to talk before they hit the property line. Conversation ebbed and flowed, and was a little stilted by the time they made it to Main Street. Still, they were talking. He needed to remember how well a ride into town worked the next time he felt like he couldn't communicate with his daughter.

Colter glanced up at the hotel as they passed. Was Willa settling in? Did she like her room? The furniture in the old hotel was in good shape, and Angie Lyon had given the pieces in the teacher's rooms a serious polishing when she and her crew came in to clean. He'd painted the rooms and spent his own money to replace the mattresses and bedding. Sylvie had chosen the sheets and bedspreads and helped him set up the rooms. On a whim, they'd picked wildflowers for the teachers, setting small bouquets on each windowsill.

Who'd have ever thought he'd be picking flowers for Willa Marshall again?

"Dad?" Sylvie tapped his arm.

Colter looked down at his daughter, then in the direction she was gesturing. The young sheriff was running into The Restaurant, her dog Greg on her heels. From half a block away Colter could hear male voices making some kind of cacophony inside.

They nudged their horses into a canter, then swung off their mounts at the hitching post in front of the café. He handed his reins to Sylvie and headed inside.

He might not be the best dad on the planet, but his daughter could handle her horses.

"I'm just asking a question." The tall teacher, who Colter remembered was named Tate, had his arms outstretched in innocence.

"This isn't a place for questions," Angie, the proprietor, snapped back.

"It's a restaurant."

"Exactly."

Tate looked in disbelief at the other teachers. Willa said something to Angie, but she had all her focus on Tate.

"If you don't like the way I run things, you can take your business elsewhere."

"Actually, I can't," Tate said. "This is the only '*restaurant*' in town."

"I'm sorry, sir, but if you keep this up, I'm going to have to give you a ticket," Sheriff Aida Weston said.

"A ticket for what?" another teacher asked. Colter was pretty sure his name was Mateo.

"Creating a public nuisance," Aida said. Her German shepherd looked at Tate and back up at his partner, not fully on board with her assessment.

"All I asked for was a substitution."

Everyone in The Restaurant groaned. Angie had a long list of don'ts in this place, and substitutions were somewhere near the top.

"After asking for a *menu*," Angie said, like a printed list of food options had been outlawed by the Geneva Convention decades ago.

Tate was still talking. "How was I supposed to know that sign—" he indicated a nearly illegible sandwich board on the counter "—was the entire menu?"

"This ain't a Denny's."

"Of course." Tate gestured broadly. "I didn't expect it to be a Denny's. But I did expect there to be more than two options."

Colter glanced at the sign. Today's offerings were breaded chicken, mashed potatoes and corn, with cherry cheesecake for dessert, *or* fried chicken, baked potato and peas, with strawberry cheesecake for dessert. It was actually a pretty good offering for The Restaurant. But these newcomers wouldn't know they'd hit the place on a good day.

Colter made a quick appraisal of the situation. An educated guess told him the teachers had broken at least six rules, and probably a few more.

One: they'd waited to be seated.

Two: they'd pulled two tables together.

Three: they asked what kind of beer she had on tap.

Four: they'd asked for menus.

Five: someone was a vegetarian.

And after all that, Tate had the audacity to ask for a substitution. It probably wouldn't do any good to tell him everything on the menu tasted the same here, anyway.

No, after their disconcerting meeting with Loretta, they were now getting caught in the cross-hairs of Angie's wrath. Their time in Pronghorn was not starting out well.

The door opened and a pair of slightly-too-large riding boots clumped in behind him.

Colter closed his eyes.

And this is Sylvie's introduction to her new teachers.

Willa placed a hand on Tate's arm and said something in his defense. Sheriff Aida shook her head and pulled her ticket booklet from her back pocket. He knew Aida well enough to understand that when she got her back up, it could take a good six months to calm her down. But she was *not* going to give this guy a ticket on his first day in Pronghorn. Not for asking to substitute corn for peas, not on his watch.

"Hello there," Colter said, treading heavily across the floor. He kept his focus on Aida and Angie. "How're you all this evening?"

"It's you!" Luci said. "Thank God. I need to talk to you about some hedgehogs."

Colter nodded politely, choosing not to roll down that particular path at this time. He looked meaningfully at Angie. "Glad to see you've all gotten to meet the new teachers."

Angie scowled. "Teachers?"

"These are the *teachers*," he reminded the woman who had three teenagers at home. The Lyon kids really needed to get out of the house. "And they're new to town, so let's give them some time to get adjusted."

Willa glanced at him briefly, a hint of gratitude flickering in her eyes. Like she *could* be grateful in another life, where he wasn't such an idiot.

Sheriff Aida protested, something about a law being a law. Tate launched into a spirited self-defense, which actually was loud enough to be construed as a public nuisance. Luci, bizarrely, was still talking about hedgehogs.

Colter held a hand up. "Everybody's got their side of this story. Let's turn the page and start something fresh. Angie, I'd like you to put their meal on my bill."

Angie rolled her eyes, but the teachers responded with gratitude.

"Wow!" Luci said, beaming.

"Thanks, man," Vander said.

"Thank you," Willa said quietly, turning her water glass on the table. He hoped to heaven she hadn't tried to ask for ice.

"Not a problem," he said. Since Angie never put her prices up, they didn't realize he wasn't being that generous. At The Restaurant, you got what you paid for, which wasn't much on either side of the equation. "Welcome to town."

Sheriff Aida sighed and slipped her ticket booklet back into her pocket. "Welcome to Pronghorn," she said. "My office is right next to the school if you need anything." Then she glared at Tate. "I'll keep an eye on you folks."

Aida waved, then followed her dog outside. Angie stomped back into the kitchen. The dining room gave a collective sigh of relief.

Crisis averted.

"Hi, there."

Willa's voice startled him. Colter looked up to see Sylvie had drifted over to the one person at the table he'd never expected to be talking to his daughter.

"Hi." Sylvie glanced at Willa, then started playing with the strings on her hoodie.

"Are you Sylvie?" Willa asked.

His daughter nodded, then shrugged, then cleared her throat.

Willa's beautiful smile broke out. "I'm Ms. Marshall. I'll be your English teacher."

Sylvie tucked her hair behind her ear. "Cool. I like to read."

"That's great. What kind of books do you like?"

Sylvie shrugged again. What kind of books did she like? The kind with words. His daughter was a voracious reader, sometimes reading two books in a day.

Willa turned from the table completely, focused

on Sylvie as she gently questioned her about what she liked to read, and what she hoped to study in school. Complicated emotions welled up in Colter's chest as he watched the exchange. Willa had always made others feel comfortable. She was smart, but also approachable. No wonder she'd chosen teaching.

In another lifetime, he would have been there to watch her make the decision to go into this profession. He could have supported her through grad school and rejoiced when she got her first job. He would have been the type of husband to make her coffee and rub her shoulders as she graded her way through a stack of essays.

He shook his head. In this lifetime, he was never going to be any type of husband for Willa.

And he wasn't completely comfortable with the idea of her getting too close with his daughter. Too close or too distant. He wanted her to teach Sylvie everything she deserved to know about literature, but without his daughter getting emotionally attached. Was that too much to ask?

Sylvie laughed, then nibbled at the end of the strings on her hoodie.

Yeah, it's probably too much to ask.

"You guys want to join us?" Mateo gestured to the table.

"Please!" Luci said, scooting over.

Colter hesitated. Pulling up two more chairs could incur the wrath of Angie *and* Willa.

"Yeah," Sylvie said, without so much of a glance to check his reaction.

Okay, if his daughter was choosing a social situation with no prompting from him, they were staying.

Colter glanced behind the counter. Angie had re-emerged from the kitchen. She kept a steady gaze on him but didn't complain as he grabbed an extra chair and set it next to the table. Sylvie did the same, and no surprise, she decided to park herself next to Willa, to whom she was expressing her feelings on optimum chapter length.

Angie returned, face grim, holding a tray with five cans of Pabst Blue Ribbon Beer. She unceremoniously plunked one in front of each of the teachers. "Beer is on the house. Just this once." She glared at Tate, who was staring at his can in wonder. "And no, I don't have any other kind of beer."

"This is my favorite." He held up the can and gave Angie a broad, toothy smile. "PBR is my go-to."

She harrumphed, but Colter could detect a smile. He had a feeling Tate would be receiving more than one free beer during his time in Pronghorn.

"You two still gotta pay," Angie said, pointing at him and Sylvie.

"Coke, please," Sylvie said.

"A Coke for me, too." Colter gestured through the window to their horses. "I didn't bring a designated rider."

Vander twisted in his seat to get a look at their mounts. "Did you ride those horses in?"

"Yeah," Sylvie said, setting a world record for

thirteen-year-old girl communication with new adults. This was all the proof Colter needed. These new teachers might not know how things worked in Pronghorn, but if they could get his daughter to sit down and join them at a table, then actually talk? He was going to do everything in his power to keep them around, regardless of the personal toll it might take on him.

"Cool. I want to learn how to ride while I'm here."

"My dad can teach you," she said, tugging at the knot in her hoodie strings.

"Would you?" Vander asked.

Colter delivered Sylvie a look, suggesting he didn't have much of a choice now. But he liked Vander. Willa might never give him the benefit of the doubt, but it would be nice if her colleagues didn't mind his company.

This was going to be hard. But no matter what havoc these teachers might wreak, Sylvie was worth it.

"You can come out for a riding lesson any time," he offered. "You're all welcome at our ranch."

CHAPTER THREE

WILLA STARED AT the machine. It had four large, fat wheels and two seats, and was painted camo.

"Is this an ATV?"

"Yep," Vander confirmed.

"So when they said vehicles would be provided for our use…?"

"They weren't lying," Luci said. "It is technically a vehicle."

A newer, more pure form of panic shot through Willa. She was already going to be late for her first school board meeting, and now she'd be arriving on an all-terrain vehicle.

It was one o'clock when Willa got the text from Loretta letting her know the school board was meeting at two o'clock. At Colter's house. She'd scurried out of her classroom, leaving it in disarray as she went back to the hotel to change her clothes and check the list of concerns the teachers had assembled. Then she'd set out to find one of the cars they'd been told would be provided. Unable to find anything with an engine, or get ahold of Loretta, she'd asked the others for help, resulting in the least fun egg hunt on record. After forty minutes, Mateo finally pushed open the slider door of a dilapidated woodshed next to the hotel. There he found a pink note attached to the steering wheel of this...vehicle.

Enjoy your wheels! Don't speed.
—L.L.

"It blends in with the forest?" Tate said, like that could be considered a benefit.

"It does." Willa pointed at a second vehicle that was somehow worse than the first. "And that one would be a—?"

"Snowmobile."

She nodded. Twenty-four hours into their Pronghorn adventure and the teachers didn't even need to exchange glances anymore. They all knew when the others were rolling their eyes.

Luci circled the ATV, arms crossed over her chest. "In all fairness, Loretta didn't specify it would be a car."

"Wild assumption on our parts," Mateo muttered.

Tate turned the key in the ignition and revved the machine using the handlebar throttle.

"It runs," he said. "So that's a plus."

Willa gave a sharp nod. "Okay, then. Do I wear a helmet?"

"Do we have a helmet?"

"Unlikely."

Willa glanced down at her outfit, a knee-length skirt and sleeveless silk blouse. This was her first school board meeting, and she was showing up with a long list of concerns. She wanted to look professional but approachable.

Professional, approachable, with a hint of *you made the worst decision of your life in leaving me, Colter Wayne.*

Unfortunately, none of those looks went with off-roading.

Was she seriously about to ride this thing to Colter's house? He was the one man she'd sworn never to forgive, and that hadn't been a hard oath to keep. But seeing him with his daughter last night had shifted her perspective. Sylvie was a great kid: smart, with a dry sense of humor she was almost too shy to share. Willa had worked to connect with her like she had with the students she'd volunteered with over the years. By the end of the evening, Sylvie was teasing her dad and dropping one-liners to rival Tate's.

Willa didn't need Mateo to do the math for her. Colter had disappeared from her life fourteen years ago, and his lovely daughter was thirteen years old.

She swallowed against the tears pressing for release. He'd cheated on her. Somewhere on the rodeo circuit he'd cheated. Someone had gotten pregnant. Rather than ask for forgiveness, or help, or anything, he'd taken off. He'd married *someone* else. And at the end of all those bad decisions, this amazing girl who loved books and horses was the result.

It was a lot to wrap her head around, and too much to even consider wrapping her heart around.

Willa brushed her bangs to one side and stepped up to the ATV.

"Wait!" Luci pulled a pack of antiseptic wipes out of her bag, because of course Luci had wipes on her. She rubbed down the seat, saving Willa from arriving with a dusty behind.

"You've got the list?" Vander asked.

"It's in my backpack," Willa confirmed, saddling up on the ATV.

"The biggest issue is the schedule," Mateo said. "We can't prepare for the school year until we know exactly what we're teaching."

"And since the school year starts in a week, that would be good information to have," Luci added.

"Yes. Our concerns about the schedule, and ideas for it, will be priority one. Then I'll try to figure out if we can get stable internet access. Luci, I've detailed your concerns about the library research offerings and added my own requests for literature. Right now, it's filled with pulp fiction and old copies of *Field & Stream* magazine."

"And you'll ask about getting equipment for the Physical Education program, right?" Tate asked.

"Right. And remind me, what do we have right now?"

"One hockey stick, six child-sized jump ropes and a deflated football."

"On it."

"And don't forget the science budget," Vander said. "It's fine if it's small, but I just need to know what I can spend on textbooks and labs. As of right now all I have is a tumbleweed."

"I will not forget the science budget." Willa turned the key in the ignition. The little vehicle jumped to life, and she gave the throttle a squeeze.

"You look like a general right now, preparing for war," Mateo said.

Willa laughed. "I'll try to keep that in mind as I cruise into battle."

"Speaking of battles, I'm going to attempt shopping at the store." Tate gestured over his shoulder in the direction of the small market. "Anyone up for going with me?"

"Somebody'd better go with you," Mateo said. "We don't want another restaurant debacle on our hands."

"All I did was ask to substitute corn for peas."

Vander laid a hand on his shoulder, imitating an officer. "High crimes and misdemeanors in Pronghorn, my friend."

Willa managed to back out of the garage without running over any of her colleagues, and get herself bumping along the main road to Colter's place.

Driving an ATV was fun once she got the hang of it and managed to get up over ten miles an hour. The town receded behind her, the landscape opening up in miles of undulating prairie grasses and sagebrush. Her heart picked up nervously as she turned off the highway and onto a tree-lined road. Possibly the best thing about the ATV situation was it distracted her from Colter. But he was going to be a little hard not to think about when she was sitting in his living room. Blood pounded in her veins as she passed under a gateway sign reading C & S Ranch.

Willa nearly flipped over the handlebars for a second time in her life when she emerged from the trees and pulled up to Colter's place. It was heart-achingly beautiful. Stables made of warm, honey-colored pine ran alongside a riding arena. One of the horses she'd seen outside the restaurant last night eyed her from a snug turnout pen. Others were grazing in the pasture, calmly enjoying the perfect, late-summer day. Beyond the stables were other well-kept outbuildings, thickets of Aspen trees, then the prairie rising up a low hill to rimrock.

A flock of birds passed overhead, inspiring her to turn as she watched them. That had her gaze landing on the house. It appeared to be custom-built, again of warm, knotty pine. A long, deep front porch looked welcoming. Every kind of wildflower bloomed in the yard out front, as though a man with little sense of how to garden had planted them for his daughter.

Willa shook her head.

Okay, so he has a nice ranch. That's legal.

She had a job to do. She needed to park this… vehicle, get inside and start the meeting off right.

She motored to the end of a line of cars: a yellow Volkswagen Bug with eyelashes, an older Subaru, a large truck, and a strange bicycle/Segway contraption painted orange and red with a big sticker proclaiming it to be a Lyfcycle.

And she was adding the camo-mobile to the mix. This was going to be an interesting meeting.

She parked the ATV but couldn't figure out how to turn it off. The key seemed to be locked and the thing was still making a lot of noise. She put pressure on the key and tried to turn it again. Why wouldn't the engine stop?

Willa fussed with the machine, inadvertently giving the throttle a nudge. It leaped forward.

"Turn off!" she barked.

Because that was super effective?

"Need some help?"

Willa drew in a deep breath and puffed out her cheeks. Did she need the still gorgeous ex-love-of-her-life to see her struggling to turn off a land vehicle most often associated with children and reckless teens? Not really.

She held her hands up in surrender. "Apparently. This is my first time on one of these."

Colter reached a strong hand in front of her and positioned it on the keys. "Hit the brake and that red button." Willa obeyed the instructions and the snarling machine finally quieted.

She could feel the absence of noise throughout her body like a wash of warm water. A breeze fluttered past, bringing the sound of swallows chirping from their nests. She closed her eyes briefly.

"Thank you."

"No problem." Colter held out a hand and without thinking she took it, allowing him to help her off the vehicle. She tried not to let her fingers fixate on how much they missed his touch. "Can I ask how you came to be driving an ATV?"

She released his hand. "Take a big guess."

Colter stopped in his tracks. "Loretta did not leave you all with nothing to drive but an ATV?"

"Oh, no. There's also a snowmobile."

He shook his head. "Willa, I'm so sorry. She's always been hard to rein in, but…"

He ran a hand through his hair. This was hard for him, too. He'd done her wrong, no doubt. Yet from what she'd seen so far, he'd done everything possible to make his daughter's life more stable than his had been at that age.

"But she promised you a school, didn't she?"

His deep blue eyes connected with hers. He nodded.

Willa could feel every hope he had for his shy, smart, awkward daughter. And his hopes were multiplied by every parent in Pronghorn. That was what mattered.

"Well, we're here. And with this thing to drive we can't exactly run away, so she made good on her promise to you, at least." Willa took long steps toward his front porch, but Colter stopped her with a hand on her arm. It was a light touch, as though *he* knew they were no longer friends, but his fingers hadn't gotten the memo.

"I want to be clear on one thing. Before we go in there."

Willa tensed. She'd expressly asked him not to apologize, not to bring up the past.

He stared at his boots for a long moment, then looked into her eyes.

"Sylvie is my *daughter*."

Willa knit her brow. "I know. I mean, obviously. I'd have recognized her smile anywhere."

He gave a chuckle, acknowledging this. Then he grew serious again. "She's my daughter. I want the best for her."

Willa couldn't track where he was going with all this. Did he think she wasn't going to treat Sylvie fairly? Or that she wasn't capable of teaching because she was new to the profession?

"I'm going to do *my* best. It's all I got."

He shook his head, like she wasn't understanding him.

Which was correct. She had no idea where he was going with this.

"No, I know." He met her gaze again. "You're gonna be a great teacher."

Willa blinked as his words settled. He meant it. He thought she could do this, and for whatever reason, his opinion still meant something to her, all these years later.

"For what it's worth, I think everyone Loretta recruited is going to be exceptional in their own way. I may be the weak link."

He scoffed. "You were never the weak link." The smile that matched his daughter's slipped out.

"Sometimes you were a stubborn link. A cranky link. Never weak."

Willa turned away, sending a clear signal. *Light flirting is not okay.*

But now she was staring at his stables, which made her think of Colter on a horse, which was not much better than gazing into his blue eyes as he teased her. But it *was* better.

"I'm serious," she continued. "Luci, Vander, Tate, Mateo and I are all real different from each other, but we all have our gifts. I can't say if it was intention or luck on Loretta's part, but we're a strong team."

"That's what I'm saying. The strong team picked you to be their leader and come out here and tussle with the school board."

There was truth in his words. She was the rock.

Colter ran a hand through his hair. "But I'm also trying to tell you, I've given everything I have to raise my kid."

Since it was the third time he'd said basically the same thing, and she still didn't understand what he was talking about, it felt like time to acknowledge a communication gap. Her guess was he wanted assurance Sylvie would be treated fairly. She placed a hand on his arm to reassure him. And yeah, his biceps had gotten bigger in the last thirteen years.

"I took this job to be part of something special. I know the kids around here haven't had a normal school year in a long time. I'm ready to show up every day and bring my best for Pronghorn—and *all* the students here."

He cleared his throat and gazed toward the barn, then gave one strong nod. "Thank you." They walked next to each other to the front porch. "You ready for the school board?"

"As ready as I can be." Willa started up the front steps, then paused. Colter was probably the best person to shine a light on a point of confusion the teachers had with the whole situation. "Quick question, though. Is Loretta...certified to be an administrator?"

Colter laughed. "Of a school? No."

"Then how did she get hired as principal?"

"She wasn't. She's volunteering."

Willa puffed out her cheeks and let out a breath. That explained *a lot*.

It also meant she really *was* in charge. A quick glance at Colter suggested this wasn't a surprise, or even something that might get labeled as a problem.

"Before we go inside, I want to let you know it can get kinda prickly in these board meetings."

"I expect it can. The other teachers and I have a list of concerns we need addressed before we can move forward."

Colter reached past her and opened the door. "You can count on my support."

Willa braced herself as she stepped over the threshold, determined to keep her reaction to his home neutral.

The house unfolded before her, a modern series of half walls and graduated levels delineating the rooms. Reclaimed wood, glossy and warm, ran throughout. The place was clean and neat, but with just the right amount of life to it. Smooth, wide plank floors were broken up with woven rugs. In a sunken living room, rich leather furniture made a cozy conversation nook. And the windows! Everywhere she looked, a window framed stunning views of Colter's acreage.

The house was beautiful, warm, friendly, and pure Colter. It was the type of home she'd imagined sharing with him.

She looked up to see him, observing her as she observed this house.

"What do you think?" he asked.

"It's great." She understated. "Is this what brought you to Pronghorn?"

He laughed. "Nah. When I bought the ranch, there was a tiny two bedroom out near the main road. I built this."

"You built—" she gestured to the walls, the floors, the open kitchen with vases of wildflowers everywhere "—this?"

Okay, that's just not fair.

It should be against the rules for your first love to grow up gorgeous and live in a perfect house he'd built by hand. And have a wonderful daughter.

"Yeah. It took me long enough, but Sylvie and me are comfortable here."

"Sylvie and I," she corrected, out of spite.

He chuckled. "Something like that. You ready to meet the board?"

COLTER WATCHED WILLA descend into his sunken living room, as though walking into a lion's den. She was confident and smiling, like she'd done coursework in large cat handling. You'd never know the woman strolling in had recently been on the losing end of a battle of wits with an ATV.

He hoped he'd been clear with her about Sylvie. She was his daughter, and he didn't need anyone's help in raising her. He needed a good school where his daughter was treated fairly. He didn't want special treatment for her, but he didn't want her to hide behind her books, either. Someone needed to draw her out, but not in an obvious way.

He'd made that clear, hadn't he?

He wasn't going to interfere in their teacher-student relationship or tell Willa how to do her job. He wanted her to teach Sylvie everything she needed to know, but not get too close to her.

Just a perfectly normal, student-teacher relationship where the teacher happened to be the woman the student's dad had once intended to marry but didn't because he got someone else pregnant. Then that woman, the pregnant one, was horrible, but the baby turned out to be the most incredible kid on the planet.

Did they learn how to handle that type of thing in teacher school?

"Hello, you!" Loretta said, jumping to her feet as Willa walked into the room. She turned to the others. "Didn't I tell you she was pretty?"

Willa didn't acknowledge the comment, but

rather took control of the situation, turning to Raquel Holmes. "Hi, I'm Willa Marshall. English teacher."

"I'm Raquel. Former teacher and mom of two girls at the high school. I represent the parent council."

This was the first he'd heard of any parent council, but Colter suspected Raquel was referring to her personal circle of friends, many of whom were parents.

"Great to meet you. Did you teach high school?"

Raquel hesitated in response to a direct question about her teaching career, then said, "I have a lot of ideas about new titles you might want to add to your curriculum. Kids should be reading engaging literature."

"I agree." Willa shook her hand, smiling.

"Pete Sorel," the grizzled rancher sitting next to Raquel said. He held out a hand and Willa managed not to wince as he crushed her fingers in his unintentional vise grip. "I represent the majority of folks around Pronghorn when I say we want some good, basic education for our kids. Nothing fancy, just straightforward information."

"I'm a big fan of straightforward," Willa responded.

"He represents *some* of the folks around Pronghorn," the fourth member of the school board spoke, her robes of orange and red unfolding as she rose from the opposite sofa. She took both of Willa's hands in hers. "I am Today's Moment. I come as a representative of every child, everywhere in the world."

"She's from the commune," Pete grumbled.

"I'm a member of the Open Hearts Intentional Community." She blinked twice, keeping Willa's hands in hers. "And we are all so happy to have you here."

"I'm happy to be here." Willa disentangled her hands from Today's Moment and chose a chair to perch on. It happened to be his favorite chair, but that was fine. She opened her backpack and pulled out a list. "I have a few questions for the board. Mind if I get started?"

The board members smiled, as though indulging her.

No one seemed to mind her starting, but for the next hour not one of them let her finish a sentence.

The meeting was mayhem.

Pete was talking in circles about the teachers giving the kids "the basics." Today's Moment argued with him, suggesting that kids could always look up facts on the internet, what they needed was to learn to think. That led Willa to bring up a concern from the teachers—reliable internet at the school. That was doable, you just needed a good router. The cell towers and broadband connections most Oregonians relied on didn't exist in this sparsely populated corner of the state. A person couldn't just open a phone and expect coverage in Pronghorn, but the teachers wouldn't know that. The school had a satellite and if the router/modem unit wasn't working, the board needed to get it fixed.

But rather than solve this one easy problem and

move on, Loretta suggested the teachers prioritize their demands. Willa tried to explain the teachers didn't have demands, they were asking questions. Then Raquel jumped into the fray, explaining that the priority was curriculum, and the teachers had to be responsive to the community when deciding what to teach. Willa said they couldn't decide what to teach until they knew what classes they were teaching. A-aaand that had Pete going off about "basics" again.

When Colter had accepted the position as school board president, he understood it was because he'd donated more money than anyone else. He knew nothing about education but was deeply invested in the success of the school. He assumed he'd host the meetings, weigh in on matters of finance, and be there to fix the boiler if it went out.

That was the difference between him and the other board members. He acknowledged he knew nothing about education; they did not.

Colter drew in a deep breath, wondering if it was time to break out the cookies.

"Can I clarify something before we go any further?" The piece of paper shook in Willa's hand. Colter knew her well enough to see she wasn't nervous, she was mad. "I have a quick question about the budget."

Yeah, this wasn't the right time for cookies. He wasn't bringing any projectiles into the room if money was being discussed.

"None of the teachers know what the budget is

for their department, nor do we know the process for making orders. Tate needs all sorts of PE equipment. Vander needs to know how much he can spend on labs, and the textbooks are so outdated they don't meet Oregon State Standards anymore."

Everyone stared at Willa like she'd just asked for five diamond-encrusted tiaras and matching scepters for the first day of class.

She swallowed. "None of us expects the budgets to be large, but we need to know what we have to spend so we can plan accordingly."

Face red and trembling, Pete leaned forward. "You can't come in here demanding funds—"

Willa cut Pete off. "I'm not demanding anything. I'm asking what the budgets are for Physical Education, Science and the library."

The board went silent, staring back at her. Everyone in the room, and most of the community, had given every extra penny they had to support the school. Because the population was so sparse, the state was able to provide online school, but anything beyond that was funded by the school district. The district was barely scraping by, already transporting young kids in Pronghorn to a grade school forty miles away. In-person high school in this area was considered extra. Colter himself had used the last of his rodeo earnings to fund the project. It hadn't occurred to anyone that it might not be enough.

Co-evils of anger and embarrassment simmered in the room. Willa raised her chin, unaware that she was poking the pride of lions in their most sensitive spots.

"Hi." Sylvie stood at the edge of the stairs, bouncing on her toes. The adults forced smiles, trying to hide their anger like kids caught with comics behind their textbooks.

Willa was the first to respond. "Hi, Sylvie. That's a cool skirt."

Sylvie glanced down, feigning surprise when she saw what she was wearing. This had to be what Sylvie described as *"like a skirt."* The asymmetrical fabric looked less like a garment and more like someone had come out on the wrong side of a tangle with a tablecloth. She wore it with a cropped sweatshirt, a puffy vest over the top of everything. "Oh. Thanks." She took a few steps toward Willa. "I made it."

"Wow! Your dad builds houses, you make clothes. What's next?"

Sylvie shrugged, then drifted into the living room and sat on an arm of the sofa, the closest seat to Willa.

"Cookies," Colter answered. "Sylvie, you want to help me serve those cookies we made?"

She didn't move. "I'm good."

He gave her a look, attempting to communicate that what he really meant was, *"Please leave this contentious school board meeting, and don't form a lasting bond with a woman who rightfully hates me."*

Sylvie chose not to receive the message.

"Well, would you look at the time?" Loretta

jumped up and glanced at her wrist where a Fitbit was displaying her steps, rather than the hour. "I have to get back to town."

"But we don't—" Willa held up the list. Not one of the concerns she'd raised had been adequately addressed.

"Rome was not built in a week, my dear." Loretta batted her eyelashes that matched the ones on her Volkswagen Bug for length and inauthenticity.

"We'll have students in the building in seven days," Willa said.

"A lot can get done in seven days. Just ask Julius Caesar."

"Please, please stop mixing metaphors," she begged.

Colter caught her eye and gave the slightest shake of his head. She wasn't going to get anything done going through Loretta. The trick there was to work around her.

Willa held eye contact, then lowered her list. Colter nodded and slipped the paper from her hand, examining it.

Loretta kept chattering. Somehow Willa's plea to stop with the metaphors only made things worse, and now Loretta was whistling on about paying the Pied Piper his pickles before the early bird snatched them up. Willa blinked back tears.

"I feel the expression of emotion in this meeting was real and powerful," Today's Moment said. Then she looked at Willa. "We've had many community sharings where we discussed the option of our emerging adults joining the school. I trust your energy and will support anyone who chooses to attend the public school. You *will* do the right thing."

"Thank you?" Willa replied.

Pete and Raquel left her with similar, vaguely threatening statements of support, and suddenly the house was empty.

Willa dropped her head into her hands.

"What were you guys arguing about?" Sylvie asked.

Willa pushed her palms against her eyes, which Colter knew was something she did to keep herself from crying.

"This school is real important to everyone," Colter said. "When everyone wants something so badly, they get kind of riled about it."

Willa peeked at him from between her fingers. "You call that 'kinda riled up'?"

He leaned forward on the sofa, resting his elbows on his knees. "It was pretty tame for a school board meeting."

The remaining color drained from her face. She looked like she was about to faint, or leave Pronghorn. Possibly both. That couldn't happen. She was the leader in the group of teachers and if anyone would make this work, it was Willa.

"Hey, Sylvie, would you make Ms. Marshall some of your chai tea?" He glanced back at Willa. "You still like chai, don't you?"

She nodded.

"And grab the cookies."

Sylvie was reluctant to leave, but her desire to show off her chai was greater than her need to stay in the room.

Colter refocused on the list. "You guys don't have a schedule?"

"Nope. We haven't gotten any information about what classes are offered, the bell schedule, or even how many kids are registered for school."

He glanced further down the list. There was a lot that needed to happen, fast. He felt foolish for not having foreseen this. He'd been so worried about his kid and so thrilled when it looked like they were getting a school he hadn't thought to ask questions.

"Okay. Let's meet with Mrs. Moran about that. I'm sure she's got ideas. You all design the schedule, then send it out to the families before the board meets again."

"You want us to design our own schedule?"

He nodded. "Can you do that?"

She straightened. "Yeah. Yes. We can."

He scanned the list. "In terms of what classes you're teaching, my guess is you haven't been told what to teach because no one knows what the kids need after three years online."

Willa nodded. "I'd been worried about kids getting misplaced. In my subject, it's not as much of an issue, but math and science are more sequential."

Colter stared at his hands, then risked a glance at Willa. She was beautiful when contemplating dire educational issues. "How could we deal with that?"

"What if—" She ran a finger across her bottom

lip. "What if we planned the first days of school as get-to-know-you days, along with placement assessments? It's a small school, right?"

"You'll have somewhere around thirty kids, depending on who shows up."

"Then assessing their skills over the course of a few days is doable." She leaned toward him. "It's actually preferable. That way we can be sure everyone is appropriately challenged."

Her eyes lit up, reminding him of the nights they'd spent scheming as teenagers.

He'd known he was in love with Willa long before he got up the nerve to say anything. When a guy was falling for his best friend's sister, he had to tread carefully. But doing anything carefully had never been his strong suit.

Colter had devised every ploy he could come up with to spend time with her alone. It was tough because Willa was responsible and even-keeled. She idolized her brother. But she was in love with Colter. One night, as he was leaving the Marshall house, he'd seen her sitting outside her bedroom dormer on the gabled roof of their house. Climbing out her window was certainly not on the approved list of activities, and Willa wasn't one to break rules without a reason. He'd stopped halfway up the stone pathway from the front porch to the street and stared at her. Then she'd grinned, and her intention finally made its way through his thick skull. He'd waved goodbye, or rather, he'd waved see-you-in-five-minutes. Then drove two blocks to the south, parked his truck, snuck back to her house along the riverbank and climbed up on the roof with her.

She hadn't been able to keep her smile at bay as he scaled the drainpipe to meet her. He remembered being suddenly shy, unable to say anything once he finally got to her side. But she'd taken charge, like she always did. Slipping her fingers through his, she'd said, *"We need to come up with a plan."* Colter, never one to think more than fifteen minutes into the future, had leaned in to kiss her, because that was *his* plan. He'd kissed her once before, after the Sisters Rodeo, and hadn't been able to think of much else since. But she signaled him to wait. The situation was complicated—even he could see that. As much as he wanted to kiss her, he wanted to let her know everything would be okay so long as they were together. He'd sat back, tapped into his tiny reserve of patience, and said, *"You're right. What are we going to tell your brother?"*

"Here's your tea." Sylvie reappeared with a frothy beverage, snapping Colter from his memory. It didn't escape his notice that she'd given Willa her favorite mug, the one with stylized mustang horses cantering around the base.

"Thank you." Willa beamed at her, then took a sip. From the little jolt she gave, he guessed Sylvie had made the beverage a touch too spicy again.

"Do you like it?" Sylvie asked before Willa had a chance to swallow.

Willa just turned to his daughter, in the warm,

caring way she had that made everyone feel like they, too, could be strong and smart like Willa. "I love it."

Sylvie beamed, returning to her perch on the sofa arm.

"Cookies?" Colter reminded her.

"Oh. Duh. Be right back." Sylvie scampered to the kitchen, and Colter figured he had less than thirty seconds to say what he needed to before his daughter rejoined them.

He pulled in a deep breath. "Please tell me you can do this."

Her violet eyes met his. Memories swarmed him as he held her gaze. The first time she brushed her hand against his. Their first kiss in the moonlight on the rodeo grounds. Their first date.

The phone call from a woman he couldn't fully remember, informing him that she was pregnant with his daughter.

"Cookies!" Sylvie called, returning from the kitchen.

"Please, Willa." He dropped his voice. "I know I have no right to ask anything of you. But you've got to make this school work."

CHAPTER FOUR

"*YOU'VE GOT TO make this school work.*"

A small request. No big deal. Just create an exceptional educational institution out of thin air with an inexperienced crew, a contentious school board and no money.

Willa would get that done right after placing in the top ten at the Boston Marathon.

The last few days had been a mad scramble of figuring out who would teach in which classroom, what supplies they had, what was essential, and what they could live without.

In spare moments they attempted to set up their lives in Pronghorn. Food was procured at the small grocery store where the primary items for sale were saltine crackers, canned soup, instant coffee and postcards. Mateo had placed a spectacular array of ingredients in an online shopping cart, only to find delivery was "unavailable at this time." So, until they could find someone to drive them an hour and a half away to the nearest grocery store, crackers and soup it was.

Unexpectedly, it was kind of…fun. Like summer

camp. Willa couldn't remember laughing this much since she was a teenager. The new recruits worked well together, finding their strengths and buoying one another emotionally. So long as the volunteer principal didn't show up, they were getting it done.

Presently, they were working on the class schedule over lunch in the courtyard. Most days they fixed their meals in the industrial hotel kitchen, then ate in the courtyard where rosebushes and boxwoods in desperate need of a trim gave the space a feeling of glamour from a century ago. As in, it had been glamorous a century ago, and if you squinted just right you could almost see it.

Tate leaned back in his chair, giving the schedule a final once-over.

"Solid." He nodded. "This is a *good* plan. I'm excited."

Vander took the clipboard from his hand and studied it as he took a long drink of coffee. "It's good."

Luci pushed her teacup to one side and leaned across the wrought iron table to get another look. Luci always insisted they finish lunch with coffee or tea, and a cookie, in a gesture of self-care. Today's selection was a small sleeve of travel-sized Oreos, served with a choice of Folgers or Lipton.

"All thirty of our students start the day with Tate in PE." Luci looked up at Tate. "It's not going to be too chaotic having freshmen through seniors all in the same class?"

"No, because morning PE is only about getting

some movement. I'll teach skills classes in the afternoons. We start the day with brisk walking or runs, do some yoga, calisthenics. When the weather gets colder, I'll augment that with games in the gym. Morning PE is short and quick, but it will get their bodies and brains warmed up for the day." He crossed his ankle over his knee. "And that's straight up brain science for you. Kids learn better when they start the day with movement."

Vander offered him a fist bump. "Word."

Mateo took the schedule. "Then students have two academic morning classes, lunch, two academic afternoon classes, and finish with elective hour."

"Our classes are going to be tiny," Luci said. "I'm kind of excited for that."

A rustling sound came from behind Willa, near the arched opening from the courtyard into the street. Willa didn't turn around for fear it was Colter, who seemed to be everywhere in this town. She focused on her coworkers. "We each teach four of the six periods, have one prep period and one administrative period."

"I still don't understand what we're going to be doing during the administrative period." Luci took a sip of her tea.

Willa set her Oreo on the edge of her saucer. "It's just a precaution. Mrs. Moran mentioned that things come up. Unexpected...things. Having at least one of us on call to deal with whatever seems like a good idea."

"And Mrs. Moran is only teaching Spanish in the afternoon, correct?" Luci asked.

"Yes. Two classes of Spanish after lunch, then an elective." Willa didn't entirely understand Mrs. Moran's role at the school, but she was calm and experienced, and as far as Willa was concerned, she could teach or not teach as much as she wanted to.

Heads nodded around the table. Tate's broad smile flashed across his face. "I think we've got a schedule."

Willa fought the urge to leap out of her chair and pump her fist into the air in triumph.

They'd done it.

Five young teachers with no practical experience had created a multigrade schedule for the whole school. Not only was everyone happy with it, they had fun hammering it out. They'd poured all they'd learned from their master's programs into the work, creating an ideal day for learners.

A tiny little voice whined in the back of Willa's head, like a mosquito. *Maybe it was the lack of experience that made it possible to come up with something so quickly?*

Whatever. They had a plan.

One step closer to *"You've got to make this school work."*

An image of Colter's blue eyes pleading for this opportunity for his daughter tripped her up. She shook her head to dislodge the image. She wasn't doing this for Colter. She was doing it despite him. Her old self would have walked away, deeming

Colter's presence too hard to deal with. This Willa was going to stay in Pronghorn, slay her personal dragons and find her own happy ending.

"I love how we have the flexibility to meet kids where they are, rather than shoving them into a rigid system," she said.

"My classes will be small enough that if someone needs to catch up on a math concept, we can get it done then and there," Mateo added.

Luci stepped on the end of his sentence, saying, "What I love is we have the kids in academic classes in the late morning and early afternoon, when their brains are most receptive. But we also start and end the day with fun, so they'll want to come on time and stay through the day."

"Hold up." Tate placed both his hands on the table. "PE and health aren't just about having fun. These classes teach people to care for their bodies, setting them up for a lifetime of health and happiness."

"Right. Sorry. I didn't mean to suggest your class was just fun. I only meant it's not academic."

"What?!" Tate leaned forward. "My classes are plenty academic. I teach the most important classes at this school."

The table erupted in offense.

"Ohhh! I see how it's gonna be." Luci pointed a finger at him. "You've got nothing on my classes, Tate Ryman. I teach social studies, the class where you learn history, current events, how to manage your money, appreciate other cultures, and *vote*.

You care about individual health. My subject concerns the health of society. Social studies is far and away the most important class."

"Wait, wait, wait." Mateo held his hand out to stop the discussion. "If your classes are so important, why do Vander and I, science and math, get all the funding? Maybe because our curriculum is actually practical."

Vander slapped Mateo a high five as Tate and Luci groaned, firing back with smack talk about STEM.

Willa grinned over the top of her coffee cup as she listened to the banter.

All their classes were important. Of course, no one could study any of it if they didn't know how to read and write first, but she'd keep that fact to herself.

The shuffling sound from the door increased, and if she could hear it over Tate's bellowing, she should probably check it out. Willa turned around. And then she screamed.

Not like a bloodcurdling outburst of fear, more of a vocalization of extreme surprise.

There were five—no six—large horned mammals walking calmly into the courtyard. Some with horns up to a foot long, others with shorter, but no less deadly horns. Each animal was a mix of brown and cream-colored fur, with darker markings on their faces. And they were all staring at the teachers.

Specifically, Willa, since she'd screamed.

Mateo stood abruptly. "What the—"

"Pronghorn!" Vander exclaimed. "I was hoping we'd see pronghorn out here."

"Were you hoping they'd join us for lunch?" Luci placed a protective hand around her cup of tea.

As though responding to her question, one of the pronghorn took long, slow steps toward a rosebush. Turning her head to the side and stretching out her lips, she sucked in one leaf, then another. In seconds she'd stripped half the bush.

Willa jumped out of her chair.

"No," she told the antelope.

The pronghorn turned its large eyes to her as it consumed the plant.

"Git. Shoo. Go elsewhere!"

Another pronghorn advanced on a decorative shrub. Yes, the boxwood needed a good trimming, but not like this. She waved her hands at the animal. It lifted its large head and eyed her pale green cardigan sweater. Willa took a step back.

"Is everything okay?" An impossibly handsome man ran into the courtyard: work boots, broken-in jeans, a worn leather tool belt slung across his hips and a T-shirt so soft and lived in it was hard not to think about what it would feel like against her cheek.

Right, her ex.

"I heard yelling." Colter was staring at her across the courtyard, as though unclear on why she had screamed. Never mind there were half a dozen antelope between them.

She pointed to the plant munchers. "There are... pronghorn."

Colter finally acknowledged the animals. "Hey. You. Get away from there."

The animal chewed thoughtfully as it gazed at him.

"I'm sorry," he said. "Pronghorn are a real nuisance around here."

Luci furrowed her brow. "You think?"

"In most places they're pretty skittish, but some of the folks at Open Hearts took to feeding them a few years back and now we've got a problem." Colter looped around the animals, his Red Wing boots heavy on the brickwork. "Y'all git on out of here," he told the animals.

One plodded slowly toward the opening, the others refusing to follow until Colter took a few steps toward them. He held his arms out, his feet wide and back straight. The pronghorn slowly realized who they were dealing with, and more out of respect than any real fear, headed to the archway.

Colter's posture and voice in herding the antelope sent Willa straight back to high school. He'd always had a way with animals, the bigger and scarier, the better. Colter and her brother had met doing junior rodeo. Holden roped calves; he was good but nowhere near competition level. Colter was a bronco rider, and a natural. He had no fear with animals, just a steady understanding of himself as an equal to any creature. Riding broncos wasn't about mastering the animals for Colter, it was about enjoying a fun challenge with them. He was relentless, joyful and steady as he rode.

That was the boy she'd fallen in love with. Quick with a smile, just on the other side of reckless. A boy who'd disappeared from her life years ago. In the interim she'd done her best to forget all the things about him she'd loved. If she could dwell on everything he'd done wrong, it helped her forget everything that had been so right.

The end of their relationship could be chalked up to his failure, rather than her inadequacy. *Colter messed up* was so much easier to live with than *Colter left me*.

Any thoughts of the sweet moments, the good before he left without saying goodbye, pelted her like a sleet storm, soaked her through with pain that could trap her in days of *why* and *what if?* Every warm, happy moment had turned horribly sour by his abandonment. If she acknowledged his good points, it made the hurt much harder to bear.

So watching him handle a herd of pronghorn the same way he used to manage cattle was *not* going to work for her.

She just had to come up with a plan for dealing with the cowboy if she couldn't straight up avoid him. The boy who'd broken her heart had become a man who loved his daughter, and championed education in a difficult situation. But that didn't mean he wasn't fully capable of breaking her heart again, truly shattering it with no repair this time. He was single, which probably meant the county was chockablock full of other, similarly broken hearts.

Willa had come to Pronghorn to create the life she always wanted for herself. Colter was an extra challenge. The key was to compartmentalize different areas of her life, set some boundaries for once. When Colter showed signs of the reckless cowboy who'd left her, like making references to their past, speaking before he thought it through, looking good herding any kind of animal, she would walk away. When he was an upstanding community member and father of one of her students, she could deal with him. It was as simple as that.

Easy.

Right up there with placing in the top ten in the Boston Marathon.

"Move it," Colter said to the male in the group. "Out you go."

What was next around here? Colter had done his best over the last few days, keeping the board and all their conflicting demands, away from the new teachers as they got set up. He'd tried to keep out of Willa's way himself, but that was hard to do when there was still so much work at the school. It was also just hard. He'd missed her so much over the last fourteen years that his joy in seeing her threatened to override his good sense in keeping out of her way. He felt like a puppy who knew not to jump up but was having a heck of a time keeping all four paws on the floor.

When he'd heard her yelling in the courtyard, his body reacted without a thought, running in to save her. Like Willa had ever needed anyone's saving. She did, however, need help with semidomesticated pronghorn.

"Can I try?"

Colter turned around to see Vander standing next to him. Did the kid really need to ask permission to yell at pronghorn? Because if so, he was going to be asking for permission a lot.

"Sure."

Vander imitated his stance. "Be gone!" he told the animals. None of them moved. The young teacher lowered his arms and looked at Colter. "I think they can tell I don't really want them to go. This is so cool."

Colter chuckled. "You'll get tired of them soon enough."

"Never."

"Well, think of it this way. The courtyard's a bad place for them. They could get trapped and panic. They'll be happier outside."

"Good point. How do I do it?"

Colter tried to keep his focus on Vander, and not turn around to stare at Willa. "Herding is in the stance and voice. You can say just about anything, so long as you make your intention clear."

Vander straightened his back, raised his arms like Colter had, and intoned, "A long time ago in a galaxy far, far away."

The pronghorn scuttled on their hooves and trotted out the door. Vander grinned, then turned back to the group. "I *love* this place!"

The last of the pronghorn broke into a run at his proclamation, speeding out into the street.

"That makes one of us," Tate muttered.

Colter checked for Willa's reaction. Her face was neutral, neither loving nor hating Pronghorn, Oregon. Withholding judgment until further evidence.

It was his job to make sure she saw the correct evidence. Pronghorn, despite its quirks, was a fantastic place.

"We should head out of here, too," Mateo said. "Now that we've got the schedule, I'm excited to get back to my classroom and start planning."

"Let's do it," Tate said, rising from the table.

Colter watched as the crew picked up the remains of their lunch, cheerfully joking with one another. For all of Loretta's faults, she really had "done good" with this crew.

"I got this," Mateo said, taking Willa's cup. "You go show the schedule to Mr. President." He nodded to Colter.

"You finished the schedule?"

Willa calmly picked up a clipboard and brought it over to him. He was almost impressed by the neutrality of her expression—not too eager, not too angry, straight down the middle appropriate for the lead teacher handing a schedule to the board president. Colter managed to get his eyes off Willa to scan the boxes and assignations.

And yeah. He didn't have a clue as to what he

was looking at. It could have been a launch plan for the space shuttle for all he knew. He asked the most important question. "Are you happy with it?"

"Yes. It's fantastic." She gestured at the page, as though its greatness was clear to any viewer. "Do we need board approval?"

Did they? That seemed like it should be a thing, a school board gravely and wisely looking over a schedule, then approving it. But he was pretty sure that wasn't how it would go down around here.

"Has Mrs. Moran seen it?" he asked.

"I was going to show her the final outcome after lunch. Although when I ran the basic premise by her she seemed to like it."

"If Mrs. Moran likes it, you're good to go."

The other teachers filed back into the court-yard, carrying backpacks and messenger bags. Luci handed Willa her backpack and they headed out into the street, toward the school. Colter followed a few steps behind them as the teachers joked about whose classes were more important. Willa bent down to give Connie the watch-cat a quick pat as she passed, then looked nervously over her shoulder to where the pack of pronghorn were advancing on The Restaurant.

An embroidered patch on the back of Willa's pack seemed to wink out at Colter. Before he could stop himself, he asked, "You still a fan?"

She glanced down at the patch. "Of Kermit the Frog? Always."

Instinctively, rashly, stupidly he lifted a hand and said, in his best frog voice, "Hi Ho! Kermit the—"

She spun around in the middle of the street and clapped a hand over his mouth. "Not funny. Not okay."

Her fingers brushed his lips, reminding him of other times she'd shushed him, in the days they kept their relationship a secret from her brother. The times he could barely stop himself from telling her, and everyone else on planet earth, how in love he was. Her fingers remembered, even if she didn't, lingering a touch longer on his lips than any imitation of a frog puppet warranted.

Willa dropped her hand. "Sorry," she said, loudly and for the benefit of the others. "I've been touchy since the death of Jim Henson."

She spun around and continued her march toward the school.

"Pretty sure he passed away before you were born," Colter couldn't help but mutter.

"Then I guess I've been touchy my whole life," she shot back.

Colter followed at her heels. Should he apologize again? Tell her it just slipped out? Try the frog voice once more in hopes she'd try to shush him again?

Or should he release the words he was desperate to share with her? *I'm so relieved you're here. Single parenthood has gripped me in fear every day for the last thirteen years, but you're here now, and you'll make everything okay.*

You have every right to hate me, but that doesn't mean I'm going to reciprocate.

Willa continued to stride across the street. It didn't take a master's degree in education to know she didn't want to hear anything he had to say. On the first day she'd told him, "Don't," which was advice he could probably use in most aspects of his life.

Could he get away with a simple *I'm glad you're here*?

As though reading his thoughts, she glared at him, then tilted her head in a challenge.

Yeah, this wasn't the moment to spill his heart out.

"What brings you to town today?" Technically, it was a polite question, but the strain in her voice did away with any pretense of sociability.

He gestured to the brick building they were approaching. "What brings anyone to town these days?"

"I don't know, that's why I'm asking you."

She *really* did not get what a big deal this school was.

"I've got a few things I need to finish up at the school before the kids arrive. Fixing a few lockers, fixing a few treads on the stairs, fixing a few mistakes other people made while fixing lockers and treads."

She gave him a brief smile, like a glimpse of sun on a rainy March day.

"Sylvie's here, helping," he added.

"Cool." She remained cool as well, turning to

walk ahead of him. He trotted forward and opened the door to the school for her.

"Willa," he said, attempting to stop her march.

"Colter," she replied, with no signs of stopping.

He followed her into the school. "There's something I've been wanting to say."

As the other teachers headed to their respective classrooms, Willa came to a standstill under a sign that read Thankful, the word bookended with a turkey on one side and a pumpkin on the other.

Her sigh was so loud it could have gotten a herd of pronghorn out of a fresh field of clover.

"I… I wanted to tell you—"

Was he going to do this? Spill it all out in a way he could never take back? Let her feel uncomfortable because he still cared about her and couldn't imagine a world in which he would ever stop?

"Colter Wayne." Mrs. Moran emerged from something he was pretty sure was a broom closet. "How's today treating you?"

Like being strapped to the front of a Mack truck driven by a rabid squirrel through Hells Canyon.

"Just fine. How about you?"

"It's nice to have another day on earth." She turned to Willa. "The school received a grant."

"It did? That's amazing. From who?"

She waved her hand, "Some math and science foundation."

"I heard that!" Mateo yelled. "Who you gonna fund?" he called to Vander, who responded with "Math and science!" at Ghostbusters tempo.

"It should cover some of Vander's costs," Mrs. Moran said, "And we can consider health a science, can't we?"

"Can we?" Willa asked.

"I can. We'll buy Tate some new equipment for his PE classes."

"That's great! Thank you. Did you apply for—?"

"Do you think he'd like soccer balls?"

"I think so?"

"Everyone likes soccer," Mrs. Moran said. "I'll order soccer balls. If anyone needs me I'll be in my office." She pointed to the broom closet.

"Your office is a—"

"Cozy little space!" Mrs. Moran opened the door and slipped inside.

Willa stared at the closed door, then shook her head. "What were you saying?"

Colter blew out a breath. This was so hard, but he needed to get it out and over with.

"Willa!" Raquel came sweeping in the front door, loaded down with a box. "I brought you books."

"Thank you?"

"I managed to get fifteen copies of *The Round House* by Louise Erdrich." She placed the box in Willa's arms. "Teach it."

"Oh, okay. Thanks. This is a fantastic book."

"I know."

Colter reached into the box and pulled out a book. It looked strangely familiar and had an award medal on the front of it.

"The Lexile level might be a bit high, but it's a

great story and will be a nice enrichment outside of the core curriculum."

For all her "teaching experience," Raquel didn't seem to be following Willa's words.

"Just teach the book."

"I'm planning on it."

"Then why didn't you say so?"

The front door clanged open and Pete Sorel ambled in. "Whoa, whoa, whoa. What's going on here?"

Willa glanced up. "Raquel brought some books in for my English class. *The Round House* is the winner of the National Book Award."

"What if I wanted to give you some books?"

"That'd be...good?" Willa looked to Colter for help. "Wouldn't it?"

"What'd you have in mind, Pete?" Colter asked.

"Well, I don't know—"

"It would be a good idea for you to have a book in mind before asking if you can suggest one," Colter said.

"I want to make sure she's not playing favorites."

"None of the teachers have had enough time to choose a favorite, much less play to them," Colter said, adopting the same stance he used with the pronghorn.

Willa might have a *least* favorite, but no favorites so far.

"Are we suggesting books?" Today's Moment materialized before them, orange robes flowing in pools around her. "Because we have a number of authors in our community—"

Pete snorted. "Pretty generous with what you call an author."

"You're pretty generous with what you call a book." Today's Moment gave a saccharine smile. "And while generosity is a value I will always champion, Ms. Marshall needs to be very careful about the values she instills in the emerging adults of our town."

Pete puffed out his chest. "That's exactly what I'm concerned about. Values."

Willa cleared her throat, a small but powerful sound. "At present, I have a library that is one quarter full. We have murder mysteries, political thrillers, the complete canon of Barbara Cartland romance novels, and a stunning supply of *Field & Stream* magazine. I need books, and I'd love to strategize. But right now, the priority is getting my classroom set up." She turned to Raquel. "Thank you for these. I loved *The Round House* when I was young and look forward to teaching it."

That was why the book seemed familiar. Willa had had her nose glued to it in the spring of her senior year. "You couldn't put that book down when you were in school."

"Yeah. It's good."

"I remember. I tried to *get* you to put it down."

"I put it down occasionally," she defended herself.

Colter grinned. "After a lot of effort on my part."

"Wait." Raquel looked from Willa to Colter. "Did

you two know each other when she was in high school?"

Willa blinked. Heat rose to her cheeks. She must remember the day she'd lain out in the sun, tearing toward the ending of her book. Colter had pulled the book down to get her attention and she'd shifted away, blocking her smile with the pages. He'd pulled the book down again and she'd snapped at him. Then he'd stretched out beside her in the sun and closed his eyes. His twenty-year-old self was slowly learning that a relationship with Willa took patience, but it was more than worth the effort of cultivating it. After a minute she'd laid her free hand on his arm as she continued to read, and soon he'd drifted off to sleep in the comfort of her company. He'd awoken to a light kiss on his cheek, the sunlight dappled by a curtain of Willa's hair falling around his face. "I'm finished," she'd whispered, then leaned in to kiss him.

A perfect kiss, lost in the wreckage of his mistakes.

The board, however, was not sharing this memory. All the noise and energy of the school seemed to intensify as they watched Willa consider her answer.

She lifted her head. With a bland smile she said simply, "Colter used to know my brother."

She dropped the sentence lightly, like a boulder on his heart.

That's what they'd come down to?

After all the years, the conversations, the family

dinners, the stolen kisses, the plans and schemes. She'd loved him. She'd wanted to marry him.

No, she'd *agreed* to marry him, and told him what he was going to wear to the ceremony.

And now it was just, *"Colter used to know my brother."*

"Was he always this bossy? Or is that a result of being named school board president?" Pete asked.

"Depends on who you're asking, people or pronghorn," Willa said.

That got a chuckle out of all three board members, and agreeing to laugh politely may have been the only thing they'd done together since the inception of the board. Colter forced himself to rally, to shove aside the sadness and get back to the business at hand.

"Okay everyone. Let's let Ms. Marshall get to work. I'll come up with a review plan for suggested materials to go over at our next school board meeting. Until then, Ms. Marshall needs this time to get her classroom in order."

The board members dissipated, but not without a few final words. Willa let out a barely audible sigh.

"Are we going to read this book?" a young male voice came out of nowhere.

Colter spun around to see Mav Lovelight standing right beside them, head drooping into the box.

That *kid*.

Mav drifted around town like a tumbleweed, showing up anywhere and everywhere, at any possible time. No, not a tumbleweed, more like a pronghorn. He was one of the kids from the commune, which meant there weren't a lot of rules at home, or homes, or however they did it out there.

"We are," Willa said, in no way fazed by the apparition of a tall, lanky student. It was fascinating how adults could throw her off-kilter, but she was always ready to talk to a young person. She seemed to have a blanket policy that anyone under the age of nineteen got her easy, cheerful best.

"Can I start now?" he asked, reaching for a book.

"You can start now, but not with this book. Your first task in my English class will be to tell me about yourself."

"Why?" Mav asked.

"Because I need to know who you are before I can determine what we're going to learn. What's your name?"

Mav loped alongside Willa, answering her questions and chatting like there was no tomorrow. Colter watched them walk away down the hall, everything he wanted to share with Willa unsaid, building pressure in his chest.

He had to keep it together, not just for Sylvie's sake, but for all the kids in Pronghorn. Colter had made a lot of mistakes in his life, but he was not going to mess this up.

CHAPTER FIVE

DIRTY WINDOWS, empty bookshelves, screaming yellow walls, dusty everything. The classroom felt like the inside of an abandoned mustard bottle.

Willa let out a breath. Then she picked up the Windex.

One step at a time. One windowpane, one surface. It might take her every available minute between now and Monday, but she could get this room organized. It would still be aggressively yellow at the end of the day, but at least it would be clean.

And as much as she didn't want to be inspired by any of Loretta's inspirational signage, this *was* her time. Colter Wayne could do his adorable Kermit the Frog voice all day long, she was still going to make good on her commitment to the life of her dreams. She was going to do everything in her power to be an exceptional teacher.

When Colter disappeared all those years ago, Willa's ambition had faltered. Her former dreams felt empty and juvenile. Over time she'd pieced together an undergraduate degree, then taken a dead-end job that paid too well to quit, but not well enough to travel or pursue many interests. She told herself it wasn't heartbreak that derailed her plans. Pining over a man was *not* her MO. But each passing day was like the pull of quicksand on her motivation. She'd wake up and make promises: *"Today I'll contact a career counselor."* But petty work drama or someone else's relationship hiccups were so much more comfortable to think about than her own life drifting off course. She'd never been good at setting boundaries, and in her early twenties she didn't even try. Every coworker, second cousin, secondhand friend found a willing sponge for their problems. Their drama temporarily filled the emptiness inside of her, the emotional equivalent of cotton candy for a woman whose soul was malnourished.

Then one day she'd run into her favorite English teacher from high school at the grocery store. Or rather, she'd run away from her.

Mrs. Bodtker had introduced her to the poet Mary Oliver. She asked her students to consider, *"What is it you plan to do with your one wild and precious life?"* as Oliver did in her poem *The Summer Day.* Willa couldn't stand to disappoint her with the answer of *"Not much."*

Rather than greet this teacher who had meant so much to her, Willa had ducked around the end of an aisle and fled the store. The minute she slammed her car door shut, she burst into tears.

That moment had spurred Willa to change. She researched volunteer opportunities with students, then made an appointment with a counselor. Five years of soul searching and hard work later, she had a master's degree, her self-confidence back, and was ready to start her first teaching job. *The Summer Day* was definitely making it into her curriculum.

Willa glanced around the room. Her own classroom. It had a lot of good points. Sturdy, built-in bookshelves lined the lower half of the south wall. Above those was an expanse of divided light windows. It was old, single-pane glass with ancient black muntins holding those panes together, but they provided lots of nice, natural light for her students.

She grabbed the back of the wooden chair, dragged it over to the wide windowsill/bookshelf and climbed up. She pumped the handle of the Windex and a narrow stream of cleaning fluid pelted the glass, splashing back on her.

Reflexively she tried to stop the stream of spray from running down the window with the brown paper towels she'd found in a supply closet. This resulted in a big smear of dust but not something anyone could consider a clean window.

"Hey."

Willa spun toward the voice, inadvertently clutching the Windex bottle and sending a spray of cleaning fluid straight into Colter's face.

"Argh! Willa!"

"I'm so sorry."

"Windex? In the face? I mean, I know I messed up—" Colter wiped an arm across his face.

"You startled me." Willa braced her hand against the windowsill and started to climb off the wooden chair. "Wait, what did you say?"

"I was trying to say, 'Hey,' but believe me, I won't be pulling that again."

"No, I—" She stopped before she could go any further.

I know I messed up.

She'd told him point-blank not to bring up the past, or apologize, or try to make up for it. Then why did those three little words, *I messed up,* feel so gratifying?

Why? Because she had no boundaries and couldn't compartmentalize two paper clips. And now he was standing there, gazing at her with those soulful blue eyes, tool belt and boots making him look like a fixer-upper fantasy. Was the man trying to sabotage her school year?

Willa set the Windex aside, then just to be safe turned the bottle so the nozzle wasn't pointing at anyone. "Hi. Thank you for your help with bookgate earlier."

"I should have warned you." He shoved his hands in his back pockets. "Problem is, I'm so used to all this I don't know what you might need a heads-up about."

She let out a dry laugh. "This town is much more complex than I thought it was going to be."

"Most towns probably are."

Her gaze connected with his. She was interacting with grown-up Colter now, the school board president who could help her get this done. He had information she needed. She was herself a grown-up, not a teenager pouting after a breakup. Willa sat on the windowsill.

"What can you tell me about this place?"

Colter leaned back against a desk facing her. "What do you want to know?"

"Gosh. Everything? Let's begin with the commune."

Colter held up a hand. "For starters, it's not a commune, it's an—"

"Intentional community," Willa said with him.

He chuckled. "You're already learning the ropes. Open Hearts is actually a pretty nice place. I don't necessarily get it, but they're good people. Vegetarians, of course."

"Does that cause trouble down at The Restaurant?"

Colter's gorgeous smile caught her off-balance. She gripped the windowsill with both hands.

"Every once in a while, but they coexist pretty well. The people at Open Hearts love their children, value community, working together, and they put a high premium on taking care of the land."

"Is it weird that those sound exactly like Pete Sorel's values?"

He chuckled. "Not at all. They have more in common with the ranching community than either side is willing to admit. But keep in mind they also believe their souls won't be liberated unless they are wearing orange at all times, they don't accept traditional marriage, and think the center of the human heart is made up of the same substance as the center of the sun."

"So, a few minor differences." She grinned at him.

"What you need to know for the classroom is that they believe kids—"

"Don't you mean emerging adults?"

"Right. Their view on emerging adults is that they should have a lot of freedom. It may make things interesting at school."

She shrugged. "Every kid brings a different perspective with them into the classroom. My job is to meet them where they are and teach them to the best of my ability."

He glanced down briefly, then raised his gaze to connect with hers. "The best of your ability is the best there is, so they're all in good hands."

She smiled back, soaking up his belief in her. The idea that the center of her heart could warm to twenty-seven million degrees like the center of the sun didn't seem so far-fetched.

So it took a moment before she could remember he'd once broken her heart and long periods of eye contact would likely lead her straight back down that road again.

It was time to compartmentalize like a boss.

Willa shook her head. "Did you need something?"

"What?" He was still staring at her with a dreamy smile.

Willa straightened her shoulders.

"Did you need something here? In my room? Or did you just come in to be attacked by Windex?"

"Oh, yeah." His face fell, the moment between them dissipating, as it should. "I need to—" He gestured vaguely around the room.

"You need to…what?"

"Fix a couple of things. I need to anchor the freestanding bookshelf to the wall. And reattach the molding around the door. And then attach the door to the frame. Fix the ceiling tiles." He exhaled. "But I don't want to disturb you."

Too late for that.

"Oh. No problem," she said reflexively. "Mind if I keep cleaning?"

"Sure. I won't disturb you?"

"It's fine."

It wasn't fine, but what was she going to say? *No worries, we can let the ceiling tiles rain down on young people because I'm uncomfortable with how good you make a tool belt look.*

"I'll keep working on these windows, then."

He stared at her, making no move to get started on the shelves, or anything else. "Oh, yeah. Sure. No problem. I don't want to bother you," he said. Again.

It felt like she'd landed herself in boundary-setting boot camp. Willa dredged up her inner drill sergeant.

"I think we're good."

"Okay."

"Okay."

He gazed at her for another moment, then pulled a hammer from his tool belt and swung it once, like a cowboy with a six-shooter. Willa turned away sharply.

She was intensely aware of the creak of the chair as she climbed back up on the windowsill to resume her cleaning. Cleaning fluid blasted the window. She rubbed the paper towel against the glass, an annoying "squeak, squeak" accompanying every movement.

Should she make conversation with Colter? No. They were here to work. She could treat him like any other mind-blowingly handsome man fixing up a dilapidated classroom.

Squeak, squeak, squeak.

Why hadn't she thought to put on music? Because the last thing they needed was a love song playing. At this point anything with a melody could be considered dangerous and she wouldn't be surprised to find herself getting emotional over "Happy Birthday."

Squeak, squeak, squeak.

Ugh. Why had she come to Pronghorn in the first place?

Willa tossed the crumpled-up piece of towel in the most subtle act of frustration she could muster. Eyes screwed shut, she threw her head back and tried to be quiet with her exasperated sigh. Behind her the sound of the former love of her life attaching a bookshelf to the wall seemed to fill the room.

Willa breathed in deeply, and when she opened

her eyes, she was gazing out one shiny clean windowpane at a tiny town on the edge of the prairie. The clear glass let in a warm beam of sunshine. One person, making steady progress over time, could make a real difference.

That was why she'd come to Pronghorn.

She wasn't here to save anyone or achieve national recognition as an amazing educator, but to work steadily to help kids gain confidence in their skills and intellect. When she'd met Loretta at the job fair, she'd known without a doubt she was meant to take this job. She couldn't explain it, but after years of drifting, Pronghorn felt like the right destination. Sure, at present she needed to veer slightly to avoid a head-on collision with Colter, but this time *she* was holding the steering wheel.

Because if she knew anything after what she'd seen so far, it was that she was born for this.

THE SOUND OF Windex spattering across dirty panes drifted across the room. Willa scrubbed at the windows, her back to him.

Squeak, squeak, squeak.

There was a definite rhythm to her work. Long, spattering spray, crumpling of bathroom hand towels, then *squeak, squeak, squeak,* followed by a longer, softer *squeeeee* as she ran the towel around the muntin.

Had he said the right thing? Was he doing the right thing, staying here and working?

He legitimately needed to get this room in order, but working in silence with Willa? It felt like the expanse of the classroom was crowded with memories. Secrets, sweet moments, private jokes stacked to the ceiling, with a narrow path between these land mines of emotion leading straight to her.

"I'm sorry." Colter stood, set down his hammer and turned to her. "I can't do this."

She glanced over from where she'd been meditating on a clean windowpane. "Do you need different tools?"

"No, this." He gestured between them. "I can't pretend like I never knew you."

She refocused on the window, cleaning the next pane with significantly more energy than the task warranted.

"We were friends," he continued.

Her hand stilled in its movement. He saw her shoulders rise and fall with a breath. Then she returned to her cleaning. "Yep. We sure were."

The hurt in her voice weighed down the words, like each syllable was so heavy it took physical labor to force them out.

"Willa, we don't have to hash out whose fault this is. I destroyed our relationship. I think about it every day."

The squeaking increased as she cleaned more furiously, smearing the dust on the windows.

"Will you just let me apologize?"

Her hands stilled, paper towel still firmly pressed against the window.

"You are the last person on earth I ever wanted to hurt," he told her. "You had to know that, didn't you?"

She remained still. He took it as a sign to keep talking. "Please let me apologize and tell you how relieved I am that you're here. If anyone can lead this school—"

"Stop it." He could hear the threat of tears in her voice. She turned around, backlit by the afternoon sun as she remained on the windowsill. "I need you to stop talking, Colter."

"Willa—"

"No. I'm not going to let you talk me into a friendship. We are stakeholders in this school. We have a common goal. Let's leave it at that."

Her words skewered him like a lance through his chest. "You're going to pretend nothing ever happened between us?"

"It's a lot easier than remembering what *did* happen."

Sadness washed through the lance wound, filling every corner of his being. She didn't remember the good times. All he was to her was heartache, while she was every sweet memory he had.

"Let's just be professional," she said, voice also professional. "I don't see why we can't keep out of one another's way."

He gestured to the bookshelf, the doorframe with no door. "Because I have work to do here, too. Because my daughter's going to be in your class. Because we're in Pronghorn."

"Then what do you want me to do?" she finally snapped at him, dropping the crumpled paper, arms flailing in the dust-filtered light. "You're *here*. I'm finally putting my life together. I took a massive personal and professional risk to relocate. And out of everyone in the world, I have to deal with *you?* I have what is arguably the biggest challenge of my life, reviving this school and starting the school year, and you want to talk about our past?"

The words came at him like a spray of buckshot, but the only sentence that really landed was *"I'm finally putting my life together."* Had Willa's life been…apart? Why? What had happened over the last decade that had her feeling like she needed to put the pieces together again?

"This isn't fair," he admitted. "But I'll do anything I can to make it up to you."

She put her hand on her hip and sighed at him, like she did when they were young and he'd come up with some crazy plan. "What do you want, Colter? Do you want forgiveness? Do you want to ensure I'm going to stick around and make this school work? Give me something concrete and I'll see what I can do."

"I want—" He didn't even know where to start. He wanted to be friends. He wanted to be allowed to make jokes. He wanted to dust off his Kermit the Frog voice and express himself through the words of a very wise, felt-covered amphibian.

And yeah, he wanted to erase a pile of bad decisions he'd made fourteen years ago, except the one that led to his thoughtful, creative daughter. He wanted the one brilliant mistake, along with Willa's forgiveness, and her love and friendship.

None of that was going to happen.

"Dad?" Sylvie's voice came from out in the hallway, reminding him of what mattered here.

"In Ms. Marshall's room," he called back.

"I'm done with the lockers." Sylvie came swinging into the classroom. She wore the tool belt he'd given her, screwdrivers and WD-40 at the ready. "Some of the hinges were pretty crusty but all the lockers now open *and* shut."

Willa blinked, then quickly replaced her stern expression with one of interest. Colter turned all of his focus on his daughter.

"Nice work." He tried to say it casually, masking his pride at a thirteen-year-old who knew enough about hinges to assess and handle problems. Willa might think he was irresponsible and impossible, but his daughter fixed lockers on her own so she could just *dwell on that*.

"Hi, Ms. Marshall."

"Hi, Sylvie. Nice to see you."

Sylvie shrugged, moving closer steadily to Willa, magnet for young people that she was. "What are you doing?"

"Trying to get this room in order," Willa said. "What do you think?"

Colter returned to his work on the bookshelf. He didn't have to stand here and watch his daughter bond with a beautiful woman who refused to accept his olive branch.

Even if it wasn't exactly an olive branch.

It was more of an apologetic bouquet of wild-flowers he had no right to ask her to consider.

Sylvie put her hands into the pockets of her hoodie and gazed around. "It's awfully yellow."

Willa sighed and sat down on the wide window-sill. "It is at that."

"Dad, do we still have some of the paint we used at the hotel?"

Colter looked up sharply. He had a total honesty policy with his daughter, which meant he couldn't *not* tell her there were gallons of pale pink and green paint back in the shed at the hotel, along with drop cloths, rollers and painting supplies.

Willa had made it clear she didn't want to spend any more time with him than was necessary. But what did she dislike more, him, or the yellow interior of her classroom?

"I don't know if we have time to repaint—"

"Dad." The statement was accompanied by her arms held out wide, gesturing at the room around them. That one word held a world of arguments.

He glanced at Willa. Her face had been full-on grim for the last twenty minutes, but talk of paint brought a sparkle to her eye.

Okay. He was officially less appealing to the love of his life than semigloss acrylic from Sherwin-Williams.

"Colter, I can paint," Willa said quickly. "You've already done so much."

Actual meaning: *"You've already annoyed me enough."*

"Do *you* have time?" he asked. "You've got a lot to do before Monday."

"For this?" She pointed at the walls, like a flight attendant on an airplane pointing out emergency exits. "I can make time for this. This is a quality-of-life situation."

Colter knew he shouldn't laugh with her, but a chuckle escaped anyway. "Good point."

"I can help," Sylvie said. "I'm really good at painting."

He glanced at Willa. Was he really going to subject her, and every student in Pronghorn, to these walls just because she was unwilling to accept his olive branch/wildflower bouquet?

Colter turned to his daughter. "You know where to find the paint."

"Yes!" Sylvie gave an uncharacteristic cry of excitement. "Ms. Marshall, can you help me get everything?"

An hour later the room was awash in drop cloths, rollers, brushes and blue tape. He had no idea how much Willa knew about painting, but she took direction from the thirteen-year-old patiently. Willa's focus on her words visibly buoyed Sylvie's confidence, like the random set of skills she had in this world were worth something.

And when the first rollers full of pale pink paint

dried over the crusty yellow, Colter had to acknowledge this was the right thing to do.

At some point Mav drifted in, getting in the way and making commentary about the color choice. Sylvie clammed up when he entered. The girl had been talking a mile a minute, but the moment another teenager got there she seemed to run out of words. Colter had witnessed this phenomenon before. His only child was much more comfortable with adults than she was with other kids.

But then Willa worked her teacher magic, getting Mav set up with a roller and instructing him to get the high spots she couldn't reach, then engaging both kids in a discussion about whether or not you could consider a hot dog a sandwich.

It was incredible to watch, almost enough to keep him from stewing about his attempted heart-to-heart with Willa.

Still, it didn't matter how open-minded a man could be, a hot dog was *not* a sandwich.

"Hey, what's going on—" Luci poked her head in the door, then froze in her tracks. "Oh hallelujah, there's paint!"

Willa laughed. "Is your room yellow, too?"

"It's beyond yellow. Who are you?" she asked Mav.

"I'm Mav."

"I'm Ms. Walker. What grade are you in?"

Mav stared at her, thrown off guard by the question. "I don't know."

Luci's eyes darted to the bright orange shirt he

wore, then nodded. "Cool. We'll figure it out next week."

"I'm not sure I can be confined to one grade," he said, with a hint of judgment in his voice. Like it wasn't his fault for not knowing his grade, but society's fault for coming up with the construct in the first place.

Colter expected the well-dressed, precise young social studies teacher to balk, but instead she shrugged. "Who can?" Then she glanced at Willa. "I'm going to help paint, with the steel-hearted certainty you'll help me paint my room when we finish here."

"Yes," Willa confirmed. "Sylvie saved the day with all this."

"You got any music?" Luci asked.

"My phone's back at the hotel," Willa said. "Do you have yours?"

"We can use my dad's," Sylvie offered, drifting over and pulling the phone from his back pocket. Colter went cold as she opened the music app. There were some choices within his playlists he didn't really want to explain.

"What do you guys want to listen to?" Sylvie asked. "Dave Mathews? Cold Play?"

"Dave Mathews?" Willa turned on him. "You're *still* listening to the Dave Matthews Band?"

Okay, apparently they could talk about the past if it involved mocking his music choices.

"Those guys are great musicians."

"So was Beethoven. But a lot of people have

added new stuff to their playlists since he was popular."

"I love Beethoven," Luci said.

"Dad only listens to old stuff," Sylvie told them.

"That's not true. I listen to your music." He turned back to the bookshelf. "When you're blasting it in your room and I can't *not* listen."

Mav and Luci laughed. His joke got a tiny smile out of Willa.

"What else is on his phone?" Willa asked. "No, let me guess. Tim McGraw?"

Sylvie burst out laughing as Willa hit the nail on the head. And that was just too much.

"You do *not* disrespect Tim McGraw." Cotler straightened and faced Willa. She held all the cards here. He knew that. If he offended her, she would walk and then there'd be no school. But there are certain lines you don't cross.

"I'm on Colter's side with this one," Luci said, coming over to look at the phone. Then she glanced at him quizzically. "Meghan Trainor?"

Colter had downloaded her albums when someone had told him Meghan Trainor recorded positive, girl-empowering music. Then it turned out to be really catchy, and fun. Somewhere along the way he'd learned all the words to the songs and wasn't entirely opposed to singing along.

Luci looked him straight in the eye, as though intuiting all of this, and pressed Play. The bright, happy music filled the room. Like the pale pink paint steadily overtaking the oppressive yellow, the music seemed to wash the tension from the room. The five of them painted, transforming the space into a clean, comfortable classroom.

In time, Mateo was drawn in by the party atmosphere, then Vander, and finally Tate. Daylight started to fade, tingeing the prairie with a dusky pink light. And if Colter sang along occasionally and people thought it was funny, so be it.

"I'm hungry," Mav said.

Colter glanced up at the clock. *How had it gotten so late?*

"Where'd the time go?" Willa asked, echoing his thoughts. She stepped down off a chair and rubbed her arm, glancing around the room. "This looks amazing."

Colter gazed at her. She had droplets of paint on her arms and a little spatter across her cheek. She'd always had this ability to speed up the clock, hours in her company passing in seconds.

"I'm hungry, too," Colter said. Then he gazed around the room. "What do you all think—should I incur the wrath of Angie by trying to order takeout from The Restaurant?"

"Dad!" Sylvie was aghast. "There's no takeout at the restaurant." Her phrase had the same intonation one would use to remind someone they can't take the Mona Lisa home for the weekend to see how it would look hanging in the breakfast nook.

"I'm not going to use the T-word, I'll just order a bunch of food and then ask for—" he glanced around the room, counting quickly "—eight doggie bags."

"Am I gonna get a ticket?" Tate asked. "Because the sheriff has it in for me, and I still don't know where I stand with Angie."

"I'll keep your name out of it," Colter promised.

Willa leaned closer to him. "Thank you." She held his gaze, acknowledging his contributions. "Thank you for everything you've done for this school. I know this is—" She trailed off, then finally gave him a wry smile, finishing with "A lot."

"Yeah, man." Vander nodded. "We appreciate it."

Colter chuckled uncomfortably. "You're the ones who uprooted your lives and moved out here. A little paint and dinner is the least I can do."

Willa's gaze skipped from Colter to his daughter, then back again. "Both of you," she said, smiling at Sylvie, then at Mav. "All three of you."

Colter didn't know how long he stood there, soaking in the one small compliment. Then he shook his head. "Okay. I'm off to brave The Restaurant. I'd asked if there are any special requests, but that's strictly forbidden."

He gave the group a salute, and allowed himself an extra nanosecond of connecting with Willa.

This was a tough situation, but Colter didn't make it to the National Rodeo Championships without developing a little grit along the way. Willa was rightfully still mad at him, but she'd also given him another clue about her last fourteen years. She felt like she needed to get her life back together, which meant it had been out of order. He might never be able to win her love again, but if he could find out what had happened in Willa's past, he could help her lay the foundation for a future on track with her dreams.

CHAPTER SIX

WILLA'S HEART THUMPED in her chest, knocking against her rib cage. If the other teachers were as nervous as she was, it didn't show at first glance.

But at second glance, she could see there was just enough tension in their broad smiles. Humor felt a little too forced. Fingers were clenched, shaken out, then slowly clenched again.

They were scared to death. The first day of school was terrifying. Why hadn't they gone over this in college? Why hadn't even one professor thought to mention that preparing to coerce teenagers into learning all day was a horrifying proposition? Two years of theory and practicum were nowhere near enough to quell the panic.

Willa glanced out the front window. Students and their parents had been gathering in front of the school for the last thirty minutes, and Willa had to admit it reminded her a little bit of a zombie apocalypse movie.

"We ready?" Luci asked. Somehow Luci looked even more "Luci" than normal. She wore more makeup than she regularly did and a pair of tortoise-rimmed glasses Willa hadn't seen before, and she had her hair smoothed back into a bun. Her clothing was aggressively preppy.

"I really don't know," Vander admitted.

"Let's do it." Tate reached out and opened the front door.

Students came streaming into the building. No, a stream was too gentle; they came rivering into the building, parents hot on their heels. Despite the signs directing everyone to the gym, kids scattered throughout the front hall.

"Which locker is mine?" a girl asked.

"Oh, uh. Just pick your locker," Vander said.

And that was when the chaos truly began. One four-word phrase set off what the town would later remember as the Great Locker Grab of Pronghorn Public Day School.

Who'd have thought anyone cared so much about a locker? But care they did. Kids pushed toward the bright yellow lockers, jostling one another and elbowing peers out of the way. A student would pick theirs, then when they saw someone choose a locker closer to the main entrance, or nearer the cafeteria, or the office, they would rethink their choice and pick a new one. Some kids stubbornly guarded their choice; others couldn't seem to make up their minds; and some felt the only reasonable choice was one already made by someone else.

"Should we have preassigned the lockers?" Luci asked.

"Too late now," Mateo quipped.

"Don't they need locks?" a mom asked, with a huff of indignation. "That would have been nice information to have in advance."

Willa was about to apologize but a man with long, flowing hair and orange palazzo pants said, "I don't see why we need to encourage greed and fear by implementing locks. This should be a space where kids learn to trust one another."

The two parents descended into an intensely polite argument while kids grabbed, abandoned, traded and fought over lockers.

"Please be careful not to slam the doors," Willa heard Sylvie say softly. "The hinges are, like, seventy years old." A loud slam prompted Sylvie to raise her voice to almost audible. "Please don't slam the lockers."

"Let's head to the gym, everyone!" Tate called. *"Everyone"* ignored him.

Luci clapped her hands, trying to get attention, but it was hard to hear over the slamming of lockers.

Vander circled the group and stood with his back to the main door. He straightened and raised his hands. "To the gym," he intoned.

Yeah, this was exactly like herding pronghorn.

Willa rose on her tiptoes to scan the crowd for Colter. He leaned against the front door, arms crossed as he watched the mayhem.

Awesome.

The plan had been for the teachers to be sitting at their stations in the gym when the kids arrived *on time*, not a full hour early. Luci had created meticulous signage directing the students to each station. There, Willa, Tate, Vander, Mateo and Luci would gather information about the kids: age, interests, career goals, specific learning needs and other pertinent details. Mateo was even going to take a school picture of each kid, since they didn't have a real photographer, and save them for the yearbook club. If anyone actually joined the yearbook club.

After they'd each met the students, Tate had a few field games planned as icebreakers. In the afternoon, students would rotate through the classrooms for assessments so the teachers could determine skill levels and place kids accordingly.

But several flaws in the plan were immediately evident.

No one read any of the signs.

Parents stuck by their kids with no indication of leaving.

All those parents had questions they felt needed to be answered before one more second ticked by.

The questions were largely about issues the teachers hadn't considered, like what was the after-school pickup policy?

So, rather than an orderly procession through the warren of tables where the teachers could calmly greet everyone, the new students and their parents stood in an educational mob in the center of the gym.

Could things get worse?

"Welllllcooooome to Pronghorn Public Day

School!" a voice boomed out over the crowd. Willa looked up to see Loretta Lazarus in head-to-toe yellow, carrying a bullhorn. "I'm Principal Lazarus, your local real-estate agent and educational cheerleader. Welcome *back to school*!"

She intoned the words so the crowd knew to respond with a cheer.

Things could *always* get worse.

"I am so happy to be standing here at the helm of this energetic, creative, and may I say, gorgeous crew of young teachers!"

People applauded again. Willa didn't know what their looks had to do with anything, but she wasn't going to pass up on a positive comment this morning.

"Now, I know you all have a lot of questions. Then I think the teachers have a few surprises in store for you." The bullhorn, at this point, was overkill, but Loretta kept using it.

A girl who looked to be sixteen or seventeen raised her hand. Willa smiled at her. Finally, a kid with something to ask, rather than a parent with something to demand.

She nodded encouragingly to the girl, who held up her phone and asked, "What's the Wi-Fi?"

Willa's stomach churned. Loretta turned to the teachers, still speaking into the megaphone, "What's the Wi-Fi?" The request reverberated throughout the gym.

Willa ignored Loretta and looked straight at the student, ready to tell her they didn't need their phones today. But Mrs. Moran placed a hand on Willa's arm.

"The Wi-Fi isn't working right now," Mrs. Moran said gently. "I'm sure it will be back on tomorrow."

The girl shrugged and pocketed her phone.

Parents started up with questions again. Some, the teachers could answer. Some were decidedly trickier.

"What's your late work policy?" a mom asked. Loretta repeated the question, the bullhorn right in Willa's face.

Luci jumped in with an answer. "All assignments need to be turned in on time, as time management and working with deadlines are important skills in the adult world. We will consider accepting late work when there are extenuating circumstances beyond the student's control."

"Did you just make that up?" Tate muttered under his breath. Luci nodded, keeping her eyes forward. The teachers exchanged impressed looks.

"Is there an open campus?" one father asked.

Tate made the mistake of letting out a laugh. "Literally, where would they go—?"

Willa spoke over him, "Only with advance parental permission."

"What time is lunch?"

"Twelve fifteen," Willa said, with confidence.

"What if I get hungry before twelve fifteen?" Mav asked, with enough of a tone to suggest he didn't trust the authority in this so-called school, and would be on the lookout for any hint of authoritarianism that might try to repress his soul, or his digestive system.

A so-called school he'd been hanging around for the last five days straight, getting in everyone's business and asking a billion questions while they tried to get their work done.

"Pack a snack, man," Tate told him.

"Are you going to allow me to eat it?" Mav challenged.

Mateo's easy smile broke out. He shrugged casually and mugged a thoughtful expression. "Should we let the kids eat, if they're hungry? Or make sure everyone is good and hangry during their academic periods?" People chuckled, and Mateo gave Mav a warm smile. "We have a break at ten forty-five. That'd be a good time for a snack."

Mav crossed his arms and gave a sharp nod, reminding everyone his question had been a serious one. That was when the situation truly hit Willa.

These kids hadn't had a structured school day for at least three years. Some of them had never had a structured school day in their lives.

Several of them hadn't been around other kids for any real period of time.

They were feral.

Many of them, it seemed, were also used to adult attention whenever they needed it. Given the alternative, it was wonderful that most of these kids had adults paying attention. But it also meant they weren't prepared for the give-and-take of a classroom setting.

"What are you serving?" a parent asked.

"I'm sorry?"

"For lunch today. What are you serving?"

Mateo, Luci, Vander and Tate all turned to Willa, with the same question in their eyes. *We're supposed to serve lunch?*

Willa took the question and lobbed it at Loretta. The principal grinned straight back at her.

Mrs. Moran materialized next to Willa. "I believe today is a sandwich bar."

"Sandwich bar," Willa repeated loudly, then she gazed down at Mrs. Moran and asked through her teeth, "Where am I getting the ingredients for the sandwich bar?"

Mrs. Moran patted her hand and smiled. "I'll meet you in the kitchen when Tate takes the kids out for the field games."

Cold sweat broke out across Willa's forehead. Behind her, their student intake stations were set up neatly, but they might never make it to those tables. All their best-laid plans seemed to be blown away with Loretta's bullhorn. This was a disaster.

Feeling eyes on her, Willa glanced up. Colter stood at the back of the crowd, watching this overturned circus wagon of a first day. But he wasn't laughing. Instead, he made eye contact with her and nodded his head toward Loretta. Willa furrowed her brow in a question. He pointed, then mouthed the words, *"Grab the bullhorn."*

She glanced back at Loretta. Could she do that? Take the principal's bullhorn?

From the back of the crowd Colter shrugged as though answering her question with *"Why not?"*

Willa didn't let herself think it through. She reached out, snagged the bullhorn and spoke into it. "We are excited to get this year rolling!" She imitated Loretta's style. "And the first step is to form a line behind the blue sign."

Luci jumped into action, racing to the blue sign to wave people over. Tate, Vander and Mateo trotted back to their tables.

"We'll meet with each student individually, and then Coach Tate has a few activities planned for everyone outside."

Slowly, families started heading in the right direction. Before Loretta could reclaim the bullhorn, Colter pulled her aside and engaged her in a series of questions. Relief prompted a joyful skip in Willa's step as she moved to her table. She glanced over her shoulder and caught Colter's eye. *"Thank you,"* she tried to communicate. A boyish smile broke over his face, and she turned away quickly.

Compartmentalize. You can appreciate a supportive community member without dwelling on his heartbreaking smile.

It was probably a million years before Willa escaped into the kitchen. The teachers had finally been able to gather information about the students after Loretta's self-proclaimed "start the school year rally." That was a fascinating experience in itself. The kids didn't know how to communicate with new adults, and certainly not with each other.

The parents had sky-high expectations, but each of them seemed to have different, oddly specific expectations. The students who came on their own seemed vaguely shocked. Layered over everything was a quiet desperation directed toward the teachers: *"Please make this work."*

They'd done their best to dismiss the parents after the intake interviews. With a brief smile in her direction, Colter helped out again, luring parents into the parking area with the promise of a budget update. But some couldn't separate from their children. Or wouldn't.

Willa sped down the cool, empty hallway. From outside she could hear Tate issuing instructions, and community members questioning his directives. The low intonation of Vander's voice rumbled as he separated kids from adults for the activities.

The cafeteria wasn't large, but it was definitely overkill for the thirty students they had in attendance. She paused, gazing around the room. What had this cafeteria been like in its heyday? She tried to imagine it crowded and cheerful. She spun slowly, thinking about the individual kids she'd met this morning. They'd have some fun times in here, wouldn't they? It was possible the school might grow in the next few years, if they did a good job revitalizing it.

Maybe Pronghorn Public Day School hadn't had its heyday yet. Maybe this year was going to be better than anything that had come before. The morning hadn't gone super well, but the last three years of no school were undoubtedly worse.

If Pronghorn Public Day School had seen its darkest hour, this morning was the dawn. And Loretta the fully yellow rooster crowing.

Willa smiled and quickened her pace toward the kitchen. There she saw Mrs. Moran, or rather the top of her head, behind a massive pile of USDA-issued foods.

"Loretta had originally planned on signing up parent volunteers to make lunch," Mrs. Moran said. "Seems as though that has fallen by the wayside."

Willa followed the voice around the blockade of food. "Well, we've got plenty to serve the kids."

"Yes, and I know Angie will want to make donations over time."

"Angie? Like, The Restaurant Angie?"

"Don't be afraid of her, darling." Mrs. Moran patted her arm. "It's fine to have a healthy fear of her vegetable soup, but as a person she has good intentions. Now, let's figure out a sandwich bar."

Willa enjoyed the calm quiet of the kitchen with Mrs. Moran. Together they lined up sandwich fixings along the counter. The serving utensils, plates and cups were from the 1950s, but like so much from that era, they were sturdy, made to survive a nuclear attack. Willa found herself enjoying the unexpected task, and Mrs. Moran had a way of making her feel comfortable. Their hour in the kitchen was a blessed respite in a maelstrom of a week.

Until Vander came running into the cafeteria, eyes wide with panic.

"Are you ready?"

"Yes." Willa gestured to the spread, deeply proud of herself for managing lunch. A low rumble sounded in the hall outside. "It was simple, we—"

The door from outside burst open, and thirty kids, half as many parents and three exhausted teachers swarmed into the room. Someone called out, "Where's lunch?"

This time, Willa was ready. Taking a note from Colter's book, she physically blocked the lunch bar and held her hands out. "The line begins on my right" she gestured "—behind Mav."

Mav, happy to be singled out as both leader and first in line, straightened dramatically.

"Hand sanitizer first, then build your sandwich. Please use the serving utensils and take only one of each item. If there are leftovers, you can come back for seconds."

Willa crossed her arms, feeling satisfied as an orderly line emerged from the chaos.

That's lunch, Pronghorn.

Her sense of pride washed away as Mav asked, "What about the shredded lettuce? Can I only take one tiny piece of shredded lettuce?"

Willa looked Mav straight in the eye, trying to communicate something along the lines of *"Would you give it a rest already?"*

But Mav needed to feel like he had a voice around here. He spent so much time away from the commune, she could guess he didn't always fit in at home. Today he was showing his people that he was on an equal footing with the newcomers, and they weren't gonna sneak anything by him.

She grinned at him. "For asking that question? Yes. *You* get one tiny piece of lettuce. Everyone else, take a reasonable amount."

The students moved through the line, then scattered throughout the cafeteria. Those with parents in tow weren't able to engage socially because making new friends was awkward enough without a mom hovering in the background. Those who came alone either sat by themselves or moved to sit near a teacher they'd connected with. One small group of kids from the commune sat together, but Mav didn't join them. Sylvie sat alone, staring at her phone, despite the lack of internet.

It wasn't exactly the cheerful, chatty cafeteria crowd Willa had been hoping for. As though sensing this, the other teachers drifted from table to table, making conversation where they could. It was awkward and stilted, but at least it wasn't silence.

A young woman in an orange jumpsuit picked up her plate and returned it to the counter.

"Thank you," Willa said, just now realizing they had no plans for cleanup.

"I'm going home," the girl announced.

Willa smiled. "Can you stay a little longer? We have placement tests this afternoon."

"That's why I'm leaving," she said. "I don't think tests are an accurate measure of my intelligence."

Tate looked up from where he was trying to engage kids on the topic of basketball. He walked over to them. "We need to know where to place you."

"Why can't I place myself?" she asked.

Frustration bubbled inside Willa. It had been a long morning of self-regulation and she didn't have much patience left. *"Because!"* she wanted to yell. *"I'm an adult. I care about your education. I have a master's degree, and you can't be more than sixteen years old!"*

She pinched her lips together, because it was all gonna spill if she didn't.

"The tests aren't optional," Tate said. "We need to know where your skills are."

The girl lifted her chin. "I'm not taking your tests."

Willa opened her mouth to explain but before her brain could send the message to her vocal cords, Luci shot to her side.

"Let's communicate," Luci said.

The girl's brow furrowed.

Luci continued, "Your name is Antithesis, right?" Antithesis nodded. "I'm Ms. Walker."

"I know. You already told us."

"Let's open up a dialogue. I'd love to hear your concerns, and I value the opportunity to express my hopes."

Willa exchanged a look with Tate. Luci was the biggest rule follower in the bunch, and the least likely of any of them to say something like "open up a dialogue." The woman wore penny loafers, for heaven's sake. But here she was, chatting away with the most defiant human in a morning full of challenges, talking about hopes and expression? And not even flinching at the name Antithesis.

But as strange as the words were coming from Luci's mouth, Antithesis seemed to physically relax upon hearing them.

"I don't like tests. And I don't like the idea that a bunch of randoms are going to place me."

Luci nodded. "This sharing of ideas will be easier for me if you acknowledged me and my friends as caring adults, rather than randoms."

Antithesis blinked. "I'm sorry. My emotional levels are high this morning."

Without skipping a beat Luci said, "Mine, too. I think everyone's are."

By this point Vander and Mateo had come closer, listening in on this strange conversation that Luci seemed to know exactly how to handle. Luci let her gaze flicker around the group, then she said, "The judgment inherent in a placement test can intensify feelings of unease and a lack of control, can't it?"

The girl nodded, tears of frustration and what Willa could only assume were high emotional levels gathering in her eyes. "Can we go outside?"

"Into the sun? Absolutely." Luci didn't acknowledge the other teachers as she led the girl out the double doors at the back of the cafeteria.

"How did she—?" Vander started.

"I have no idea," Willa said.

"Ten bucks says she has that girl back in here,

taking every placement test possible within fifteen minutes," Tate said.

A parent with a sullen-looking boy in tow appeared at their side. "For the record, my son will take the placement test, and any other assessment you deem necessary."

Willa nodded at the woman, but there was something about the statement that sounded like less of a vote of confidence for the school, and more of a condemnation of the Open Hearts community.

Tate leaned in toward the others and said quietly, "Pronghorn parents are a lot more contentious than I expected."

Willa grinned at him. "Safe to say, nothing in Pronghorn was what I expected."

"AND EVERYONE REALLY loved the lockers," Sylvie said, chopping a carrot long past recognition. "Like, that was one of everyone's favorite things, getting a locker. And then we had an assembly—"

Sylvie had been talking a mile a minute ever since Colter had picked her up after school. She chattered the whole way home and was still at it as they made dinner together.

"Coach Tate taught us some games outside. And they were kinda confusing at first, but fun. And then we had lunch. Lunch was in the cafeteria, and it was sandwiches. But a lot of the parents stayed, and the teachers hadn't planned on serving the parents, so they had to make rules about how much you could put on your sandwich the first time through, but I didn't want ham anyway, so it was fine." Sylvie popped a piece of carrot in her mouth. "And Ms. Marshall had us take a reading test, and it was really easy. So I think I might get to be in the higher-level English class."

Colter looked up from the stir-fry. "But wouldn't that put you in with older kids?"

Sylvie shrugged. "Maybe. And then we had the math assessment—"

At thirteen, Sylvie was already young for high school. Intellectually, she was ready, and the school was small. But he didn't love the idea of her being with older kids in all her classes.

That said, she needed to make friends, and with only thirty kids in the school it was natural that some of those friends would be older than she was.

"Did you meet anyone new?" Colter asked.

Sylvie focused on the carrot, chopping the already small pieces into smaller ones. In the face of a direct question, she went silent.

Why did he open his mouth? She'd been chattering like a magpie, then he had to go and ask a question.

But in her rapid-fire speech, she hadn't said one word about the topic he was truly curious about. *Did you make friends?*

The vast majority of her words were about Ms. Marshall. Occasionally her monologue veered toward Ms. Walker, there was a spirited retelling of an exchange between Mateo and Mr. V, some evaluation of Coach Tate. And a little eye rolling about Principal Lazarus.

And while Colter loved hearing Sylvie's take on her teachers, and learning that teachers these days went by a variety of names beyond Mr. and Ms., he was concerned about what she wasn't telling him. She hadn't said one word about the other students.

He changed his tack. "Were there any problems with kids getting along?"

"No."

"How was Mav?"

Sylvie shrugged.

It was like pulling really long, entrenched teeth. And since he wasn't a dentist—no extraction tools, no skills in carrying on a conversation no matter what someone's ability to reply—he gave up and switched topics.

"Which class do you think is going to be the most challenging?"

"Ms. Walker's class. Definitely. She's really passionate about teaching social studies. She was like, *'If you don't learn this, the world will fall apart.'* But it's going to be fun. She had us fill in a map—"

Aaaand, she's off again.

Colter added Sylvie's minced carrots to the stir-fry. He'd thought about seeing if Sylvie wanted to eat in town to celebrate the first day, but he didn't really want to celebrate at The Restaurant. What he wanted was to be in town to possibly run into a beautiful English teacher and check in on *her* first day. Making it about himself wasn't fair to his daughter. So he let Sylvie pick the menu, and suggested they cook together.

His phone buzzed on the counter. Colter fought the urge to lunge for it. Willa would *not* be calling him to report on her day. On the off chance she was inclined to call him at all, it would be because something went wrong. Plus, without the school internet, she didn't have cell service.

The phone buzzed a second time. Sylvie picked it up. "It's Loretta Lazarus. Should I answer it?"

The phone quit buzzing before he gathered the strength to say yes. But, as phones do, it immediately started buzzing again. Sylvie gave him a wry look and held out the phone.

Fine.

"Hello Lo—"

"I'm calling an emergency board meeting, effective immediately."

That a board meeting would ever be effective, immediately or not, might be a topic for debate.

"Loretta, I'm sure we don't need to—"

"Pete, Raquel and T.M. are already on their way to your house."

"I don't think Today's Moment would appreciate having her name abbreviated."

"If she appreciates having a voice in this community, she'll be at your house in less than five minutes."

Less than five minutes? Open Hearts was a twenty-minute drive from here, and who knew how long it took on the electric bike/standing thing she used.

Which meant Loretta had called this meeting and invited everyone to his house at least twenty minutes ago.

On cue, Pete's truck pulled up by the door.

"Loretta, I'm about to sit down to dinner with Sylvie."

"Well, I hope you made enough for everyone, and that you have a vegetarian option."

Colter glanced out the kitchen window to see Pete and Raquel talking as they made their way to the house. Arms crossed, eyebrows furrowed: yeah, it didn't look good at all.

"This is serious business," Loretta scolded into the phone. "It was mayhem at the school today."

And that was pure Loretta. Flatter the teachers to their face, rip them apart behind their backs, and do nothing to help the situation.

"Well, I disagree. And I think my student would disagree as well, but I guess we'll discuss it when you get here."

"Oh, I can't make it. I'm showing a property near Hart Mountain."

Colter didn't take his phone and beat it repeatedly on the poured concrete countertop. That was proof he was growing, wasn't it? If only Willa could see him now, not smashing his phone at such provocation. She'd have to concede he'd become a better man in the last fourteen years.

Oh, wait. *Willa*.

"Did you contact the teachers, and let Willa know about the meeting?"

"No," Loretta said, as though he'd suggested she invite the Pope. "Those poor teachers are exhausted."

Colter shook his head sharply. "You want the board to meet without a teacher representative, to talk about what a terrible job the teachers did today? Not happening. Not at my house."

"I want the board members who weren't there today to be aware of the situation."

"So this is a meeting for gossip?"

"This is a meeting to air concerns and plan for the future."

"It doesn't make any sense to air concerns we're not going to tell the teachers about, and we can't plan for the future without the people who are in charge of that future."

"Look, if you saw what I did this morning—"

"I did see what you saw. I was there."

"—you would not be arguing with me right now."

Colter rubbed his forehead with his free hand. Stir-fry was sizzling in the wok and Sylvie shuffled over to stir it. There was a knock on the door, then Pete called out, "Hello?" as he and Raquel entered.

"Loretta, I'll say this to you now, and to the board. School went fine today." Sylvie nodded emphatically as he spoke. "My guess is there'll be a few bumps as we get up and running."

"And I'm saying it's good to talk about those bumps. Ciao!" Loretta ended the call.

Cotler set the phone down carefully, intentionally, on the counter. He ran both hands through his hair.

Who stirs up drama on purpose? Life was already unpredictable and messy—what kind of person went looking for problems rather than solutions?

The same person who didn't show up to the meeting.

"Hello?" Pete called again, then he stuck his head into the kitchen. "Oh. I didn't know we were invited to dinner. Can I get the plates?"

Colter welcomed the older man, because getting mad that he'd shown up to a meeting he was invited to wouldn't do anyone any good.

He glanced at his daughter to share a smile at the unexpected turn of events, only to see the color drain out of Sylvie's face.

"Everything okay?" he asked.

Sylvie put on a brave smile and nodded. Everything was not okay, and it surely had to do with their dinner being invaded.

"That's an interesting outfit," Pete said, eyeing the conglomeration of fabric Sylvie had painstakingly put together for her first day.

Colter bristled. His daughter's outfit was indeed interesting, fascinating even. But he was not going to subject her to the judgment of a man who'd worn the same style of Wranglers for over five decades.

"I took my girls school shopping at N'Style in Klamath Falls," Raquel said.

Colter drew in a deep breath. The moms of this town had been dropping off-handed comments about his parenting since he'd rolled into Pronghorn. He knew they meant well, but it was hard not to take it personally. He thought his daughter was great. No, not just great. Some of her getups could be a little off the wall, but Sylvie was the best, smartest, most creative thirteen-year-old on the planet.

"Well, my girl makes a lot of her own clothes," Colter said, putting an arm around Sylvie.

Raquel seemed to recognize her mistake. She smiled at Sylvie, so it was clear she was judging Colter for allowing her out of the house that way, not Sylvie for being raised by someone who would do so. "That's great. What did you think of the first day?"

Sylvie croaked out a response. "Good."

"I was furious about the way the teachers handled the lockers. It was chaos."

Colter groaned inwardly, as Sylvie was protective of both the teachers *and* the lockers. Why couldn't Raquel get judgmental about the inspirational signage?

"Assigning lockers probably isn't something they cover in education programs," Colter said. "That's the type of detail normally handled by an administrator or office staff, neither of which they have."

Pete grumbled something about how they should have known better, then Today's Moment was at the door and asking Colter to cook the beef in a separate pan. Pete questioned the movement games Coach Tate had led, but his worries were drowned out by Today's Moment's concern about the science curriculum, and Raquel's general fear that none of the teachers really knew what they were doing in the first place.

Somewhere in the fray Sylvie said quietly, "I have a stomachache. I'm gonna go lay down." She slipped past him and headed to her room.

Colter abandoned his guests and followed Sylvie into the hall. "Are you okay?"

"I'm fine. It's just my stomach."

Colter was torn. His instincts told him to kick everyone out of the house. He needed to care for his daughter so she'd be well enough for school the next day. But if he wanted a school for her to be well enough to go to, he had to keep the board here so he could calm their fears.

Sylvie seemed to sense this and gave him a weary smile. "I'm pretty tired. It's been a big day."

"You weren't tired twenty minutes ago. Is it because Pete said something about your outfit?"

"What? No."

"Do you want to go shopping at N'Style in Klamath Falls?"

Sylvie rolled her eyes. "No one wants to go shopping at N'Style in Klamath Falls except for forty-year-old moms."

Colter laughed. *That* was his daughter.

"Thrift shopping in Outcrop, on the other hand…" Sylvie suggested with a hopeful rise of her eyebrows.

Colter kissed the top of her head. "Sounds like a good birthday present. Why don't you go lay down while I deal with the board. I'll bring you some dinner when it's ready."

"Maybe some toast?"

"Okay."

"Thanks, Dad. Make sure they know the teachers are really good."

He touched two fingers to his forehead in a salute, then headed back into the fray.

Colter managed to calm the board over the next hour. Today's Moment and Raquel both had kids in attendance, so it was likely they'd gotten a similar, positive report. Pete's grandchildren were at the school, and if he could ever get past wanting education to be exactly what it had been in *his day*, he'd see they'd gotten lucky with this crop of teachers. And Colter had to admit, feeding everyone did improve the mood.

But he was concerned with how quickly the other board members had taken Loretta's bait. That the community felt justified in judging the new teachers within the first twenty-four hours of the school's existence worried him.

And that they seemed to be judging his daughter made him furious, and nervous. He knew he was prickly when it came to people's commentary on Sylvie, but he'd done the best he could with her.

Question was, was his best enough?

CHAPTER SEVEN

WILLA PEEKED INTO Vander's classroom. His biology class of eight students were gathered around a model of the human heart, spellbound as he explained its functioning. Rather than paint his room in a mad dash along with the others, he'd begun to transform his yellow walls with a mural. A seascape slowly emerged from the back corner, and "Mr. V," as the kids called him, was always willing to pass out an extra paintbrush if a student or two wanted to stay after school and help him. Vander's tumbleweed had a prime position on the shelves lining the back wall, now joined by an unidentified amphibian fossil, an ever-growing collection of bird feathers, and a pronghorn skull, complete with horns.

She stepped back into the hall, then passed Mateo's room. Warm pools of light spread out from the table lamps he'd borrowed from spare rooms at the hotel. The desks were arranged in cozy pods where students worked, if not exactly together, at least near each other. Mateo sat next to Neveah. The pale, anxious-looking girl's brow was furrowed.

Mateo smiled easily, cracking a joke that brought some relaxation to her face before she returned to the problem. As she came up with the correct answer, her relieved smile was nearly hidden by the hair falling into her face.

A hum of chatter and negotiation spilled out of Luci's room, as it often did. The woman really did put the *social* in Social Studies. A quick peek through the door showed students moving from one table to the next, negotiating...something. It was a simulation Luci had taken hours to set up the previous two evenings, and now the kids breezed through, no idea how much they were learning as they engaged in the activity.

Willa slipped around the corner and looked up and down the hall to make sure no one was watching. She allowed herself a brief, stealthy jump of sheer joy, whisper-yelling, "Yes!"

Then she brushed her hair back and continued her walk down the hall.

Five days in, and their school was working.

It wasn't perfect. There were still a lot of little things cropping up, most of those being procedural issues they hadn't known would be among their responsibilities in the first place. But they could handle the details.

The only problem she was truly worried about was student socialization. The kids still weren't interacting easily with each other, or interacting at all unless an adult was facilitating the conversation.

Willa kept up her pace toward the main office. It

was her administrative prep period and she'd been assigned the job of responding to parent emails, which were abundant. But the internet, which had briefly sputtered to life Monday, had been out for the last two days. Today she'd sweep the main hall since there was no janitorial staff, then help set up for lunch. Tate had the job of planning menus. They had a big supply of USDA foods, along with a random smattering of supplies from The Restaurant.

Day one had been a sandwich bar, the next day a salad bar, then a tater tot bar, followed by a noodle bowl bar.

Okay, there were a lot of bars.

But Tate explained that between the vegetarians from the Open Hearts community, the allergies some students suffered, and the general preferences of kids, choice of toppings made sense. He had an extra prep period, since he started the day with everyone in PE, so he used that time to make lunch until they could find some parent volunteers.

At the last board meeting, when Willa had asked if they knew anyone who might be willing to help with lunch, Today's Moment had responded enthusiastically. Two days ago several Lyfcycles from the Open Hearts community had showed up at the double doors leading into the cafeteria. Tate was thrilled, until he saw what they were towing, at which point everyone was just baffled. The orange-clad parents flooded the cafeteria with flowers. Not any old flowers but big, expensive-looking bouquets of roses, snapdragons and peonies: blooms that were not in season and did not seem likely to grow naturally among the sagebrush and prairie grass of Pronghorn. They made the cafeteria look like it was being set up for a Kentucky-derby-themed prom.

Colter might be able to explain it. Asking him wouldn't be breaking her compartmentalizing rule, right? In fact, utilizing Colter's knowledge about the community was a sign of progress. She was a professional doing her job, working with a colleague. A handsome, reckless colleague with the power to shatter her heart into a million pieces, but still a coworker of sorts.

Willa clipped along the main hall, past Loretta's inspirational signage.

These Are Your Good Old Days.

She stilled.

These Are Your Good Old Days.

Willa had sacrificed her twenties to her heartache. She'd taken what should have been a fun, exploratory decade of her life and spent it wallowing in how Colter had done her wrong. But when she finally collected herself and moved forward, she'd learned from the experience. There would be no *good old days* unless she made them good.

That was what she wanted the kids to know. This was their time to explore, to connect with one another. The teenage years were brief but formative. She and the other teachers had to find ways to help these kids connect.

The front door opened. Willa glanced up to see

Colter's silhouette dark against the bright landscape beyond. She fought the impulse to skip over to him and share the news. *We did it! We made a school!*

But she kept her cool. Almost.

Okay, fine, she picked up her pace and called out, "Good morning!"

It was slipshod compartmentalization at best.

"Hey." Colter gave her a big smile, his pace quickening, too. Then he stopped an awkward two feet away because, yeah, they were heading for a collision. Or a hug.

Seriously, some days it felt like the only part of her anatomy that could remember they weren't teenagers was her frontal lobe, and it was napping on the job.

Colter grinned at her, as though he were having the same issue.

Time to remind both of them of the state of their relationship. "It's always nice to see a school board member on campus."

Her words seemed to jolt him back to earth. "Is it?" He tucked his hands in the back pockets of his jeans and glanced around. "I just stopped by," he said, somewhat unnecessarily because...duh.

"Great. Are you here to have lunch with Sylvie?"

"No," he said quickly. Nervously? "No. I imagine she'll want to have lunch with her friends."

The hope and concern in his voice echoed her own. No doubt Sylvie would want to have lunch with her friends, if she'd made any yet.

"Then what brings you in?" she asked.

"I stopped by to check on things."

Okay, he was definitely nervous. Colter had changed over the years, but hands in his pockets, glancing around, repeating himself? Something was up. "Anything I should be worried about?"

"No," he said, firmly. His gaze connected with hers, warm and powerful. "I don't want you to worry about anything. You keep doing what you're doing."

Willa attempted to stuff the balloon of emotion rising within her into a compartment labeled *"The school board president is just doing his job."*

It didn't fit.

"We've heard a few rumblings from the other school board members," she said.

"They're a rumbly group." He straightened, casting his glance back out the main doors. "I've got it under control."

"Thank you," she said. "They can rumble away while we teach."

He grinned. "Sounds like a plan. Sylvie is loving school. She can't stop talking about your class."

"She's doing great."

Colter's expression tightened. He started to speak, fumbled, then tried again, "Does she…is she making friends?"

Willa pressed her lips together, then told him the truth. "No one is making friends yet."

His expression fell. Willa reached out to comfort him, placing a hand on his forearm.

"Friendships will come," Willa said. "It's a lot

for these kids, returning to a structured, in-person day after several years online. We'll get there."

Colter kept his gaze on the floor between them, absently running his hand over hers. His touch felt so easy, so right, like snuggling into clean sheets on a summer's night.

Willa joined him in studying the floor, because if she wasn't looking at their hands, it meant they weren't touching, right?

"Sylvie will make friends," she promised. "Everything takes time."

He exhaled, closing his eyes briefly, then finally seemed to realize he was trying to interlace his fingers with hers. He stepped back, refocusing on the wall behind her. A wry smile spread across Colter's face, and he pointed.

Willa couldn't figure out what he was grinning about.

Until she realized she was still staring at his smile, rather than the item he found amusing.

All Good Things Take Time.

She laughed. "Exactly. Truer words were never written decoratively on a piece of distressed plywood."

Colter chuckled, the familiar sound and expression sparking a kaleidoscope of memories in her belly. The sheer joy of making him laugh made her want to laugh, too. Long before they started dating and she had what felt like a hopeless crush on her brother's friend, Willa had carefully plotted out ways to get his attention without making her crush too obvious. When he came to family dinners, she'd monitor the conversation, choosing just the right moment to make a joke. When he turned his brilliant gaze on her, or laughed at something she said, it felt like winning every conceivable lottery, all at the same time.

"Colter!" Tate waved as he trotted down the hall. "How's it going?"

"Good." Colter tucked his hands back in his pockets, then looked around. "How are you?"

"I'm heading in to fix lunch. Wanna help out?"

"I…uh…sure."

Colter clearly had some other business to attend to. She tried to give him an out by saying, "I'm sending Mason in to help you today."

"Mason?" Tate pulled his head back. "I kicked the kid out of class this morning for being disrespectful and refusing to participate."

"Right."

"I don't want his help. The kid was giving me a headache all morning."

"Lunch duty is his punishment for misbehaving in your class."

"Says who?"

"Me?"

"Okay, obviously. But why do I have to deal with him?"

"He has to have some consequences. Mason didn't want to be in PE, so he misbehaved and got out of PE. This way he'll miss the end of math class, which he's good at, then have to finish his lunch period cleaning up. You have a better idea?"

Tate crossed his arms and studied the ceiling. Then he wobbled his head. "That's about all we got, isn't it? Lunch duty."

"It was all I could think of at the time."

"That's fair." He picked up his pace and headed on toward the kitchen. "Another perk of small schools, right? See ya in the kitchen!"

Colter gave an impressed nod. "That was well done."

"Tate's reasonable. And Mason's a headache, but he'll settle down."

"Just like his momma, Angie."

Willa smiled. He smiled back.

It all felt way too familiar. And good.

Time to get moving.

"So, I actually do need to help Tate set up lunch." She gestured with her thumb, as though she might be hitchhiking to the kitchen. Then she repeated the action, just in case he hadn't realized how foolish she looked the first time around.

Colter pulled in a long breath, like he needed to say something. Then he shook his head. "I'll help. You can catch me up on what's been going on around here."

WELP, HE'D COMPLETELY botched his mission at the school, but what else was new?

He'd come here to have a serious conversation with Willa about the concerns of the board, and the community at large. While he got daily enthusiastic reports from Sylvie, he also fielded nightly calls from Pete, Today's Moment, Raquel and others.

When are fall sports going to start?

Is the science guy going to offer Advanced Placement classes?

Why can't I see my kids' grades online?

Why is everyone concerned about sports, but no one's talking about a music program?

When are they going to post the curriculum online?

Why can't I get the head teacher to answer my emails?

Colter responded to nearly every question with one of two answers, often both: "They're less than a week into the school year," and "The internet's been real spotty."

He advised all callers to give the new school a month. Wait and see how things shook out after everyone had a chance to settle in. Bombarding the teachers with requests to do more, when they were already doing so much, didn't seem like the best approach.

What he hadn't counted on was that when a community rallied to fund a school with money from their own pockets, they saw themselves more as shareholders than supporters.

Not that there weren't plenty of offers to volunteer. But all of those offers were highly specific, and generally came with ulterior motives.

"I'd like to help out in Ms. Walker's Social Stud-

ies class," meant *"I want to see what that young firecracker is teaching my kids about history."*

"I'm volunteering to be an assistant volley-ball coach," meant *"Where's the volleyball team? I've been waiting three years for my kid to get the chance to play my favorite sport."*

Most of the offers of help, though, came from a more desperate place of wanting to keep an eye on their kids in this new situation. Colter got it. It had been hard to watch his daughter negotiate this new realm. He worried pretty much from the time she got out of the truck until she got back in it at the end of the school day.

But his job as board president was to mediate between the teachers and the board. One look at Willa and he'd gone from mediator to loyal defender in a beat of his own traitorous heart.

Did she really need to know about all the drama brewing in the community? She was so excited about school. From everything Sylvie said, things were going great.

Colter followed Willa into the kitchen, accepted a cutting board and knife from Tate, who proceeded to manage a sullen teen, a brilliant English teacher and a misguided rancher into creating lunch for thirty. The concerns of the board could wait.

At some point Tate allowed Mason to play music on his phone. The kid grumbled about the punishment but got comfortable in the kitchen atmosphere pretty quickly. The four of them set out dishes, warmed up foods and set out a buffet of items for the kids to choose from. Colter had to admit the rice bowl bar looked pretty good, definitely more appetizing than what he remembered from his school cafeteria back in the day.

"Good work," Tate said to Mason as they finished up.

Mason shrugged.

"And next week, you need to participate in PE. Even if it's only walking laps, it's good for you, gets your brain ready for the school day."

Mason glowered at Tate. The kid had been pretty pleasant, even seemed to be having fun, until PE was mentioned.

Tate continued, "You don't want to get stuck on lunch duty again."

"I'd rather have lunch duty than PE," the kid mumbled.

Tate looked at Willa, concern evident on his face. Some communication seemed to pass between them. Willa nodded briefly, and Tate, rather than get angry, said, "I think we can figure something out. Let's get out into the cafeteria. I need your help serving."

The confident teacher led the way through the swinging double doors into the lunchroom.

"What was that about?" Colter asked.

"Mason's having a hard time with the mandatory morning PE," Willa explained. "It's a great idea in theory, but there are a number of kids who are pretty uncomfortable in their bodies."

"I don't get it."

"I wouldn't expect you to. You're an athlete. You've always seen your body as a tool to get you where you need to go, so you take care of yourself."

It took pretty much all of Colter's limited self-control to keep from casually flexing in response to Willa's observation.

"These kids haven't had sports or any structured activity in three years. Some kids work with their parents on a ranch, like Sylvie does. The kids from Open Hearts get a lot of physical activity. But most of the students are uncomfortable with activity, while at the same time they're inundated with social media telling them they need to have perfect bodies and mad sports skills. Upon reflection, we should have figured out a way to ease them into physical activity, rather than have it be the first thing they face every day."

Colter stared at Willa. "I'm impressed," he finally managed. "Not everyone is willing to pivot when a decision doesn't work out."

But the board wouldn't be thrilled. Pete was upset because he'd been told there'd be fall sports and so far, there was just some *"Mickey Mouse walking class"* at the start of the day. Colter tried to explain that a full football team really wasn't in the realm of possibility this year, but it had been hard to get a word in edgewise. As Willa spoke, Colter realized they were much farther from team sports than he'd imagined.

She picked up a cutting board and carried it to the sink. "Tate's on a mission to make everyone feel comfortable with some kind of physical activity. He'll make it work." She turned around and gave him a grin. "But yeah, five new teachers with no practical experience made one mistake in setting up their school. Other than that, we're perfect, right?"

She was perfect all right. Smart, brave, humble, and getting more beautiful by the minute. This would be the time for Colter to tell her about the board's concerns. She knew problems would crop up; she was amenable to feedback.

Colter opened his mouth to tell her about Today's Moment. She was furious, or as furious as a spokesperson from the Open Hearts community could get in public, because Vander was teaching about the human heart without sending opt-out emails for the kids at the commune. Then he'd start in with Raquel's nitpicky list of things she noticed "as a former teacher," from concerns about the brand of hand sanitizer they used to the lack of unity in the way teachers had students write their names at the top of their assignments.

But instead, he stared into Willa's pretty, violet eyes and said, "We all make mistakes."

She held his gaze. The professional veneer slipped and he could see the wash of emotion in her expression.

Then she turned her back to him and busied herself gathering up dishes.

"The kids have a full fifty minutes for lunch," Willa said, depositing them in the sink and turning on the water. "Because Mrs. Moran is only teaching in the afternoons, she supervises lunch, which flows into a study hall." Colter took slow, measured steps to join Willa at the sink. He took a clean pan from her hands and rinsed it as she kept talking. "Most days Mateo, Luci, Vander, Tate and I head across the street and have lunch at the hotel. It's a nice break, and Luci is really big on making sure we all take breaks."

"Sounds smart."

She smiled, if not directly at him, at the dishes they were washing together. "This job can get pretty intense. Not unlike the rodeo."

He chuckled. "But I only had to stay on for eight seconds."

"That's about how long the school day feels, with so much going on." Willa finally looked at him, point-blank asking, "What are you doing here today?"

Colter drew in a breath. He couldn't bring himself to tell just yet. Instead, he asked, "Have there been any…problems?"

She froze, as though he'd tapped into something big.

Okay, so maybe she did know about the board's concerns.

"How much has Sylvie told you about the non-academic school day?"

"Like lunch?"

"Lunch, morning break, elective hour."

A frisson of fear shimmied down his spine and she confirmed his suspicions. "Almost nothing."

"I'm really worried." She shook her head. "The kids are doing fine in classes. I can't tell you how great it is to teach such small groups. Everyone gets all the attention they need, and we can remediate for kids in the moment, or tweak an assignment for someone who is ready for more of a challenge. In that way a small school is optimal."

"But…?"

"But the kids don't know how to be around other kids. They're not interacting with each other."

His concern intensified. This was why he'd been so desperate for a school in the first place. Sylvie was a good student and could learn everything she needed from the dullest packet sent home. What she needed were friends.

"I gotta say, to me, that's the most important thing."

"It's essential. So far, the kids are connecting with their teachers, but they struggle to open up with one another."

Colter closed his eyes briefly. He needed to hear this. "How bad is it?"

"Come with me."

Willa took off the apron and hung it next to the door. Colter followed her into the lunchroom. It looked like all thirty kids were present, but the room was less than a third full and practically silent. The students were spread out, some long tables holding only one or two kids. In some cases siblings sat together, and there was a small cluster of kids from the commune.

Nearly every kid had a phone out and was staring at it. Those who weren't looking at phones had books or homework out.

"This is *not* how I remember a school cafeteria."

He gazed around the room until his eyes landed on Sylvie, wearing his old plaid jacket, the cuffs dripping past her wrists as she took a sporkful of her rice bowl. His heart constricted at the loneliness of his daughter, at this room full of lonely kids.

His instinct was to fight. "Can't we take their phones away? I've read the studies on social media. It's addictive—"

Willa placed a hand on his arm. Arguably, also addictive.

"That's part of what makes this so unsettling. The internet isn't even on right now. They're not staring at anything new."

A lump rose in his throat. This was so much worse than he'd thought.

"Staring at a phone is like putting your head under a blanket. Everyone understands it as a universal symbol of 'don't talk to me,'" Willa said. "They don't know how to interact."

Colter took a decisive step toward his daughter, intent on confiscating her phone. Willa's hand tightened on his arm and held him back.

"There's no simple fix."

"I think taking her phone away is pretty simple."

"Then she stares at a book, or a reading from class. I grant you that's better, but what we really want is for all these kids to be sitting together and talking."

"They have to talk some, right? Like in class?"

"We've figured out ways to make it safe for kids to participate in class. But they don't have the ebb and flow it takes to be social in a setting like this. When we planned the long lunch, we imagined the kids eating together, then hanging out here, or outside. Instead, they just finish their lunches and wander into the study hall."

"They never talk?"

"We've had a couple of mild altercations, the occasional polite comment, but no chatter."

Colter stared out at the kids. *This* was why Sylvie wasn't talking about friends. The heavy quiet of the cafeteria felt stressful, oppressive.

"But some of these kids know each other." He gestured to Raquel's girls. "Taylor and Morgan hang out with June because their moms are friends. The kids from Open Hearts have known each other since they were born. Why aren't they talking?"

"It's different when they're all together. I'm guessing Taylor, Morgan and June have well-established patterns, but those fly out the window when other kids are thrown into the mix. School adds pressure on top of that."

"We weren't like this in school."

"The world has changed substantially. It's natural for teenagers to fear the judgment of their peers, that's not new, but that fear has intensified along with the fishbowl of social media. These kids second-guess everything they might say or do and feel judged even when no one notices them. Add in three years of online school, and this isn't much of a surprise. I'm just glad we haven't had any arguments today."

Colter hadn't thought about the added pressure of the internet. He'd done his best to connect Sylvie with other kids, but the parent-arranged social gatherings were always awkward. Sylvie felt at ease with her teachers because they were literally professionals when it came to connecting with kids.

"The tensions between different factions in this community probably doesn't make it any better," he muttered.

"It does not," she agreed.

A metal bench squeaked softly as Oliver Sorel stood and picked up his tray. The kid tried not to draw attention to himself as he headed to the lunch counter. He glanced at a group of kids from the commune, eating together in silence as he passed by.

"What'd you say?" Mav asked. The phrase was defensive and pure Mav, though he had to clear his throat first because he hadn't spoken in a while.

Oliver turned around, bewildered. "What?"

"You said something."

The kid furrowed his brow, looking exactly like his grandfather Pete. "I didn't say anything. I'm just going back for seconds."

"You were staring at my shirt."

Oliver rolled his eyes. "It's *orange*."

Mav stood, his anger catching. "I'm sick of being stared at all the time."

"What if I'm sick of having my eyes assaulted by bright orange?"

The confrontation seemed forced, as though both boys knew their communities weren't supposed to get along and they were doing their part. Colter took a step toward them, but Willa held him back, saying, "Let me get Luci."

"Why does this place have to cater to a bunch of meat eaters, anyway?" Mav asked.

Oliver dropped his tray on Mav's table. "If you don't like the way things are done in Pronghorn, you can leave. Go back to Mars, or *California*, or wherever you're from."

Mav took a step into Oliver's space.

Colter might not know anything about education, teen isolation, or what had or hadn't been said about Mav's shirt, but two hotheads getting into a fight? That was his wheelhouse.

Colter jumped out of Willa's reach and ran in between the two boys. He knew from experience that this was a good way to get hit, but better him than one of the students.

He dropped a hand on each of the boy's shoulders.

"He started it," Mav accused as Oliver said, "I wasn't doing anything." The frustration and confusion on their faces was palpable. They didn't know how to handle this any better than the adults in this town.

"Unless both of you want to be bucking hay all fall out at my place, I suggest you drop it."

Mav gave his best glower, but the fierce look was tempered by the relief in his expression. Oliver crossed his arms tightly and stared at the floor.

"Mav, you've got to stop thinking everyone in this school is out to get you. Your teachers put in a lot of hard work. Oliver, a quarter of the people around here have been wearing orange since before you were born. Don't make a big deal out of it."

Colter glanced over his shoulder to see Willa watching him. She had a healthy dose of *"What are you doing!?"* in her eye, tempered with *"But I guess it's working, isn't it?"*

He was familiar with the look, and before he could stop himself, responded with a wink, asking, "Cleanup duty for these two?"

She nodded, the glimmer of a smile in her expression.

Willa was right, these kids didn't know how to be together. And the contention between the adults in their lives was not helping. The school board had a host of demands, but as far as he could see, what the school really needed was the community's unwavering support.

CHAPTER EIGHT

WILLA AWOKE TO light streaming through the window. She readjusted herself in the cloud of soft white bedding. Curtains fluttered on the cool morning breeze, and the pale pink walls glowed in the morning sunshine. Anticipation warmed her as she stretched, propping her head up against the pillows.

Why did she feel so good?

Willa pulled her phone off the bedside table and glanced at the date and time.

It was Saturday!

She sat straight up like it was Christmas morning and threw off the covers. Saturday! They'd made it through five days and now she had two whole glorious days off. Two days where she didn't have to be in charge, or know the answer, or worry about how the cafeteria was going to play out.

She popped out of bed and walked over to the open window. Outside, the town was stirring ever so slightly. Tate was doing a workout on the field behind the school, the sheriff watching with suspicion as she and her dog headed to the store. Angie was setting her illegible sandwich board in front of The Restaurant.

Willa pulled on a pair of jeans and a T-shirt, then headed downstairs. She might do something wild and crazy today, like spend the entire morning reading a book in the courtyard. Or take a long, slow walk. The possibilities were endless.

Admittedly tame, but endless.

"Good morning," Luci called as Willa made her way into the industrial kitchen of the hotel, following the scent of warm cookies and Folgers instant coffee. "Have you recovered from the rager we threw last night?"

The rager had consisted of the five of them sprawled out in the hotel lobby, watching the hedgehogs explore the room. At some point Mateo had got an internet signal and decided to watch *Madagascar*. And by watch, that meant fall asleep to, in Willa's case.

"I slept for eleven hours last night," Willa said.

"You earned it," Luci said. "I slept until seven, which is very late for me."

Willa wasn't at all surprised to see Luci up, showered, dressed impeccably, and industrious in the kitchen. Sure, she occasionally checked on the box of sleeping hedgehogs, but other than that, the behavior was totally on brand.

Luci pulled a tray out of the oven.

"Are you making cookies?" Willa asked. "I mean, obviously, you're making cookies. I guess I'm asking, where did you get the ingredients?"

Willa grabbed a hotel cup and saucer set and made her way to the jar of instant coffee. "I'm also asking if I can have cookies for breakfast."

Luci laughed. "I guess since it's the weekend I won't bug everyone about routines. But just sayin', you should have some protein, too."

"There's eggs in the cookies, right?" Willa stirred milk and sugar into her coffee, making a surprisingly drinkable beverage, then grabbed an oatmeal cookie off the cooling rack.

This was literally the best morning.

Yes, next week would be as hard as this one. Yes, they had mountains of work to do. Yes, she was still stuck in a tiny town with the man who'd broken her heart. But right now, she had cookies and coffee and the entire day ahead of her.

"Did you get the ingredients at the store?"

Luci delivered her with a dry look. "Oatmeal? At the store? No." She pulled a second tray of cookies from the oven and set them on the counter. "Colter dropped them off."

Willa choked on her cookie. She set the treat down on her saucer and cleared her throat. "Colter?"

"Yes, and I have you to thank for it. Apparently, you told him I always insist on cookies after lunch. He figured the selection of travel packs at the store might get old, so he and Sylvie dropped off everything they thought I might need to bake."

"That's so—" *sweet, thoughtful, adorable* "cool. They came this morning?"

"No, last night. You were asleep."

Willa closed her eyes briefly, imagining what she looked like passed out on the sofa, hair plastered to her face, mouth hanging open while *Madagascar* played in the background. Not the powerful, independent teacher image she hoped to portray.

"It was sweet. Sylvie had put everything together in a basket, and was really excited to show me what she'd brought. And you know how Colter has this way of like, doing things before he's thought them out? Like he just reacts to a situation."

Willa nodded. Yeah, she'd noticed.

"So when he sees you sleeping, he strides into the room and without even pausing in conversation he picked up a blanket and tucked it around you. Like that's just what the board president does, tucks in exhausted teachers while dropping off baking supplies. He's so great."

And what compartment does that go into?

Willa changed the subject. "Why *do* you insist on cookies after lunch? You have my full support, naturally. But I'm so impressed by the way you stick to your civilized routines. I always feel like I'm barely keeping my head above the water. You remind us that the details matter."

Luci paused, as though she was weighing her words.

"In my life, I've come to appreciate structure. I can't predict what others will do or say, or what crisis will pop up next. But I can control my habits. A cookie and tea after lunch is a powerful signal to myself. I matter. I am worthy of small delights on a daily basis. Taking time with my appearance, scheduling time for pleasure in this unpredictable life helps me find balance." Her expression flipped from serious to irreverent as she said, "And why wouldn't I want cookies after lunch? What's even the point of lunch if there are no cookies?"

Willa laughed, even as she sensed there was something deeper in Luci's adherence to structure.

"Well, I for one can use your routines. I appreciate your insistence on them."

As though on cue, Mateo wandered into the kitchen. His hair was sticking up at the back, and he wore the same T-shirt he had on from the day before. "Hey. 'Mornin."

"Good morning," Willa said. Luci busied herself with the cookie dough. It looked as though she was still smarting from the argument she and Mateo had had the day before about excusing kids from class early and/or late. Mateo tended to keep the kids until they'd learned the concept at hand, and the clock didn't figure into his dismissal policies.

"Do we have any soup leftover from last night?"

"Tomato soup is not breakfast," Luci said.

Mateo opened the massive, mostly empty fridge. "It is if I eat it for breakfast."

"Leftover soup is no way to start the day."

"It's no way to end the day, either, but until we can get into Lakeview to buy some groceries, we're stuck with it."

Willa had only spent two weeks with Luci and

Mateo, but she had a pretty good idea where this conversation was going. She finished off her last sip of coffee. "Speaking of shopping, I'm heading to the store to grab a few postcards. I figure if I can't text my family regularly, I'll send some actual mail."

"That's a fun idea," Mateo said. "My niece would love a postcard."

"I'll pick some up for you. Luci?"

Luci used a spatula to lift cookies from the tray and set them on a cooling rack.

"Luci, can I grab you some postcards to send to family?"

"No, thanks," she replied. "But see if they have a can of breakfast soup for Mateo here."

"Breakfast is nothing more than a construct—"

Willa slipped from the room before the argument about food consumed prior to 11 a.m. could go any further. She strode through the dining room and into the courtyard. Vander sat in a wrought iron chair, playing a slow, soulful melody on his guitar. He nodded to Willa as she passed through, smiling but not taking a break from the music.

Willa exited onto the street. Since it was Saturday, Connie was stretched out flat on the pavement napping, rather than sitting up watching the comings and goings of the school.

Sunshine washed through the town, making it more quaint than bleak. Willa's heart lifted. Saturday at the end of the first week of school felt incredible, like she'd been banging a cast-iron skillet against her head all week long, then stopped.

"Willa Marshall."

She glanced up to see Raquel barreling down the street toward her, hand held up in something that could be a wave, or a signal to stop.

"Raquel—"

"Heading into work?" Raquel asked.

"Uh…no I was going—"

"I always worked weekends when *I* was teaching."

Willa's smile dropped. She'd worked harder during the last two weeks than she thought possible. Was one day off too much to ask?

"I cared about my students."

Apparently, it was.

"What subject did you teach again?" Willa asked, expecting her to say something like astrophysics, which would, indeed, demand more outside prep time.

Raquel ignored the question. "Now, I know you've been getting a lot of flak from the other parents, but I wanted to let you know I'm here to support you."

Flak? Willa hadn't heard a peep out of any parent other than Colter. Were people complaining?

She thought back to Colter's visit the day before. He'd been decidedly nervous. What was he not telling her?

On the other hand, Raquel was on point with the judgy statements and backhanded compliments. Despite all the teaching experience she claimed to have, and all the support she purported to give, she was a serious busybody.

Willa glanced up at the blue sky overhead, the

ANNA GRACE 169

cool, easy feeling of Saturday dissipating. The question was, were other parents honestly upset, or was Raquel just looking to stir up drama? Both?

"I'm on your side," Raquel said. The phrase rested between them, Willa unwilling to pick it up and Raquel determined that she would.

"You can count on me." Raquel leaned in, as though this fact were best kept a secret. "If you want advice or for me to run interference with the other parents, I'm always available."

The parent she needed help dealing with was standing right in front of her. Willa met Raquel's gaze and summoned all her strength not to let the woman's words sap her confidence. Which was probably why she didn't notice a truck barreling down Main Street, swerving around Connie, and parking haphazardly along the curb.

"Willa! Raquel. What's going on?"

Willa looked up to see the man who was arguably her most problematic parent climbing out of his truck. Yeah, if Raquel was willing to run interference on her behalf, Colter was the one she needed help with.

COLTER SLAMMED HIS truck door and ran over to Willa and Raquel. He'd been clear with the board: *he* would take on the job of communicating any concerns or discontent with the teachers.

Not that the board was under any obligation to do as he said. Also, he'd done a terrible job communicating their concerns.

When he and Sylvie had dropped by the hotel the night before with cookie supplies, he'd thought maybe he'd sneak off with Willa for a few minutes. He could tell her about the phone calls he'd been getting. They'd laugh at the community's unreasonable demands, and she'd come up with one of her perfect, Willa solutions to the whole situation.

And sure, he'd also imagined her forgiving him for cheating on her and not being honest fourteen years earlier, and then smiling at him again the way she used to. But he was clear on what part of the whole imaginative experience was hope, and what part was wishful thinking.

When he'd arrived, he'd found the teachers exhausted, sprawled out on the antique furniture in the hotel lobby, watching a kids' movie. Willa was fast asleep, curled up in a wingback chair. She looked so peaceful, but still powerful, like a napping jaguar.

And from the look of the current situation, Raquel was getting into the jaguar's space and spewing some nonsense about being on Willa's side in all this. He might have done a bad job explaining the community's concerns to the teachers, but what Raquel would make up and exaggerate was considerably worse.

"Good morning," he said, like he always swerved to the side of the road and joined in on random conversations.

Willa nodded to him, her neutral look firmly in place. Not too happy, not too surprised, just appropriately pleased to greet the school board president on a Saturday morning after he'd hurled himself from his truck to protect her from the town gossip.

"Good morning, Colter," Raquel said. "How's Sylvie feeling? Did her stomachache go away?"

Colter bristled. Sylvie's stomachache had gone away as soon as the board vacated his house Monday evening, but she hadn't been feeling great Thursday or Friday. He'd had to coax her into school Friday morning, but once the day was over, she was home packing up baking goods to take to the teachers.

"She's doing great."

"Wonderful. And please don't hesitate if you need help. Girls sometimes just need a mom."

Some combination of what he logically understood as insecurity and fear washed through him, but his physiological reaction was all anger. He took a step toward Raquel, ready to defend his daughter's right to an upset stomach without getting called out for *his* lack of a wife.

Willa seemed to sense his frustration, shifting slightly so she blocked his advance, "Sylvie did amazing work in class this week." She smiled at Raquel. "Taylor and Morgan are delightful students, too. Overall, I'm really impressed with the progress everyone has made so far."

Raquel ignored her, saying to Colter, "And Sylvie's always welcome to tag along the next time we make a trip to N'Style."

This time it was pure anger bubbling up inside

him. Sylvie was fine. She liked the clothes she created, even if no one else around here did. Colter clamped his mouth shut before he could tell Raquel that N'Style was for forty-year-old moms.

Because, of course, Raquel was a forty-year-old mom and probably wouldn't find it much of an issue.

Willa stepped in again, patient and undisturbed. "Raquel mentioned there have been a few parents with concerns about the school. Is this something we should discuss with the board?"

Colter used the same look on Raquel as he did when one of his rescue horses hadn't yet figured out who was in charge at C & S Ranch.

"I know you have so much to do," Raquel said. "I wouldn't want to call extra meetings to take away from your planning and prep time." She turned to Colter. "I was a little surprised to hear Willa wasn't heading into the school this morning. When I taught, I *always* worked weekends."

"Right," Colter put his hands on his hips and glanced down at the cracks in the sidewalk. He'd used up all his patience with Raquel for the week, possibly the year. "And you taught part-time in Bend for—was it one year or two?"

Color rushed up Raquel's neck. Colter continued, "And that was sixteen years ago, correct? I imagine things have changed a bit since then."

Raquel started sputtering out excuses, and Colter knew he needed to back off. Then again, so did Raquel. "Do you have a degree in education?

Or was that job a temporary thing? Because Willa and the other teachers have all prepared for this, so I imagine the need to work on weekends isn't as great. And even if they have extra work to do, I'd rather see them taking a few days to rest up before they get in there and do it all over again."

Raquel was now livid. She was so angry she couldn't speak, which was really saying something.

Maybe he shouldn't have exposed her in this way, but he wasn't going to see a woman who'd fallen asleep at eight o'clock on a Friday night be bullied back into her classroom on her day off.

He glanced sideways at Willa, his mood lifting as he saw the effort it was taking her not to laugh.

"Teaching has always been a challenge," Willa said generously. "And working part-time has its own ups and downs, like any job."

Raquel glanced at Willa with something close to gratitude for her grace in the situation. Raquel liked to be the Queen Bee, and her strategy had always been to make others feel like drones. If she was going to work with Willa, she'd need to learn that wasn't going to fly.

"Well, I'll let you get on with your Saturday. As I said at the start of our conversation—" she gave Colter a look, reminding him he hadn't been there for the beginning "—you can count on me for support, Willa. Colter can fill you in on what the others were saying." With that Raquel nodded, then disappeared into The Restaurant, no doubt on her way to repeat her version of the conversation to anyone willing to brave Angie's breakfast offerings.

With Raquel off the street, Colter and Willa were the only two out on this Saturday. Willa quirked an eyebrow. Colter steeled himself for her wrath at not telling her about the board's concern, but she just said, "She seriously only taught part-time for one year?"

"I think it was at an experimental arts elementary school."

Willa let out a breath and shook her head. "Wow."

"Maybe I shouldn't have called her out in front of you?"

She gave him a wicked grin. "Maybe I should have been working in my classroom by six a.m.?"

He laughed. Willa's reaction to his laugh was interesting. She reddened slightly, then looked away and resumed her walk. Colter caught up and matched his strides to hers.

"She means well," Colter continued. "She's annoying and always trying to tell everyone what to do, but she means well."

"I think most people mean well. And this situation is tricky." She glanced up at him, then out at the empty town. "Thank you. I don't know where that conversation was going and I'm glad I didn't have to find out."

She brushed her bangs off her forehead, then slipped her hands into her jeans pockets. She wore a University of Oregon T-shirt and sneakers. The simple outfit and lack of makeup somehow amplified her confidence, like she didn't need to impress anyone. But she was impressing him all the same.

"Where are you headed?" he asked.

She gestured to the store. "I'm picking up post-cards to send to the family."

Colter's heart stuttered at the mention of her family. "You gonna tell them I'm here?"

"I already did."

Colter felt the sidewalk shift beneath his feet, as though the cement had been replaced with knee-deep mud.

Willa continued casually, "Mom says hi."

Colter caught her eye. She didn't look away. The tiny word of greeting from Mrs. Marshall felt like a bar of stability in a world where he couldn't find footing. If Mrs. Marshall could forgive him enough to offer a one-syllable greeting, what did that mean for the rest of the family?

Probably nothing more than what he already knew: Willa was willing to work with him, and Mrs. Marshall was a kind and forgiving person.

But Mr. Marshall? And Holden? They probably had a heck of a lot more to say than "hi."

Willa dropped her gaze. "So, Raquel mentioned that a lot of parents have been unhappy. Is she exaggerating or is there something we need to discuss?"

Colter gave himself a mental slap. There were more important things going down around here than his feelings. "Well—" He took a long moment to consider the correct way of starting this conversation. He didn't need to be running off at the mouth again.

"Ouch. The pause says it all."

"It's not that bad." Or it *shouldn't* be that bad.

She crossed her arms and looked up at the sky like she was trying to hold back emotion. "I'm just surprised. The week felt pretty good on our end. I mean, not without its hiccups, but we feel like we've done some good work. I know the social situation still isn't optimal."

"Willa, the school is fantastic. You all are exceptional."

"Then the parents are complaining about—what exactly?"

Everything would be the answer there, but Colter wasn't going to lay their concerns on her shoulders. He truly believed that if everyone just sat back and let this school get rolling the kinks would work themselves out.

He scrambled for something that was close to the truth but that wouldn't ruin Willa's Saturday. "Pete is still hoping you'll offer fall sports."

Willa furrowed her brow. "Sports may take a while. As of right now there aren't a lot of kids interested. But Tate looked into it, and the league is pretty flexible. If interest emerges, we can register a team after the start of regular season."

"Oh. Well, great. I'll tell Pete."

He could already predict Pete's response, something along the lines of how are the kids supposed to know they're interested if the teams don't exist?

Upon reaching the store, Colter took a few steps ahead and opened the door, gesturing for Willa to enter. All conversation inside Mac's ceased as Willa walked inside. She paused on the threshold, the three other patrons and Mac staring at her as though she was a rock star with a wild reputation.

"What else?" she asked, unaware of the attention she was drawing.

"Not much." Or not much he was going to tell her about here, with four curious Pronghornians listening in.

Willa picked up a can of soup, examined the ingredients, then set it back on the shelf. "There has to be something else."

"Just a few curriculum questions." Like a million, and most of them from a furious Today's Moment, who'd accused Vander and Mateo of "wooing the emerging adults to normalcy."

Her eyes lit up. "We should have a curriculum night. We could invite families to see what we're doing. Do you think that would help?"

Colter had been distracted by her bright eyes, and it took a minute for her words to get through his thick skull. "Yeah. Yes. That'd be great. That's exactly what the board had in mind."

To be fair, the board had proposed something more on the lines of *"Let's grab torches and surround the school until those teachers let us look at the curriculum,"* rather than the civilized evening of discussion Willa was suggesting. But this would do the trick.

"Okay, then, let's get it on the books."

Willa came to a standstill at the dusty postcard rack. Colter had never understood why Mac sold postcards. It wasn't like they got a ton of tourists through here in the first place, and he didn't think people sent a lot of postcards these days. But the rack had been here as long as Colter had been in town, and was finally getting some attention. Willa selected cards efficiently, going for images of Hart Mountain, herds of pronghorn, panoramas of sagebrush and several unrealistically flattering pictures of the old hotel. She'd send them back to the family he'd naively assumed he'd be a part of one day.

But Willa didn't need him bringing up the past. She needed his help negotiating the future. Instinctively, he reached out, took two of the postcards from her hand and set them back on the rack.

"What are you doing?"

"It's time for Pronghorn boot camp. I'm gonna teach you how to fit in."

She laughed, encouraging him.

"For starters, you never stock up on anything in this store. You only come here for immediate needs."

"Is that so they don't run out of goods?"

"No, it's because people come to the store to chat and catch up on what's going on around town. If you stock up, it's seen as antisocial."

"Seriously?" Willa glanced around, just now noticing how much attention they were drawing. "So when Tate and Luci came in and bought eight cans of soup and two boxes of crackers—"

"—they were accused of not having any manners."

Willa clapped a hand over her mouth to keep from laughing, then leaned in close to him and whispered, "In the future, should at least one teacher stop by the store to pick up our evening soup and crackers once a day?"

"That would be best practice, yes."

"Okay then. Done." She set back three more postcards. "What else?"

"Don't bring undue attention to yourself."

"Undue attention?"

"Like, try to blend in. You want to be a solid, good citizen, but not too flashy. For example, if someone brings up my rodeo career, I downplay it and act like it was no big deal."

"Is that healthy? Downplaying your own accomplishments to try to fit in?"

"Probably not."

"Wait." She muttered in an undertone, "How does Loretta get away with being Loretta?"

He laughed out loud, breaking the very rule he was trying to teach her. "I think she's tolerated because she generates a lot of gossip."

"That's fair. Personally, no attention at all would be my dream." She glanced around at the other patrons. "I can't wait for the day when I stop being interesting to everyone in town."

Well, that's not gonna happen. She was always the most fascinating woman in the room as far as he was concerned.

"What's next?"

"You've learned most of the rules governing The Restaurant, but there are a few more unspoken expectations."

"Such as?"

"Most people stop in for a meal about once a week."

"People like Angie's food that much?"

"Oh no. No one really likes The Restaurant. But they want Angie to stay in business."

Willa furrowed her brow. "If they don't like it, why does it matter if she stays in business?"

"Because no one wants Angie to lose her livelihood."

"So people like Angie, rather than her food?"

"I didn't say that. Angie's hard to like."

Willa's laughter filled the small store, along with every crack in his weary heart. Without thinking Colter plucked the postcards from her hand and pulled out his wallet.

"I can buy my own postcards," she said.

"Generosity with newcomers." He winked. "That's another Pronghorn rule."

"Even newcomers without the sense to stop by the market once a day?"

He grinned at her, taking one step closer than was prudent given there were four people watching them carefully. His smile, tone and proximity to Willa were all in direct violation of the "don't bring undue attention to yourself" code. "Especially those newcomers."

CHAPTER NINE

CHATTER WAS STREAMING out of the school's kitchen when Willa poked her head in. Tate had music playing on his phone as three kids worked together to prepare lunch.

"Ms. Marshall, check it out!" Antithesis called, holding up a tray of artfully arranged chopped veggies.

"Beautiful."

"Look at mine." Greta held out a tray where she'd arranged her veggies to look like a rainbow.

"This is going to be a gorgeous lunch," Willa confirmed.

"You guys, keep chopping," Mason said. "Lunch starts in ten minutes."

"Who's got an eye on the tortillas?" Tate asked.

"I'm on it," Mason responded. "Greta, can you chop up one more pepper?"

"It'll mess up my rainbow."

Three kids, all working together in the kitchen, occasionally squabbling like normal teenagers. Who would have thought lunch duty was the answer to social anxiety?

Witnessing the tense, quiet cafeteria from Colter's point of had been eye-opening. The teachers couldn't *make* the kids be social. When they tried get-to-know-you games or icebreakers, the kids were on to them, clamming up in the face of adult-sponsored friendship. It was only by accident they'd discovered lunch and cleanup duty were surprising sources of connection. The first day, Mav and Oliver were both so mad about being sentenced to the chore they'd formed an alliance of sullen conversation in the kitchen. That conversation had led to the discovery of a mutual appreciation of chess, and dislike of arbitrary authority.

Mason, on the other hand, enjoyed the kitchen. So much so he'd asked to come back the next day. Tate had agreed to let him keep helping prepare lunch, but had brought in a couple of other students and allowed Mason to run the show so the kids had to talk to one another.

In the lunchroom itself, Luci had placed signs on half the cafeteria tables that just said *NO* in large letters. When kids took their trays to sit down, the only choices were four crowded tables. If anyone complained, which someone always did, they got cleanup duty and another opportunity to socialize.

And the big event of the week? Antithesis asked if she could start a creative writing club. She didn't have any potential members, but a club of one person was better than no clubs at all. The teachers had celebrated the small victory with dinner at The Restaurant, which they'd now committed to patron-

izing once a week. There, they'd run into a couple
of families and convinced two more kids to join
the club. Three kids in the same place at the same
time in Pronghorn was definitely a party.

Willa slipped out of the cafeteria. She had time
to answer a few emails before she and the other
teachers headed over to make their own lunches
at the hotel. The internet was randomly working
today. They'd done everything they could to figure
out the rhyme and reason of the fickle modem but
the thing seemed to have a mind of its own. It was
like the internet knew when it was well and truly
needed, and graced them with its presence accordingly. When it flipped on this time, Luci switched
up her lesson plan and had her kids working on a
research paper. Willa always tried to take advan-
tage of the internet to write back to parents.

Willa glanced out the front window at the sound
of hoofbeats. A horse and rider were galloping full
speed down Main Street, headed straight for Connie. The cat had survived several years of lounging
in the middle of the lonely highway, but the horse
was coming fast and Connie was intently cleaning her paw.

Willa's gaze skipped to the rider.

Oh. *Colter* was galloping full speed down Main
Street.

The man was born to ride. He handled animals
beautifully, somehow managing to stay in the saddle of the wildest horse, or get the most stubborn
one to run wherever he wanted. She'd analyzed the

reasons endlessly, coming up with a combination of physical strength, intuition, telepathic communication with the animal, and a completely unfounded, yet ultimately true, belief that he wasn't going to fall off.

Yeah, Colter Wayne, on a horse, recklessly heading toward her at top speed? Totally her catnip.

But this wasn't a rodeo, and he probably wasn't out for a fun ride down the center of town. Connie stood and stretched, not even annoyed. Willa glanced in the other direction to see Loretta Lazarus bustling down the street from the store. As Colter reached the school, Pete's truck pulled up.

Willa's heart began a slow, painful, plummet. It seemed to sink into her stomach, dragging everything it was attached to with it.

Colter swung out of the saddle as he maneuvered around Connie, already talking. Pete was red-faced and yelling. Colter tethered his horse to the railing, then raced up the steps to block the front door.

Today's Moment materialized and Loretta joined her on the steps, also red-faced, also shouting. When Raquel popped out of her Subaru, the entire board was assembled on the front steps, with Colter actively blocking the door.

This could not be good.

Willa stepped back from the window, weighing her options. Whatever was happening outside, her students did not need to see it. The problems they faced in the school were a mirror of the community, and the kids didn't need any indication that it was okay to shout and make demands. Priority number one was to keep the board away from the students.

The English teacher in her appreciated the irony, if not the reality of the situation.

As the lead teacher, she should go out and calmly discuss...whatever it was. What on earth could they be so upset about? She glanced back out the main window.

The argument had intensified, angry arm gestures now entering the fray.

Willa did not like conflict. She generally didn't see the need for arguments when reasonable discussion was an option. But she was shaping and directing her own life now, and she was willing to fight tooth, nail and any other calcium-rich appendage to salvage the social gains they'd made in the school.

Willa opened the front door.

"You can block the door all day long, cowboy—" Loretta was saying.

"Hi." Willa waved awkwardly. Everyone ignored her.

"—but I have a thing or two to say to those teachers."

"Hi," Willa said again.

"I'm calling an assembly." Loretta waved her bullhorn.

"Loretta, for the last time, let's meet this evening and talk it out before we make any more rash decisions," Colter said.

"I'll enter through the cafeteria to make my announcement." Loretta bustled down the steps and took off around the side of the building. The other board members followed like a group of angry, self-important ducklings.

Willa felt like she was stuck in a nightmare, one where she wanted to run but couldn't move her limbs. She looked at Colter, who seemed, for once, as panicked as she was.

"Announcement?" she asked.

"Very bad," was all Colter could get out.

On instinct she grabbed his hand, just as he said, "Through the school."

Colter and Willa ran through the main hall, into the kitchen, and burst into the lunchroom just as the other board members entered through the double doors at the back.

Thirty kids sat at four tables. One chess game was underway. The creative writing club sat together, if not talking, then at least writing together. Because the kids were all packed in next to one another, and in many cases actually talking, no one noticed the board members. It was beautiful. A week ago they were all sitting alone, staring at phones that didn't work. Today they were acting like normal teenagers, and ignoring the adults. Yay!

"May I have your attention please?"

Loretta didn't seem to find the lack of interest as exciting as Willa did.

Oliver looked up from his chess game with Mav. Antithesis glanced over but didn't set aside her pen. The rest of the writing club, both of them, followed suit. Mason gave Loretta a brief glance, then gave directions to kids wanting seconds.

"This school day is canceled, effective immediately."

That got their attention. Thirty young people all stopped eating and stared.

Mav, bless his heart, looked up suspiciously. "Why?"

Loretta Lazarus, bless her heart, didn't really have an answer, but kept talking anyway.

"The board has serious concerns about the education you are receiving at the hands of your teachers. We have tried to communicate with them repeatedly, but they refuse to make adjustments. We have a list of concerns the teachers are required to address before we open this building back up. If we open it up."

The words knocked the breath out of Willa's chest. They'd finally gotten the hang of things around here. Kids were talking to each other; classes were running smoothly. Sure, there were a few problems, but what school didn't have a few problems?

Strong, work-worn fingers laced between hers and gave her hand a squeeze.

Oh. Was she gripping the hand of her gorgeous ex-boyfriend, the school board president? He gave her a confident nod, then released her hand and stepped into the cafeteria.

"Hold up here, Loretta. I'm not sure we need to cancel school."

"I'm the principal of this school, and I say we need to shut down, now."

The kids exchanged confused glances.

"I thought Ms. Marshall was the principal," Mason said.

"They share principal," Antithesis said authoritatively.

"*I* am the principal, and I do it for free—"

"You get what you pay for..." Mateo muttered.

"I have volunteered countless hours to this endeavor, and I have serious concerns about where it is heading. Until these teachers make several serious improvements, classes are suspended."

"But the internet's working," Antithesis said. "We have social studies research."

"Classes are canceled immediately," Loretta snapped.

"You want everyone to go home?" Tate asked.

"Yes." Loretta looked around at the kids. "Go home."

"My mom won't be here to pick me up until four o'clock," Oliver said. "We live forty minutes away."

"I can take you home," Pete said.

"Can I finish my chess game first?"

Pete seemed to realize for the first time that his grandson was playing chess with a boy dressed in orange. He exchanged a look with Today's Moment, both horrified the kids were getting along.

If either of them interrupted that chess game, Willa wasn't going to be responsible for her actions.

"Okay, those of you with the option to leave

should leave now," Loretta said. "The rest will remain here, in the cafeteria. You are not to return to class."

"Who's going to supervise the kids?" Tate asked.

More evidence that Loretta had clearly not thought this through. And heaven forbid she supervise the teens.

"One of you will stay here with the remaining kids, but you are not to teach them anything."

Vander glanced at Loretta, then widened his eyes at the kids. Several students stifled a laugh.

"Wait a minute." Luci stepped forward. "I can appreciate the board is angry, but I don't know anything about your concerns, or the improvements you want us to make."

"Whose fault is that?" Loretta asked.

"I don't know," Luci said, in a tone similar to a very bad actor pretending to be unruffled. "But I'd love to go over the changes you'd like us to make before you shut down the school because we didn't make them."

"I'd say you're a day short and a dollar late. The school is closed."

"But—" Luci held out her hands, pleading "—we have internet today!"

"Dad?" Sylvie left her table and came to stand next to Colter. He wrapped an arm around his daughter as she asked, "What's going on?"

Colter rubbed Sylvie's back and planted a kiss on her forehead. Then he stepped forward and looked at each of the teachers. "I think I can offer a little more information. Is there a place we can talk?"

"Back at the hotel?" Tate suggested.

"I'll stay here with the kids," Mateo offered, glancing to where the board members had assembled into a knot. "You all can catch me up on the bad news later."

"I'll stay, too." Mrs. Moran came shuffling over. She held several large stacks of playing cards in her hands, as though she'd been prepared for Loretta's nonsense and was ready to make the best of things.

"Thank you," Willa said, taking solace in Colter's warm gaze. This school wasn't going down without a fight. And for all his faults, Colter was the first person she'd want on her side in any altercation.

"THIS IS MY FAULT," Colter said. He hadn't been able to bring himself to take a seat, instead pacing the courtyard.

"Yeah, I'm not feeling that," Tate said.

"This is all Loretta's doing," Willa said.

Vander furrowed his brow. "I try to understand her, but I don't get how she can be so nice to us one minute, then shut the school down the next."

"Loretta is creating drama because she loves drama. It makes her feel important," Luci said. She held up an old teapot. "Tea, anyone?"

Willa held her cup out, seeming much calmer than Colter would have expected. "I love that even in the most dire moments you still insist on your elegant routines, finishing lunch with tea and a cookie."

"Routines and habits are essential, especially in dire moments." Luci stirred sugar into her tea. "Like the way you still direct focus to people's strengths, no matter how badly the world is crashing down around our ears."

Colter's heart surged as he watched Willa blink back tears at the unexpected compliment. Then he had to blink back his own tears because Luci was right: the world was absolutely crashing around their ears and if he didn't get the board in line, Pronghorn Public Day School was over.

"That's Willa," Colter said, allowing himself a moment to smile at her. Then he looked around the table. "You all bring so much to this school. But I don't think it would have mattered who they hired, this community..." He blew out a breath, unable to finish the sentence.

"Is struggling?" Tate guessed.

Colter closed his eyes and nodded. He loved this place. He wanted the school, and Pronghorn, to work so badly.

"The board and the community have sky-high expectations," he explained.

"And I don't know if anyone else feels this," Luci said, "but it seems like the sky is actually higher here than it is in other places."

"That's partially because of our altitude, and the lack of light pollution," Vander said. "There are fewer molecules to scatter light at higher elevations, and less water vapor. So it's easier for the short wavelengths our eyes register as blue to scatter. The sky is actually bluer here, giving the appearance of more height."

Luci gestured dramatically toward Vander. "Okay, how would you not want that for your science teacher?"

Colter sighed, then reached into his back pocket, pulling out the list he'd been avoiding sharing with the teachers. *"Mr. V"* was one of the biggest areas of concern.

"Vander has been teaching a philosophy of human anatomy at odds with certain belief systems."

"A philosophy of human anatomy?" Vander asked. "There is no philosophy. There's just…human anatomy."

"Not according to the Open Hearts Intentional Community."

Vander's expression fell. "I thought all that stuff about the heart and the sun was a metaphor."

Colter shook his head as he consulted the list again. "The other complaint is that you're such a good teacher you're wooing kids over to your philosophy with such compelling lessons."

"This is bad," Tate said. "This is so much worse than bad."

Colter held up the list. "There are thirty-two demands from the board. I didn't share them with you earlier because I don't think they're reasonable. The board knows I haven't shared the list with you, but they are still accusing you of not meeting their demands." He studied the flagstones beneath his feet. "This *is* my fault. I decided not to tell you all about it. I thought I could get them to see this list is unreasonable." He let his gaze connect with Willa's. "I thought I could change their minds. I wanted to spare you all from—" he held up the impossible list "—all this."

It was the same thing he'd done the last time he'd found himself in serious trouble. He hadn't told Willa, thought he could protect her from the hurt and solve everything on his own. Instead he'd just wound up hurting her more, and ended up in more trouble than when he started.

Willa stood and walked toward him. For a second his unreasonable subconscious thought it might get a hug. But no. She plucked the list from his hands and scanned it. Then she laughed out loud.

"This is incredible." She shook her head as she read out the title of the typed list. "Immediate concerns and accompanying solutions for the continued operations of Pronghorn Public Day School."

"Should the fact that it was clearly typed up on an old-school typewriter concern me?" Luci asked.

"The entire thing is concerning."

"Lemme see!" Tate reached out for the list. He stared, slowly tilting his head to the right before finally sputtering out a laugh. "We're supposed to offer football, volleyball, soccer and cross-country?" He looked up from the paper. "We've got thirty kids. Less than half have any interest in sports. We've barely got enough athletes for two sides of a pickleball game."

Luci snatched the list from his hands. "They want me to post ten-page lesson plans for every class I'm teaching on the school website, a week in advance? I have four different classes to prepare for every day. I'm literally teaching myself econ as we go along."

"And Vander has to post his lessons, too." Tate pointed to another spot on this list.

"And my lesson plans are what, chopped liver?" Willa asked. "Why doesn't anyone care about literature?"

Vander patted her shoulder.

"Where do they think they're going to get a music teacher to run an after-school program?" Willa asked.

"Oh no," Vander said.

Colter pointed to a subpoint under demand number twelve: *Vander Tourn arrived with a guitar, we can assume he plays the guitar and he can use it to lead music.*

"No." Vander looked panicked. "I don't play in front of other people."

"But can you teach other people to play in front of people?" Luci asked.

"I can't even read music. I just play the guitar to relax."

"I think we can all agree there are few things less relaxing than an after-school music program," Tate quipped.

"I took this job for the kids," Vander said quietly. "There are four people on the board, but thirty in our classrooms. We should be asking the kids what they want."

Willa turned to Colter. Despite the situation, it didn't escape his notice that she was very, very close to him. She made everything better, inspired him to find solutions to what seemed like an unsolvable puzzle. Again, the rightness of Willa washed away every concern or trouble.

"Colter, this isn't possible."

He knew it wasn't possible. He'd known the moment Sylvie's mom called to tell him she was pregnant that he'd ruined any future with Willa. She was impossible, but that didn't mean he would ever stop wishing she wasn't.

She waved the paper in front of his face.

Oh, she was talking about the school board demands.

"Right." He shook his head and chuckled. "These demands are not possible."

"In a larger school with more funding, sure. But we don't have the resources or even the interest from students to do all this."

Colter knew Willa took her position of caretaker of this eclectic group seriously, protecting them like a mother hen. She didn't want to be saved. She wanted the tools and information to successfully fight on behalf of others.

"We're already working twelve-hour days. We expected long hours and signed on for an intense beginning to the school year. But we cannot do more. We can drop some things to focus our energies elsewhere, but we can't do more work on top of too much work."

"You're absolutely right," Colter said.

"If they want after-school sports and a music program, Vander and Tate either need to be compensated, or do less work during the day." Willa was so confident Colter found himself nodding, even though he knew there was no extra money to pay anyone anything, and didn't understand the first thing about their duties during the day.

"If we could get someone else to take care of lunch, it would free up my time," Tate said. "I'm happy to coach if we have kids who want to participate."

"Parent volunteers should be our first priority." Willa said. "We need people to take over the basic jobs like fixing lunch and taking out the trash. Then we can add extra duties to our schedules."

"But how are we going to get volunteers if the community doesn't trust us?" Luci asked.

Colter let out a breath. "I have an idea, but it would take more time on your end." He glanced at Willa. "Maybe even include working a few Saturdays."

She rewarded him with the glimmer of a smile. "Let's hear it."

"The grapevine has blown you all out of proportion. Most of the parents have no idea who you are, or what's going on in class. It would be a nice gesture, and give you some insight to the community, if we did a few home visits."

The group stared at him like he'd suggested they each donate a lung to Loretta.

"I can go with you. We'd call ahead and arrange to have a quick visit with each of the families. I think once people get to know you, they'll feel more comfortable. We'd only have fourteen stops, since there are siblings in the bunch, plus the five students from Open Hearts. We could get it done pretty efficiently."

All the teachers nodded, except for Luci, who looked as though she'd been asked for a second lung. The color drained from her face.

"I'm not going to the commune," Luci said abruptly.

"No one *has* to do any home visits," Willa said gently. "But you're so good with the kids from Open Hearts."

"Seriously. It's like you speak their language," Tate said.

"I'm not going." She gestured broadly. "I'm not meeting with anyone who accuses Vander of teaching so well students start to believe his controversial theory of human anatomy." Her words were intended to be a joke, but everyone could sense the tension behind them.

"I'm happy to go," Willa said. "The list has the fewest demands of me—it's only fair that I take on the home visits."

Colter couldn't stop himself from smiling. Fair?

Making this amazing woman spend an entire day with him to save a job she was already crushing.

It wasn't fair at all. But it was exactly what he was hoping for.

WILLA'S HEART THUMPED ERRATICALLY, knocking into her rib cage as she and Colter led the teachers back across the street to school. Had she just agreed to spending Saturday driving through Warner Valley, riding shotgun to Colter Wayne?

She glanced at him as he advanced on the school, head high, ready for battle.

Okay, there were worse people to ally with when saving an educational institution.

"What do you suppose we're going to find in there?" he muttered as they separated and came back together to avoid stepping on Connie.

"I don't know. Most of the kids don't drive, and it will take a while for the parents to get here. I hope Mateo and Mrs. Moran are doing okay." She glanced nervously at the parking lot. Pete's truck and Loretta's Bug were still there.

Colter picked up his pace. The five of them bypassed the front door and looped around to the cafeteria.

It took a hot minute to wrap her brain around what she was looking at.

Pete Sorel was at the back of the room, scrolling through Facebook. Loretta was in the middle of a phone conversation in which the words, "charming fixer-upper" and "seasonal creek" were being pelted at the recipient on the other end of the line. The woman had the gall to wave at them, like she hadn't shut the school down an hour ago.

But as weird as it was, it was nothing compared to what was happening at the other end of the room.

Students sat in groups of four, each gripping large fans of playing cards, murmuring in low voices about meld and suits.

"Mateo?" Sylvie called out, holding her cards for him to see. He pointed out something in her hand, and she nodded. "Trump is clubs," she said.

"Awww!" Mav groaned.

"Careful," Mrs. Moran warned him. "You don't want to let your opponents know what you have. Or don't have. Besides," she continued, standing behind him and pointing something out in his fan of cards, "all hope is not lost."

Mav nodded earnestly.

Sylvie set a card down in the center of the table. Mav studied his hand, chose a card, then reconsidered. Finally, he placed a card on top of Sylvie's. Mason played next, then Antithesis.

All the students of Pronghorn Public Day School, even those who lived in town and could easily walk home, were still in the cafeteria, brows furrowed as they played a complex card game.

"What is going on?" Tate asked.

"Pinochle," Oliver said.

"I thought it made more sense than poker." Mrs. Moran winked at them.

"Right. Because we don't want to add gambling to the list of evils we're teaching these kids," Luci said.

"Oh, you can gamble on anything," Mrs. Moran responded. Willa wasn't entirely sure she was joking.

"All righty, then." Loretta disconnected her call and marched over to them. "I hate to be the one stepping on anyone's parade. But we have repeatedly warned you and you have not responded to our concerns."

Colter held up a hand. "Loretta, I've said it before and I'll say it again, the teachers need to get settled in before we start making changes."

"Be that as it may, it's time to take this school by the horns and the buck starts with me."

Willa's eye twitched as Loretta recklessly abused common idioms.

"We're giving you two weeks," Loretta said.

"Two weeks?" Tate asked, incredulous.

"That's right." Pete ambled over to them. "In two weeks' time we expect you to hold an open house, and invite the community in to see what you can do. If Community Day goes well, we'll keep the school open. If not, you can start looking for other jobs."

"We have contracts," Willa said.

"You can't work at a school if it doesn't exist," he said, somewhat obviously.

"What do you expect us to do?"

"Your jobs. I told you the first day, you should be teaching these kids basic information."

Willa swallowed hard.

Information?

There was plenty of basic information she could point out in this situation. The board's demands were unreasonable. They represented personal agendas and interests, rather than the real needs of the students. Memories of their own school days took precedence over information about the current circumstances. The demands were based on a fantasy about education, as opposed to an understanding of educational theory and practice.

Another fact worth considering: she'd grown to care deeply for her coworkers, for her students and for Pronghorn itself. She didn't want another job; she wanted this one.

Willa glanced at Colter. He stood with his back straight, arms loose but spread wide, ready for action.

Fact: Colter Wayne had grown up considerably. His intuitive, impulsive, reactive nature had refined itself over the years. He was willing to fight for this opportunity for his daughter, and for Pronghorn.

And as much as Willa disliked arguments, she was willing to fight for it, too.

CHAPTER TEN

WILLA WAS *NOT* going to get excited about climbing into Colter's truck. She released his hand quickly, refusing to fixate on the familiar smell of leather and coffee. All focus went to snapping her seat belt into place, so as to not catch a glimpse of Colter jogging around the front of the truck, giving the hood an affectionate pat as though the vehicle were an old friend. This wasn't a date. They weren't kids. The situation was serious.

Her nervous system wasn't buying any of it.

"You all set?" Colter asked, climbing into the driver's seat.

"All set."

His grin flashed as he leaned forward and started the ignition.

"Thanks for the ride. I wasn't relishing the thought of taking the ATV out for home visits."

He laughed. "It would get you some serious street cred around here."

"Until I tried to turn it off," she reminded him.

He glanced at her from under his Stetson, eyes shining. "It's a tricky vehicle," he offered.

"It's an ATV," she said dryly. "Seven-year-olds drive them."

"Around here that's about right." Colter pulled out onto the highway and around Connie, who didn't bother to move. "I think it's probably best I accompany you, anyway. People need to know it's only a segment of the board that's upset."

She nodded. They were on school business. It wasn't a date.

The truck rumbled out of town, Warner Valley stretching out beyond them on either side. Sagebrush and prairie grass flashed by. Occasional thickets of quivering aspen trees signified a creek bed or lake. Low clouds filtered the bright sun, but from what she'd learned about the weather so far, the sky would be a vivid blue by midday.

Pronghorn was situated in an isolated stretch of land between Hart Mountain and the Coyote Hills. As Colter drove farther from town, the lonely highway climbed up through the rimrock. The land seemed to subtly shift color, from muted reds to coal black.

"This is gorgeous," she said.

"You like it?"

"Who wouldn't?" She glanced at Colter, imagining him at twenty-one, choosing this place to raise his daughter. "I can see why you settled here."

Colter's brow twitched. "At the time I didn't think of it so much as settling. Hunkering down was more like. The ranch was inexpensive, and there was a lady who ran a day care out of her house in town. That was all it took."

"Then you had one meal at The Restaurant and knew you were home?"

His loud, hearty laugh warmed her. "I don't know if you remember, but my parents weren't much for cooking. The Restaurant is like my home on a holiday."

Colter's parents hadn't been much for cooking, and certainly not eating together. He'd show up at the Marshall house like a curious pronghorn at mealtime, and any time, really. Colter had been drawn to the stable, loving atmosphere of their home.

"Nah, it seemed like a good place to raise Sylvie. Until they closed the school down." He kept his focus on the road, eyes growing serious. "I just kept telling myself it was temporary, but then a month turned into a school year, and one school year turned into two."

The landscape flashed by, changing like her conflicting emotions as they climbed in elevation. In the end, this was what mattered, not her complicated past with Colter, but the uncertain future for the kids in Pronghorn.

"You were right," she told him. "It was temporary. School's back in session and we're not giving up."

He gave a strong nod.

Willa gazed out the window. In the distance a herd of pronghorn picked their way across a grassy slope. How did the families living out here balance the love of this land with the challenges of modern life? The vast open spaces and landscape were breathtaking. Just being here loosened the tightness she'd held in her heart for years. A few weeks in and she felt as if she never wanted to leave. What was it like for people who'd been here for generations? The last families standing as towns like Pronghorn, and their schools, died.

"How'd the rest of the week go?" Colter startled her out of her thoughts.

"Fine? The kids were a little shaken, but the next day we picked back up where we'd left off."

"Except now everyone knows how to play pinochle?" Colter guessed.

"Everyone is *obsessed* with pinochle."

Colter laughed. "That was a brilliant move, by the way."

"It was all Mrs. Moran and Mateo."

"I asked Sylvie if she could teach me, and she said you have to have four players." He gave her a respectful nod. "Which means she *has* to play with a group of her peers."

"Mrs. Moran is incredible. Never underestimate a woman with five decades of teaching experience."

"I wouldn't dare." He slowed the truck to observe a stop sign that had to represent the literal middle of nowhere, looking both ways as though there might be traffic. Or more likely antelope. "Okay, first stop of the day is the Open Hearts Intentional Community. From there we'll drop by Oliver's place. His mom is pretty supportive, and we're meeting a group of parents there. They're not against the school, but they'll have questions."

Willa nodded, allowing the nervous fluttering in her heart to prepare her for the challenges ahead.

"We'll finish up at the home of Neveah Danes. I don't know if anyone will meet with us. Her mom never answered or returned any of my calls, but it's on the way, so we'll give it a shot."

Neveah was the quietest of their students, and her attendance was spotty. She'd only been in class three full days this term, one of which had been the first day.

"Is it weird that I'm so nervous?" Willa asked.

"We're going into the homes of a community that hasn't been real appreciative of all your hard work. Anyone would be nervous." He gave her a sly grin. "You, on the other hand…"

Instinctively, she swatted his arm.

"You're going to be fine," Colter said. "I should have suggested this the first week. People are wary of strangers around here."

A truck appeared on the highway, rattling toward them. Colter lifted two fingers off the steering wheel as the truck passed. The other driver responded in kind.

"What was that?"

"What?"

"The finger-twitch thing?" She imitated his gesture. "It looked like the world's least enthusiastic greeting."

"That's the rural wave."

"The rural wave?"

"Yeah. It's like an acknowledgement of the other driver. I see you, I respect that we're both out here in the middle of nowhere."

"So it's like the bro nod of the lonely highway?"

Colter laughed. "What do you want me to do? Roll down the window and slap him high five?"

"With your rodeo training, it wouldn't be too hard to pull off. And it would be way more awesome."

Colter took his eyes off the road and gazed at her, all the power and energy of his rodeo days sweeping through the cab, filling the space between and around them.

"You remember—" He swallowed, turned his gaze back out the front window. "You remember coming to my rodeos?"

Willa looked out the front window as well. "That's not something I'm likely to forget."

He was so free, so completely confident and joyful on the back of a bronco. And it didn't matter how the ride ended, if he got thrown or he jumped off on his own accord after eight seconds—the minute he was on his feet in the arena he would scan the stands until he found her. Then he would smile at her, lighting up her heart as though she really did have the molten core of the sun at her center.

"So, the commune?"

"Intentional community," Colter corrected her.

"And we have arrived." He pointed to a large sign reading Open Hearts Intentional Community, Where Love Finds Love. Underneath it a surprisingly accurate drawing of a human heart had wings, flapping in front of a stylized sun.

"Would it be okay to ask them about the heart-sun connection? I want to be able to explain it to Vander," she asked as they turned off the highway and onto a gravel road lined with bamboo trees.

"You can ask them anything you want, if you want to get converted."

She laughed. "Maybe on this first visit I'll let them ask the questions."

"Good call."

They rolled through the gate, emerging from the bamboo into a well-kept complex of buildings. Everything in Pronghorn and the surrounding area looked a little run-down, but some of these buildings were brand-new.

"This is significantly more...posh than I expected."

"There's quite a bit of money here," Colter said.

"How?"

"Most of the people who join come from wealthy families. When you are initiated, you give all your worldly possessions to the community. Those worldly possessions are then handled by an investment manager who builds wealth for the community in the international market. The commune itself has its own economy, and they grow and sell high-end hothouse flowers."

He gestured as they drove past a series of large greenhouses.

"So all the bouquets in the cafeteria—?"

"Are leftovers." His bright blue eyes connected with hers, a conspiratorial grin crossing his face.

Willa laughed. "Wow. This town just keeps getting—"

"Better and better?" he filled in for her.

Willa gazed at Colter. Here he was, a rancher and former rodeo star, calmly and willingly driving a teacher to the local commune so she could better understand the community. Only Colter Wayne.

A loud, whooping sound drew her attention away from Colter's bright eyes. Mav was running alongside the truck, waving.

Her most mistrustful student was loping along like...yes, like a pronghorn, waving at her.

"He's excited to see you," Colter commented.

"Seems that way." People began to emerge from buildings, smiling and waving as they moved toward the truck. "They all seem a lot more enthusiastic than I thought they'd be."

"Hospitality is one of their keystone values." Colter reached over and squeezed her hand. She looked up at him, shocked. Colter seemed to remember they weren't the hand-squeezing type of friends, but was already midsqueeze, so he didn't know exactly how to proceed. Slowly, he removed his fingers from hers and gripped the steering wheel.

"This is so weird."

"Oh, hey. Don't use that word. They take offense—"

"I mean this, Colter." She gestured between them. Mav was still whooping, and others in orange flowed toward the truck, all appearing very happy to see them. Despite this unexpected reception, being back in Colter's truck was what struck her as odd.

"I know. And I wish…well, it's hard to say what I wish." He kept his eyes on the road, emotion deepening his voice. "I wish my small-town drama wasn't mucking up your first teaching experience. But out of every teacher in the world, I'm so glad you're the one in charge here." He swallowed hard. "You're up to this, Willa."

"Ms. Marshall!" Antithesis was waving an orange scarf, skipping toward the truck.

What she couldn't bring herself to say was that out of everyone on earth, she was glad he was here, too. Colter had always made her feel capable, like anything was possible. His abrupt departure had thrown her. As though without him standing next to her, affirming her worth, she forgot how to find it on her own. As an adult, her task was to know her own worth, and allow Colter to buoy her confidence, rather than define it.

But as Today's Moment strode toward the truck, expression forced into one of welcome, Willa needed all the confidence she could get. If a little of that came from Colter, she'd take it.

COLTER HAD ALWAYS loved to sit back and watch Willa shine, but today was like the national championships of intelligence and charm. She'd been brilliant at Open Hearts. Willing to listen, but firm on the school's position. In the end, she'd invited several community leaders to tea at the hotel where they and Vander could talk. They responded enthusiastically, then pressed bouquets of flowers on her in gratitude for her "open and heartfelt dialogue."

The stop at Oliver Sorel's home was pretty much what he expected. Four sets of parents, desperate to get their kids out of the house and off online school, but fearful of supporting the new teachers because there was so much gossip going down around town. Fifteen minutes in and they were all staunch Willa supporters, *and* they'd agreed to coordinate volunteers for lunch duty.

As much as he was trying to not make any references to their former relationship, he couldn't help but give her a fist bump over that one.

His knuckles were still happy about it.

Now they were headed to the last stop of the day.

He'd debated taking her to the Daneses'. They weren't real supportive of the school in the first place, and certainly weren't ones to get involved in either keeping it open or shutting it down. But the plan had been home visits for every student, and Neveah was a student.

"How's Neveah in school?" he asked.

Willa considered this, frowning. "It does not seem to be her happy place."

Colter didn't think Neveah had a happy place at all.

On the horizon a collection of old trailers and mobile homes appeared on a dry chunk of land. Colter slowed the truck. Willa sat up straighter as she scanned the complex.

"Is this where she lives?"

Colter nodded.

They pulled onto the dusty plot of land. A dilapidated trailer home stood at the center of the property. Windows were all covered with curtains, or boarded up, or blocked by piles of stuff. The front door and side doors were cracked open, letting fat extension cords out of the main house to fuel the ring of old campers and outbuildings. There were five dwellings on the property. Each one held some segment of the Danes family. Dogs barked at the truck, and the flicker of a screen could be seen through an open door. The only beauty was a plaintive, a cappella country song drifting from an old camper. No one came into the yard to greet them.

Willa had both hands on the door handle, but didn't make a move to get out of the truck. "This is where Neveah lives?" she asked again.

Colter nodded. "Yeah. And I'd love to tell you places like this are an anomaly, but they're all over rural Oregon." He pointed to the main house. "That's the legal residence. The others are abandoned trailers and mobile homes."

"How did they…come to live like this?"

"Most of the people on this property started out

this way. It's a cycle that's almost impossible to get out of. It's hard for the kids to get anywhere, literally since they're so far from town. There's not a lot of encouragement or even role models of what's possible, and a lot of misconceptions about the outside world."

Tears appeared in Willa's eyes. She quickly blinked. "Intellectually, I understand rural poverty."

"But it's a lot bleaker to see it face on," Colter finished for her. "I worry about Sylvie, but it's kids like Neveah who truly rely on the school."

Willa took a deep breath and opened the truck door. For all he'd been the rodeo star, Colter always thought of Willa as the brave one.

He hopped out the other side and moved to stand next to Willa. She glanced around at the campers and trailers. "Which door do we knock on?"

The screen door to the nearest camper banged open and a woman stepped out. She wore a nightgown and settled a ball cap over her hair as she approached them. She glanced behind her, then folded her arms over her chest. "You're wasting your time."

"Are you Neveah's mom?" Willa asked.

"Aunt," the woman said. "And I don't mean to be rude, but you may as well get back in your truck. We're not interested."

Willa smiled and took a few steps toward the aunt. "We're here to get your opinion. I know families have a lot of questions about the school—"

"My opinion is you need to get back in your truck. We know the rules, the lady from the county explained it all real well. Neveah will come to school when she comes to school, we don't need you hounding us. She's sick today, that's why she missed."

"Today is Saturday."

The woman's confidence faltered, a flicker of embarrassment across her face quickly turning to anger. "She's sick all the same."

"I'm so sorry to hear that," Willa said, with no trace of irony. "It's no fun being sick or having a sick teenager around the house."

"Okay. I know you have to do this." The woman flicked her wrist at the truck, then the property. "It's your job. We all do what we gotta do.

The song from the trailer ended, prompting the woman to mutter, "Oh Lord, here we go."

Willa glanced around the compound. If she was scared, it didn't show. If anything she looked more confident. "I'm Willa Marshall—"

"One of the teachers from the city, I know." She started backing up toward the trailer, just as a door opened.

Colter wouldn't have recognized Neveah. She was pale, her hair lank, her posture unhealthy. She glanced at her aunt, then at Willa. Colter got a quick, suspicious look, but no curiosity.

"Hi, Neveah," Willa said. "It's great to see you."

"Hi."

Neveah's aunt let out a frustrated breath and looked over her shoulder at the trailer, as though annoyed that she was the family member who had to take care of all this.

Willa focused on Neveah. "We're doing home visits today, getting to know families better and asking about what you'd like to see happen at the school."

"School's fine," Neveah said.

"I'm sorry to hear you've been sick."

Neveah glanced nervously at her aunt. Willa continued, "We missed you this week. Mr. V wanted me to tell you he's holding off on the Oceanography unit until you get back, because he remembered that's what you said you were most excited about studying."

A shy smile lit Neveah's face. The connection Willa created with her was palpable, as though with her kind words and interest she was inflating a life raft for Neveah to return to school.

The aunt made short work of letting the air out of it.

"Honey, she don't mean that," the aunt said. "She has to say nice things. Mr. V don't know your name."

Neveah's smile disappeared, replaced with a practiced look of disinterest.

Willa bristled. "There are only thirty kids in the school. I assure you Vander, and the rest of her teachers, know her name and miss her when she's not in class."

"She's only goin' to school 'cause she has to. She don't like it." She looked down at Neveah. "You said it's boring, right?"

Neveah didn't respond. Her aunt continued, "I don't see how the government can tell her she has to be in school anyway. She's just gonna flunk all her classes, like last time."

Willa's face lost all color. She had to clear her throat before saying, "She's doing well—"

The aunt interrupted her, "And you can tell that school bus guy to stop coming around every day. He can just stop by once a week and if she's feeling okay, she'll go."

With that she turned around, a sharp wind kicking up dust that clung to her nightgown. She put a firm hand on Neveah's shoulder and led her back into the trailer, leaving Willa and Colter alone.

Willa was shaking as he helped her into the truck. She wasn't scared, she was mad. Questions and long tirades seemed to work across her face as he trotted around the front of the truck. She started to speak as soon as he climbed in, then stopped several times.

They were a mile down the highway before Willa finally spoke. "What are we going to do? The purpose of public school is to give every kid the skills and opportunities they need to shape and direct their own lives. I'm not here to save anyone, but school can give Neveah options so she can choose what she wants."

It was a complex situation. The Danes weren't bad people, and he understood their desire to protect their own against a system that had failed the family in the past. But he'd seen the way Neveah looked at Willa. She wanted to go to school.

"We're going to keep showing up for her. And keep trying."

Willa nodded, pressing her palms against her eye sockets. Then she dropped her hands and looked up at him, questioning. "Also, we have a school bus?"

"By law, we have to provide transportation. Pete does it."

"Pete's the school bus?"

"School truck, I guess, but yeah. He drives about four hours a day, picking up and dropping off kids. There are only three riders, four if you count Neveah. But he comes here every day. And if I know Pete, he won't give up on her."

"We're talking about Pete Sorel, the board member."

"Yep."

"*Just teach kids basic information'* Pete."

"Same one."

Willa blew out a breath, then leaned forward and cradled her face in her hands. When she finally re-emerged he could see tears.

"This matters."

"I don't mean to criticize your word choice by suggesting that's a bit of an understatement, but yeah."

She closed her eyes and leaned back in her seat. "They didn't issue superhero capes in ed school."

He cracked a smile. "Who needs a cape? You've got a team of misfit geniuses and something very similar to the bat cave, if Batman ever had to deal with semidomesticated antelope."

She laughed. "And a sweet all-terrain vehicle."

"And me," he said, before he could stop himself.

"And you." She gazed at him, then nodded. "We couldn't do this without you."

He tried to make a joke. "Since I'm the founding donor and all."

"Founding donor?"

"Uh...yeah. Please don't get mad, but this whole school was... Well, I guess you could call it my idea."

She turned in her seat, tucking her left leg under her as she faced him, like she'd done so many times when they were young. "Your idea?"

He shrugged. "It was either that, or send Sylvie to boarding school. I mentioned it at a city council meeting and pledged a pretty good sum. Loretta got real excited, and I guess the rest is history."

"Huh." She nodded appreciatively, impressed even.

Colter couldn't stop himself. He reached over and gave her shoulder a playful tap. "See? I've made a few good decisions. I'm not a complete wreck."

She furrowed her brow. "No one said you were a wreck."

"No one has to say it. I'm impulsive. I make bad decisions."

She shifted, tucking her leg further underneath her, leaning toward him. "Who says you make bad decisions?"

"Really? You're asking that question?"

She studied the seat between them, then brushed her bangs out of her face and looked up at him. "Colter, you hurt me. We're clear on that. It happened. It's over. But you've made a hundred good decisions since then."

"Like not telling you how upset the board was? That turned out great."

She rolled her eyes. "No one blames you for the board's unreasonable demands, and you told them to hold off on them until we'd settled in. And that's *one* thing. Okay, maybe you could have handled it better. For the most part you make fine decisions, even good ones."

He kept his eyes on the road in hopes she couldn't see just how much her faith meant to him, her words again building the life raft he so desperately wanted after years of treading water.

"Let's start at the top. You've raised a smart, creative girl all on your own."

"You think so?"

"Please. She's amazing."

"I got lucky."

Willa tilted her head to one side, considering his comment. "You did get lucky, but you're also making good decisions. I've watched you parent. She has a lot of structure and unconditional love. You hold her accountable but give her room to experiment. You're a great dad."

Colter didn't take his eyes off the road now. If

he looked at her, his gratitude would come rolling out in the form of big fat tears.

"And I have to say, I love her sense of style."

"You do?" he asked. "She gets all these ideas off Instagram."

"She's a little fashion-forward for Pronghorn, but she'd fit right in in the city. Then there's your ranch. You're running cattle and raising horses, just like you always wanted to. Accomplishing a long-term goal is proof of good decision-making."

Colter let her words sink into his bones. He hadn't felt this capable in years. He hadn't felt this way since—

Since he was twenty-one, and in a relationship with Willa Marshall.

"You see what you're doing here?" he asked.

"What?"

"You're making me focus on the good in myself, helping me feel more confident as you draw attention to my strengths. That's your superpower."

She looked down at her lap, color flooding her face as he pointed out *her* strengths. "Okay, so I'm good at helping people see the positive. It doesn't mean you deserve any less credit for the decisions you made."

He shook his head. There was one bad decision he was never forgiving himself for. Gesturing between them, he said, "I destroyed us."

She turned away, staring hard out the window.

"I know you asked me not to bring it up, but I've never forgiven myself for what I did. I never will."

"You don't need to beat yourself up about it."
Then she muttered, "I've got that covered."

He laughed.

"Look, this is hard," she acknowledged. "But I've learned to separate the boy you were from the man you've become. We were kids. I had a huge crush on you."

Colter shook his head. He wouldn't let her minimize what they'd had. "It was more than a crush. We were going to get married."

"We were young, not much older than the students I'm teaching. There was no ring, just two kids with unrealistic dreams."

Her words shot through him. He'd never once thought of marriage to Willa as unrealistic. Their dreams of being together felt like the only thing that ever mattered.

He didn't love the feelings her understanding stirred up in him. It was harder to stomach than her anger, confirming his secret fear: he'd never meant half as much to her as she did to him.

But she was here now, and she respected the life he'd built for himself. He glanced at Willa to find her violet eyes fixed on him. If he couldn't rekindle their past, there was always a chance he could create something new.

She smiled. He smiled back.

Yeah. Pursuing Willa now, when they were two adults with a common goal, felt like a very good decision.

CHAPTER ELEVEN

"WHY IS THE grasshopper moving its jaws from side to side?" Mav asked, looking up from the poem about three seconds after Willa placed it on his desk.

"I want everyone to finish reading before we discuss *The Summer Day*," Willa said quietly.

"But why is—" Mav picked up the paper to read the author's name, "—Mary Oliver talking about his jaw?"

Willa opened her mouth to redirect Mav's attention to the poem, but Greta cut in. "The grasshopper is a *she*." Greta pointed to the pronoun in the poem.

Mav slapped his hand down on the poem. "How would she even know that? There's no way to tell if a grasshopper is a girl."

Willa pulled in a deep breath. "I love that you're questioning the author's intentions and perspective. While you finish reading the poem, I'm going to write your questions on the board."

Willa grabbed a piece of chalk and turned to the board, well aware of Mav's sigh and the dramatic rustling of his paper. Silence descended over the room as the students focused on Willa's favorite poem.

What was she doing with her one wild and precious life? *Teaching.*

"The grasshopper is washing its face?!" Mav exclaimed. "Come on. She's just making this up."

Or trying to teach, anyway.

Snapping at Mav to *"Read the dang poem!"* wasn't going to get her what she wanted. Tempting, but ultimately ineffectual. Willa drifted by his desk and redirected his focus by gently tapping the paper. He returned to reading.

"Wait," Greta's voice cut through the nanosecond of stillness of the room, "is this about death?"

"No, it's about life," Mason said. "Read the poem."

Greta turned around in her seat, her tone somewhere between flirting and fighting as she said, "Everything about death is really about life. Duh."

Mason blinked once, reddened, then grinned as he recognized the spark in her eye. He did his sixteen-year-old best to return the banter. "No, it isn't."

"If it's about life *or* death, why is she going on about the grasshopper chewing?" Mav asked. "Why can't the author just be like, 'Life is short! Appreciate it.'"

Willa wanted to remind her students that this class period was short, and she'd appreciate it if they'd all read the poem before voicing their opinions.

"I'm going to set a timer for three minutes of silence," she said. "If you finish the poem early, mark up the page with questions—"

"The internet is on!" Tate's voice rang down the main hall, interrupting class and ensuring *no* minutes of silence. "I repeat, the internet is working. If you need connection to the World Wide Web, now's your chance."

A cheer rose in Willa's class, echoed by the cheers coming out of other rooms. Internet access at Pronghorn Public Day School was always cause for celebration.

Welp, so much for sharing the most important poem of her life. That said, around here, internet connection was as short and precious as the life of a grasshopper. She'd try again with the poem next week, and every other week of the school year if she had to.

Willa stepped into the hall for negotiation. Mateo leaned out the door of his classroom. "I've got a math module I'd love for my intro and intermediate classes to try."

"So Neveah, Ricky, Audrey, Antithesis and Ben?" Luci clarified, crossing her arms.

"Yeah."

"Is Neveah here today?" Vander asked.

Willa shook her head. They hadn't seen her all week. "Both Neveah and Sylvie are out." Vander's expression fell.

"Everyone else is here," she reminded him, then turned back to Mateo. "And I'm good with you taking that crew."

"I'm with you for most of it," Luci said, "but Antithesis is really into the online geography game, and she needs it."

"Conceded." Mateo gave a firm nod.

Luci continued, "I'd like my Global Geography students, so everyone under the age of sixteen, except those Mateo called."

"Everybody okay if I take Chemistry for an online lab?" Vander asked. "Kids love it."

"What if I want to finish reading my poem?"

Everyone looked up to see that Mav had joined the knot of teachers, gesturing with the poem he'd been complaining about forty seconds earlier.

"No more poem today," Willa said, on a hunch. "We're going to finish up our discussion on Monday, so I'd like to save it for then."

"You can't make me not read it," he muttered, drifting away with his eyes glued to the page.

"You are *good*," Vander whispered.

Willa grinned. "Okay, Global Geography, Basic and Intermediate Math, and Chemistry—" Willa thought through the students those classes encompassed, then threw up her hands. "Who does that leave me with?"

Her coworkers turned on her.

"What? Have you got an online Emily Dickinson simulation your kids would benefit from?" Luci teased.

Tate came trotting down the hall. "Hey, if it's not a problem I'd love to have Mason, Sammy and Cece. They're coming along in PE, but they're still feeling awkward about physical activity, particularly in front of their peers. I've got a fun agility exercise we could do and it's gorgeous out today. With just the three of us there's less pressure."

"But the internet is on," Luci said.

"Exactly. While their peers are staring at screens, there's no chance anyone will see them as they get comfortable, and maybe even good at a lesson I'm going to use next week. Then next week rolls around, these kids lead the others and boom! Three more kids feeling better in their bodies. What do you say?"

"I have no students!" Willa cried.

"You go run the school," Vander responded, without a hint of sarcasm.

Willa sighed dramatically. "Fine. I'll respond to parent emails while you all have fun on the internet."

Cheers went up from the younger teachers, and they scattered down the hall, calling to the kids they'd claimed for their classes.

Internet hours always had a bit of a holiday feel, as the kids, unsure of what they would be doing, waited with anticipation to be called. The hallway quickly filled—students, voices, confusion—then cleared as the different groups materialized like schools of fish and followed the teachers into classrooms. At the end of the hallway, the double doors leading outside opened, and Willa's heart warmed at the sight of Tate leading three students out into the sunshine. He would encourage them, day by day, until they could embrace physical activity as something they were good at.

And if Loretta shut this school down, and the teachers were scattered to the wind, these three kids would have this day. They would know an adult valued this skill for them and believed they could do it. That was priceless.

Willa turned back to her classroom, just in time to see the door to Mrs. Moran's office close. The older woman never got into the fray for internet time, preferring an old-school, conversational-style Spanish class for her students. It was amazing how they'd all come from nationally ranked education programs with the latest innovations and ideas, and Mrs. Moran could teach circles around them. She had a calm, unhurried, unbothered persona. Everything was going to be okay in Mrs. Moran's world, and she helped Willa feel like everything was going to be okay in hers, too.

With a sigh, Willa returned to her classroom. While she didn't love that everyone else had internet fun time and she was stuck with parent emails, it did make sense. The vast majority of parent correspondence was addressed to her. She was seen as the face of the school, especially since the home visits. The community ran a gamut of emotions, but under every interaction there was baseline respect for Willa.

So yeah, she could take on public relations. That said, if she finished up these emails early, she was totally going to scour the internet for an Emily Dickinson simulation.

Willa opened up her bottom drawer and pulled

out a laptop. It was funny to think how for the last eight years she'd been glued to this machine. With the internet being so spotty in Pronghorn she'd learned to live without it.

She logged into the email and was greeted by a phalanx of unread messages. Every fourth email was from Loretta. Her correspondence was a bewildering mix of demands, actually useful information and backhanded praise.

The machine pinged, signaling a new message.

Sender: Loretta Lazarus
Subject: Hedgehog Care

Okay, that solves one mystery. The hedgehogs are from Loretta.

Leaving a second mystery of why?

The machine continued pinging as more emails populated the inbox. Subject lines like What's that tall guy teaching my kids? and List of Helpful Ideas for Luci Walker were bizarrely addressed to her.

Willa let out a sigh as she scanned the list.

Ugh. What to open first?

Willa's gaze stuttered on an email. She read the subject line again, then a third time.

Sender: Colter Wayne
Subject: Invitation

Willa's fingers hovered over the keyboard before she finally clicked on the email.

Hello teachers of Pronghorn Public Day School,
Out of gratitude for all you've done for our community, and in apology for all the trouble our school has given you, my daughter and I would like to invite you out for a day of fun at C & S Ranch. Several of you have mentioned wanting to learn to ride, and we'd like to make good on the promise. We have every lawn game imaginable, and Sylvie is hoping to get a pinochle game going. We'll serve a barbecue supper, where you'll be allowed to ask for substitutions and will have more than two beverage choices. So you can be prepared, we plan on breaking out real spices, which do exist in Pronghorn.

Please let us know if Saturday works for you.
Colter Wayne

Willa leaned back in her seat. The others were going to love this. She couldn't count the times Vander had said he wanted to learn to ride a horse. He was fascinated with ranching. And Mateo talked endlessly about how much he missed the food he'd grown up with in Portland. Everyone loved Sylvie and liked Colter a lot, given all he'd done for them. It was a sweet invitation.

But did she really need to be spending any more time with Colter? She'd done her best to compartmentalize the man she was getting to know from the boy she'd been in love with. It was the overlap that was giving her trouble.

"Ms. Marshall?"

She looked up to see Mason, a sheen of sweat already on his forehead from the physical activity.

"What's up?"

"Coach Tate wants to know if you can help out with the drill. He says there has to be an even number of people."

Willa looked at her clogged email inbox, then back at Mason.

"It's fun," he said, "and the poem was like, life is short so you should go outside."

She laughed at his simple, but reasonable, interpretation of *The Summer Day*. As a teacher, she would always be pulled in several directions at once. She needed to learn to focus on the most important aspects of her job first.

"I'd love to. Can you explain it to me as we head out?"

"Sure."

Willa rose to go run the drill, but something pulled her back into her seat for a moment. She dropped her fingers to the keyboard and typed, "We'll be there!" pressing Send before she had the chance to reconsider.

Sylvie emerged from the back room, carrying an old shipping box. "What's in here?"

Colter kept his focus on the sink he was scrubbing. "What are you doing with that? We're supposed to be cleaning."

"I was organizing the back room."

Colter managed to keep himself from grabbing the box and whisking it back to safety on the top shelf in the furthest reaches of the least-used room in the house. "Why?"

"In case one of the teachers goes in there."

Colter sighed and set down his sponge. Sylvie had been on a cleaning/reorganizing/outfit-creating spree ever since he received Willa's brief acceptance of their invitation. While he appreciated his daughter's anticipation and nervousness surrounding the event, he felt like his own apprehensions were a little more deeply rooted.

The day on the ranch for the teachers was intended to be his second first date with Willa. Sure, his daughter and four other adults would be present, but everything, from the food, to the horseback rides, to an evening by the firepit was planned with Willa in mind.

Not that he was going to share that with his daughter.

"Why would one of the teachers be in the back room, digging through a closet?"

Sylvie shrugged, as though it wasn't her fault her imagination had Coach Tate or one of the others rummaging through their personal belongings. "What's in the box?"

He shook his head. "Just some old junk. Go put it back and help me."

Sylvie started to pull back one of the interlocking cardboard flaps. Colter lunged for the box. She blinked up at him, surprised.

"What is it?"

He tried to shrug casually. "It's nothing." Colter

lifted the box from her hands and took long steps toward the back room.

"Is it about my mom?"

Colter stopped abruptly.

"No. No, sweetie. Everything I know about your mom, I've told you." He set the box down on the poured concrete countertop. "There are no secrets."

"Then what's in the box?"

He gave a dry laugh. "Old things. From when I was a teenager."

That did *not* assuage her curiosity. "From the rodeo?"

"Yeah. Yes. This has some stuff from the rodeo."

Sylvie reached to open the worn cardboard box. The box had been opened and reclosed so often the flaps were barely hanging on. Colter's heart beat steadily.

May as well get this over with, and under a time limit.

"Okay, ten minutes. Then we get back to cleaning up around here."

The house was already pretty clean. Early on he'd realized the less stuff he and Sylvie had, the easier it was to keep house. Cleaning days around C & S Ranch were largely about dusting, and at this time of year replacing the ubiquitous bouquets of wildflowers Sylvie brought in.

Colter opened the box as Sylvie perched next to him on a stool. He knew the contents and arrangement by memory. His plan was to distract her with the big ticket items up top, then shut it down before she could unearth the small, cedar box at the bottom.

Sylvie pulled a folded poster from the top of the box and spread it out on the counter.

"This is you?" Sylvie glanced up from the advertisement for the Pendleton Round Up. "This is you!!" She turned the old poster so he could see it. "This is you."

He chuckled. "Your old dad was pretty good in his day."

"Wow." She stared at the image.

Looking at the poster made Colter feel as though he were existing in an alternate reality. He knew the young man hanging onto a bronco was him, but it felt like someone else's life. Someone reckless and free. Someone who believed everything would always work out for the best.

Sylvie set the poster down and had her hands back in the box. She made a face as she pulled out a large belt buckle.

"I got that for winning at my first pro rodeo." He lifted it and examined the lettering. He could feel the rush of confidence as he rode, the excitement, the inevitability of his career taking off as he signed with his first major sponsors.

"What's this one?"

"It's from Cheyenne. That's the one that paid for this land."

Sylvie nodded, impressed. Then her expression shifted.

"Did you quit because of me?"

"I quit because the rodeo is a great way to get your neck broke. Any rodeo career is going to be short, and the trick is to end it on your own terms. When you were born, I had a good reason for keeping my neck intact."

Sylvie spread the poster out on the counter and set the buckle next to it. "Do you miss it?"

Did he? To some extent. He missed the anticipation, the crowds, the fun of being around a lot of other reckless young people.

He missed landing on his feet in the soft dirt after eight wild seconds, scanning the stands and finding Willa. He missed the look of relief and pride on her face.

"The rodeo developed out of ranching. It used to be a bunch of cowboys just showing off, and somewhere along the way someone started charging admission. Everything you do in the arena comes from the work we do here. If I want to rope a calf, or get thrown off a horse, I've got plenty of opportunity."

Sylvie smiled and reached back into the box, pulling out another buckle. "What's this one from?"

"The Sisters Rodeo."

The first night he kissed Willa.

Her whole family had driven over from Junction City to watch him ride. He'd won, and the thrill of winning with her there watching had made him determined to move this relationship forward. At eighteen he already knew he was going to marry

Willa and he'd figured he might as well get headed in the right direction.

It was nearly midnight by the time he'd managed to grab her hand and pull her behind a horse trailer. She'd grinned up at him, then risen on her toes, bringing her lips to his. The magic of finally kissing her, of her anticipating the kiss as much as he had, flushed any sense out of his head. He'd been trembling in anticipation, barely able to steady his hands on her waist.

"It's my favorite." Sylvie held the buckle up to her outfit. He could see her mind spinning, thinking of ways to make the garish buckle into a stylish accent.

"You can have it."

"I'm not going to take your buckle," she said. "You should wear it."

Colter laughed out loud. "I am not wearing any of these buckles."

"Why not?"

"They're half the size of my head."

"This one's twice the size," Sylvie said, reaching for a buckle from the National Rodeo Finals.

The night he got drunk with a woman he'd never met before. The night he'd made the worst mistake, with the incredible consequence of Sylvie. Colter took the buckle from her, then he ran a hand over his daughter's hair and kissed the top of her head.

"Okay, time to get back to work." Colter dropped the buckle back in the box and reconfigured the lid. "We can look through this box another time."

"We should frame the poster," she said.

"This place is going to be crawling with teachers in less than two hours. Let's get it cleaned up."

Sylvie rolled her eyes and pushed away from the counter, looking so much like a normal teenager he nearly whooped with joy.

The image of Sylvie sitting alone in the cafeteria still haunted him. He knew the teachers were doing their best to encourage student interaction, but over the past week Colter had begun to worry again. Sylvie had missed two days of classes. She said she had stomachaches, but they seemed to clear up pretty quick when he agreed to let her stay home. He hadn't invested the last of his rodeo earnings and endured hours in the company of the cranky board members to let his own daughter skip school.

"I'm going to get flowers," Sylvie said, grabbing a pair of kitchen shears. "This is going to be so fun."

Colter felt some relief as she headed out the front door to cut flowers. Maybe it really had been just a stomach bug. He grabbed the box and took heavy steps down the hall. Rather than turn into the back room, he kept walking through the sleeping porch and onto the back stoop. He sat on the steps and placed the box next to him. Dry prairie grass spread out before him, undulating down to the basalt rimrock shading the creek. As the land rose beyond the creek, occasional boulders dotted the landscape, reminding him of the ruins of some great civilization of the past. Those rocks seemed to echo his regrets.

Twelve years ago, driving from Reno toward some approximation of home, with a ten-month-old in a secondhand car carrier, he'd seen a For Sale sign on the highway.

Impulsive, he'd pulled off and bought the land and cattle from a family selling out after generations in this spot.

Colter opened the box and dug past the posters, programs and buckles until his hands came to rest on smooth cedar.

He'd made the pencil box for Willa to mask the real gift inside. He'd imagined her unwrapping it and exclaiming over the craftsmanship. She'd love that he'd made it for her to hold all the pens and pencils she was already reaching for. He'd imagined that every time she reached for a pen, she'd think of him, which would mean she'd think about him all the time.

Colter pulled off the lid and studied the contents. Sticky notes she'd left him. A little sketch she'd drawn of the two of them. Her senior picture. A hair tie he'd found in his truck that he could still convince himself smelled like the coconut shampoo she used.

In the corner of the box was a small velvet bag. He lifted it, shifting his fingers against the velvet, feeling the shape of the ring inside. Tears pressed against the back of his eyes. All his hope and longing contained in one small box, at the bottom of another box, tucked away with all the feelings he'd had for her.

CHAPTER TWELVE

Sylvie came busting out the door the moment Colter pulled up with a truckload of teachers. Willa and Luci would arrive separately on the ATV, but the guys had gotten it in their head that it would be fun to ride in a truck bed. They'd started the day by loading into the back of the truck, hooting and hollering when Colter drove over the smallest bump.

It did not take much to entertain these city kids.

Sylvie waved as they approached. From the driver's seat, he could see she'd placed no fewer than four mason jars of wildflowers on the porch rail. No doubt she had them in the barn as well, and who knew what the inside of the house looked like by now. Knowing his daughter, she'd put flowers in the broom closet, just in case.

Vander launched out of the back of his truck, then reached back in to grab his guitar. Tate engaged Sylvie in a complicated high five, and Mateo smiled as he held up the deck of pinochle cards he'd brought.

Yeah. This had definitely been a good idea. And

the next time he invited these teachers out, he'd have Sylvie invite some friends, too.

A faint but distinctive puttering sound drifted through the air. Colter turned to see a cloud of dust rising in the wake of an ATV. He noticed Mateo tracking the vehicle as well.

"Come inside!" Sylvie said. "We have cookies."

Colter lingered on the porch. Not because he was overanxious for Willa to get here. Not at all. It was more that she might have trouble turning off the vehicle again.

The cloud of dust turned from his access road and across the front field toward the house. Willa sat up front, sunglasses, jeans and boots giving her the vibe of the stunningly beautiful leader of a rough biker gang. He was aware that Luci was on the machine, too, but it was hard to see anyone but Willa.

It always had been.

Colter offered up a hand in greeting.

Well, in greeting and as a signal that he was there to turn off the ATV as needed.

She pulled up next to his truck, determination crossing her brow as she wrestled with the ignition. Knowing Willa, she'd practiced turning the machine off late into the night, just so she could beat it.

"This is gorgeous," Luci said. "I cannot believe this property."

"We were lucky to get it." He glanced over at Willa as she dismounted the camo ATV. She gazed around at the stables and arena, like she had on her first visit.

"Did you win it in a card game?" Willa asked abruptly.

Colter furrowed his brow. "No."

"On a game show?"

"No."

She gave him an indulgent smile. "Then maybe it wasn't luck, but good decision-making on your part."

"You call it a good decision when a twenty-one-year-old drops a quarter of his life savings on a piece of property he's been on for less than thirty minutes?"

"Does it have a creek?"

He laughed. "Yeah, actually. Year round."

"Then no, not if you can afford it." She was still and quiet for a few minutes, then her gaze connected with his. "You make a lot of good decisions, Colter, even if they're made quickly."

He soaked in the compliment like a spring rain, letting it run through his dry and cracked self-image.

"Wait, who was your real estate agent? It wasn't—"

"Yeah. It was Loretta."

"Then I take it all back. What were you thinking?"

He laughed, then headed to the front door, holding it for her.

What had he been thinking?

If memory served, his primary thought was, *"Willa would love this."*

WILLA RAN HER hand under the mane of the beautiful mustang. The gelding twitched, then turned his eyes on her. Anticipation shot through her. It had been years since she'd ridden. Fourteen, to be exact.

"You need help?" Colter asked.

"I think I remember how." She placed a foot in the stirrup and grabbed the horn of the Western saddle. Colter put his hands on her waist, giving her an extra boost up.

Willa settled back. It felt good. And Colter standing next to the horse, communicating with the animal about taking care of her? That felt good, too.

"Do you breed mustangs?" Vander asked.

"These are all rescue horses," Colter said. "Out here, when some folks find they can't care for an animal, they turn it loose. The horses join bands of wild horses and reproduce. While it sounds romantic, and in some parts of the country wild horses fare just fine, around here they're an environmental disaster. They displace native species, overgraze and put pressure on water sources. Like dogs and cats, they can do okay on their own, but most are happier in a home with humans to adore and feed them. I do my part to take in and care for wild horses, and train them up so people who are able to give them a good home can adopt them."

"I want to do that," Vander said. He pointed at Colter. "I want to rescue and train horses."

"Do you know much about horses?" Luci asked.

"Absolutely nothing. You are witnessing square one." Vander put the toe of his high-top sneaker into the stirrups and swung into the saddle with more enthusiasm than grace. "What's next?"

"Next" turned out to be a riding lesson from Sylvie, while Colter ducked into the tack room and returned with an extra Stetson for Vander, one of probably thirty he'd been given during his rodeo career. Willa rode around the snug arena, enjoying the movement as it came back to her. The stables and arena were tidy, evidence of Colter's rodeo days winking out at her sporadically: brand-name gear, the saddles he'd earned in various rodeo payouts and, of course, formerly wild horses now enjoying a happy life at C & S Ranch.

"Ready for a trail ride?" Sylvie asked, racing between the teachers like a sandpiper, making sure everyone had what they needed. She was so quiet around her peers, but like a lot of only children, quickly grew comfortable with adults.

"I'm ready," Willa called back encouragingly.

"Let's go," Mateo said.

Sylvie swung onto her mount. Colter clicked his tongue and muttered in communication with his horse. Vander gave the sounds his best approximation and his horse kindly chose to understand him. The group trotted out of the arena and into the open expanse of the ranch.

They spread out as they rode the fence line. Cattle were scattered across the low hills and took shelter under the occasional copse of aspen trees. Boulders rose from the landscape like giants. A rimrock-lined creek cut through the sagebrush and prairie grass. Willa could understand why Colter had bought the land at first sight.

"Check it out!" Tate called, urging his horse into a canter.

Mateo let out a whoop of encouragement as he followed suit.

Luci, categorically incapable of watching any sort of competition without joining in, leaned forward in the saddle.

Off to one side, Sylvie rode next to Vander. Rather than waving the reins and hollering like the others, Vander had quickly noticed how Colter and Sylvie maneuvered their horses with subtle sounds and movement in their legs and core. He was soaking up every bit of information, like one of the sea sponges he was so fond of discussing.

Willa leaned back in the saddle. A breeze lifted her hair, pushing it across her face. Colter glanced over at her.

"Can I join you?" his posture and sheepish grin seemed to say.

Before she could stop them her shoulders rose, and she smiled in a very clear communication of *"Why not?"*

"I think they're having fun." Willa nodded at her coworkers.

"A little bit."

"Thank you. We needed this. It's been a tough few weeks and it's nice to be away from everything. Back at the hotel we try to take down time, but there's always work to do."

"I thought we agreed, no working on Saturdays."

"Yes, but I'm afraid there's been quite a bit of worrying on Saturdays."

His bright blue eyes connected with hers. "I don't want you to have to worry about anything."

Warmth rose in her face as the connection lingered. Which reminded her of another thing she *should* be worrying about: Colter.

"Vander's really taking to the horses," he said.

"He's taking to everything. Of all of us, he seems the most comfortable here."

"Even more comfortable than you?"

She raised her brow. "What makes you think I'm comfortable?"

"Because you're a universally respected teacher who all the students love."

She laughed dryly, but the words managed to make their way into her heart. She worked hard to be a good teacher. It was nice to think people were noticing.

The breeze picked up, a steady warmth scented with sagebrush. Sylvie and Vander overtook the others, flowing with the speed of their horses like they were born to ride. Colter readjusted his hat and kept his eyes on the horizon. "Earlier you mentioned you came here to get away from something back home. Are you...away? Is this working?"

"I'm finding my way."

He nudged his horse with his knee, drawing closer. "Willa, I understand if you don't want to talk, but will you tell me about you? What—what have you been up to?" He looked away as he asked. "What did you do, after I left?"

"Cried."

He closed his eyes.

"Seriously. It wasn't pretty."

"I'm so sorry."

She shrugged. "It's all in the past now."

He glanced at her, as though asking if it really was all in the past. Then he shook his head. "I'm such a jerk."

She didn't respond, but he wasn't exactly right. What he'd done was jerk-like. But she had chosen her reaction. She wasn't special in having her heart broken. Relationships ended all the time. People got over it.

She'd let life stall out.

Colter's actions were those of an impulsive young man, but her reaction wasn't any more mature. At nineteen she had resigned herself to unhappiness. She let "heartbroken" define her personality. Colter's bad decision had become her excuse for not moving forward with her life.

"You may remember I have this bad habit of trying to solve other people's problems, getting in other people's business. I'm not very good at setting boundaries. In my twenties, I allowed myself to drift, telling myself other people's issues were more pressing than my own. My life floundered as I focused on others." She let out a breath and turned a bright smile on him. "But I got it all together, finally picked a career path and here I am, with my first real job."

"You're telling me that your problem was spending too much time helping other people, and your solution was to go into teaching?"

She laughed. "Yes, I do see the irony in my career path."

"You've done nothing but solve other people's problems since you got here." He grinned at her. "And you're doing a great job."

She studied the reins with some mixture of embarrassment and pride. "Let me try to explain it. Teaching is the right balance for me. I can be a leader and help others, but in a reasonable context, you know? And a big part of my job is teaching kids to solve their own problems and build practices that will lead to success. I help them create the habits now that I didn't develop until well into my twenties. It feels good."

"It's the perfect fit for you."

"I hope to do the responsibility justice. And little-known fact, teaching is fun. We read so much about underfunding and low teacher salaries and the stress of working with trauma-impacted kids. Nobody talks about the fact that most days, teaching is a blast."

Colter shuddered. "It's hard enough for me to be around one teenager."

"Says the man who domesticates wild horses."

Colter caught her eye and grinned. "I guess we all have our talents."

"WE HAVE BRAISED BRISKET, short ribs and tofu skewers over here. Then I made a salad," Sylvie pointed to a massive bowl of mixed greens topped with nasturtium blossoms. "Dad roasted vegetables, and he made the potato salad. I made all the cookies, but we bought the rolls. So," Sylvie clasped her hands in front of her, then raised them in a question. "Hopefully there's something here everyone likes to eat?"

Colter had been worried the extensive menu might be overkill. After listening to Sylvie's long-winded description, he was pretty sure it was. That said, this was his second first date with Willa. If a guy was going over the top, his second first date had to be the right time to do so.

"This is so good," Mateo said, grabbing a plate and stepping up to the buffet. "This is the best food I have ever eaten."

Colter laughed. "You haven't tried anything yet."

"No, I mean it. You have no idea how much I've missed real food." Mateo began to fill his plate at the kitchen island, and the others followed suit.

"Canned soup and a sleeve of crackers isn't your favorite meal?" Tate asked, loading his plate with brisket, short ribs *and* tofu skewers. "Because somehow I just assumed it was everyone's favorite."

"We should take the ATV to Lakeview and buy groceries," Willa said. Then she gave Colter a conspiratorial grin. "Is it okay to stock up there? It's only the local store we need to visit regularly, right?"

"Yes. And I'll drive you," Colter offered, well aware he was widening his stance and crossing his arms like he was some kind of great provider of groceries. "We can go the weekend after Community Day and stock up."

"Thank you," Willa said. "I'd love that."

Sweet. Their second, second date was on the calendar!

"If we're still employed the weekend after Community Day," Tate muttered.

"You shush your mouth," Willa said. "We are going to make it through this."

"You better," Sylvie said.

"Community Day will be fine," Willa predicted. "Pete and Today's Moment will grumble, Raquel will remind everyone she was always on our side, Loretta will act like she single-handedly saved the school, and the show will go on."

Sylvie directed their guests outside and got them seated on the stone bench Colter had constructed around the firepit. He watched Willa's reaction as she examined the patio he'd built. She seemed to appreciate it, and snuggled into the seating surrounding the small fire like she belonged there.

As everyone got situated and Colter poured drinks, Sylvie kept bopping back and forth between the firepit and the kitchen, bringing out extra food, letting people select from a variety of glasses.

They really needed to entertain more often.

Willa caught his eye. Her smile told him it was

okay, there was nothing wrong with having an overly enthusiastic hostess for a daughter.

Which was good, because if he was going to have guests out more often, he already knew who his first choice for a tea party would be.

"Want to sit by me?" Willa asked Sylvie, scooching over. Sylvie scrambled between Willa and Luci, finally digging into the meal it had taken the two of them forty-eight hours to prepare.

Conversation was fast and easy, the teachers quickly absorbing Colter and Sylvie into their banter. They were all so fun, and it had been a long, long time since he'd enjoyed the easy camaraderie of friends.

"Seems like you all got lucky, winding up here together," he said. "Can you imagine what this would be like if you didn't get along?"

The teachers glanced at one another.

"Not liking each other just wasn't an option," Luci said. "Even if some members of our group eat tomato soup for breakfast."

"It helps that we're all at the same point in our careers," Tate said. "We don't have any practical experience, but we're all excited to be here."

"I feel that," Vander said. "I never really fit in at school or in my grad program. But here—" He gestured to the others, and to the landscape around them.

Mateo grinned. "We're lucky. The school board hates us and we may not have jobs in a week, but

I can't imagine a better group of people to be un-employed in Pronghorn with."

Willa batted him on the arm. "We're not losing our jobs. Yes, this has been hard, but we're going to look back on this as one of the best years of our lives." The others groaned, but she continued, "I hate to quote one of Loretta's signs, but these are our good old days."

Mateo grinned and held up the cola he was drinking. "To the good old days."

"The good old days," the others repeated, clinking glasses.

Luci grinned at Colter and Willa. "You guys want to explain to the board that we're all going to look back on this and laugh?"

"Do they know how to laugh?" Tate asked.

"You know who Pete and Today's Moment remind me of? The old guys from the Muppets," Mateo said. "The ones who always complain."

"Statler and Waldorf," Willa said.

"Would that make Loretta Miss Piggy?" Luci asked

Willa laughed out loud. Colter caught her eye, a sly grin spreading across his face. Willa had always been a Muppets fan. She'd seen every episode and knew most of the films by heart. As a kid, if you'd asked her to name a favorite celebrity, she'd say Kermit the Frog. So Colter had learned, a long, long time ago, to do a perfect Kermit voice.

Reading his mind, Willa held out a hand.

"Don't you dare, Colter Wayne," she told him.

Why couldn't she remember never to use the words *Dare* and *Colter Wayne* in the same sentence?

"Hɪ! Hᴏ! Kermit the Frog here," Colter said in his best frog voice. Willa laughed so hard wine threatened to spew across the firepit.

"Stop it right there," she said, before remembering that only encouraged him.

He gazed at her soulfully, then began to sing "The Rainbow Connection" in a voice so much like Kermit's she was tempted to look around for the famous frog.

Everyone was laughing now as Colter did what had to be the world's most attractive Kermit imitation. Willa had half a mind to clamp her hand over his mouth, but that urge was coupled with a desire to park herself next to him and laugh with him as he wrapped his arms around her.

Which was decidedly *not* what they were invited out for.

"Dad! I didn't know you could do a Kermit voice."

"Oh, your dad does the best Kermit voice. He can even sing 'It's Not Easy Bein' Green,'" she said, then waited for him to sing the funny, but deeply moving, frog song.

Colter started to speak but was cut off by Sylvie as she asked Willa, "How do you know that?"

Colter clamped his mouth shut, shocked. It wasn't a look one often saw on Colter Wayne.

Sylvie looked from her dad, to Willa, and back

again, waiting for an answer to her perfectly logical question.

"Yeah," Mateo chimed in. "How do you know about the board president's Kermit voice?"

Colter, who could and had talked himself out of every kind of trouble growing up, couldn't seem to speak.

"Is there something you two aren't telling us?" Luci asked.

Willa's gaze connected with Colter's. There was so, so much they weren't telling them.

Colter finally seemed to come to his senses. His easy smile reappeared, with just a touch of nervousness.

"Do you want to tell the story?" he asked Willa, offering her a chance to frame the narrative.

She let her eyes flicker meaningfully to Sylvie. He should tell the story he wanted his daughter to hear. He gave a slight nod.

"I knew Ms. Marshall when she was in high school," he said. "I was...very good friends with her older brother."

"You knew my dad?!" Sylvie exclaimed.

Willa nodded. "I knew him pretty well." She didn't want to get Colter in trouble but she was not going to lie. "I was surprised to find he'd settled in Pronghorn, but nice to find an old friend here."

Colter's gaze connected with hers. She smiled. It *was* nice to find him here. Hard, confusing, and requiring major training in compartmentalization, but yeah, after she made it through the growing pains, nice.

"What was he like?"

"He was…" Willa considered the words carefully. "He was charming. So funny. Amazing with animals."

Sylvie stood. "Dad, we should get the box."

"No." Colter moved quickly, blocking her path to the door.

"But Ms. Marshall should see all the rodeo stuff."

"No box," he said firmly.

All of which made Willa really, really curious about the box.

Sylvie sat back down. "Did you ever go to one of his rodeos?"

"A few." Willa kept her eyes off Colter. She glanced around at the other teachers. "You all know Colter was a bronco rider?"

"How have you not told us this?" Vander demanded.

"The board president was a bronco rider and you never mentioned it?" Tate asked.

"It never came up."

"Loretta's former life as a circus clown has never come up either, but I'm assuming if you knew something you'd have told us," Luci said.

Willa and Colter exchanged a glance. She could feel heat rising to her cheeks. To staunch the attack, she turned to Sylvie and said, "Your dad was great. He was like he is now, only…he was more impulsive. Sometimes he made rash decisions."

"Like when he met my mom," Sylvie said matter-of-factly.

Willa's heart constricted, like a fist had closed around the organ and was steadily tightening, drawing blood from every corner of her body.

"Like when he met my mom." The sentence had come out so naturally, as though Colter and Sylvie had discussed it a hundred times. This wasn't painful to her. She knew the truth about her parents and didn't begrudge it.

"He made a bad decision," Sylvie continued calmly, "but then he got me. So it wasn't all bad, right?"

Tears pressed at the back of Willa's eyes. Colter turned his face away to hide the emotion.

That was it, right there. There was no other way to look at the situation. Willa swallowed hard.

"I support any decision that resulted in you," she said.

"Hear, hear!" Mateo raised his drink, clinking the edge with the others around the firepit. Colter tipped his glass to Willa's, the chime of his rim hitting hers ringing out around them. She held his eye. He was an incredible father who'd told his daughter the truth about her origins in a way she could understand and even feel good about. Willa took a sip of her wine, using her glass to mask the emotion moving across her face.

"So, did you have a crush on him?" Luci asked.

Colter choked on his beer.

"Luci!" Willa exclaimed.

"What?" Luci gestured toward Colter. "He must have been cute. Did you?"

She glanced at Colter, then Sylvie. She blushed so hard her scalp burned. It was taking way too long to answer, so long that there was only one possible answer. Willa set her glass down on the edge of the firepit and looked straight at Colter.

"The worst crush."

Everyone erupted in laughter. Willa held her hands up in admission. "It was bad. I used to follow Colter and Holden—my brother—around. I went to every rodeo. I was smitten."

Colter's face reddened. "It was my smooth demeanor and style, right?"

"Oh no." Willa turned to Sylvie and winked. "It was the Kermit the Frog voice."

THE STRAINS OF Vander's guitar floated from the house as Colter tidied up around the firepit. Through the kitchen window, he could see Sylvie, Tate, Mateo and Luci seated around the table, deep in a pinochle game while Vander lost himself in the music. Willa was at the sink, washing dishes like she owned the place, laughing with her friends as they played cards.

Colter had gone outside under the guise of bringing in the last of the dishes, but the truth was if he spent one more second next to Willa at the sink he was going to make another rash decision and kiss her in front of everyone.

Then go grab the box at the bottom of the other box and get down on one knee.

He let out a breath and sat down at the fire. Pink rays of light began to filter across the land as the sun dipped toward the mountains. Colter closed his eyes.

"I don't see any dishes."

Colter looked up to find Willa leaning against the kitchen doorframe.

He gave her a slow smile, admitting, "There aren't any."

"Should I leave you alone?"

He held eye contact and shook his head.

Never.

"I just came out to say…" Her voice trailed off. "I don't even know what to say. Did I handle that correctly?"

"You handle everything correctly."

"I wish you'd stop saying that." She took a few uncertain steps toward him.

"I'm not gonna lie." He patted the stone bench next to him. Willa glanced back into the kitchen, then settled next to him.

"I've handled a few things pretty poorly."

"I hate to disagree, but I think if you ask any one of the people in the kitchen right now, they'd say you do pretty well in this world."

"I'm doing okay now." She tucked her hair behind her ear and focused on the fire. "Your mistakes are big and flashy, out in the open. Your mistakes resulted in a fantastic human being and this incredible ranch. Mine were quiet, lasting years, eating away at my confidence and sense of direction." She gazed at him. "I've made plenty of mistakes, you just can't see them."

"Maybe I'm better at making mistakes than you are."

"No doubt."

Colter shifted closer. To the west the sun dipped to the horizon, a spectacular display of pink and red. Willa leaned toward him, her shoulder touching his, eyes on the stunning beauty of the sunset. He moved his arm so it was exactly around her, but his hand rested behind her on the bench. Which was likely as close as he was going to get to hugging her.

"Do you have any idea how much I've wanted to watch this sunset with you?" His voice was deep with regret.

Her gaze skipped from the land in front of them to his face. She started to speak but he cut her off. "I know you don't want to hear it, but Willa, I missed you so much. I missed you every day."

"Can you tell me what happened? Or, I guess, how it happened?"

He cleared his throat. "I imagine you've got it all pretty well figured out by now. I...uh. I got drunk after the National Championships."

"You won," she reminded him.

Colter nodded. He'd had about three hours to enjoy his win.

Call Willa. Entertain new sponsorship offers. Ruin the most important relationships of his life.

"I got drunk. I cheated on you. That's kinda how the night went." He blew out a breath. "Her name was Angel. Five weeks later I'm being served papers in a paternity suit." Tears gathered in his eyes. Willa placed her hand on his back, soothing him. "I was so scared. I didn't know how to tell you, or Holden, or your parents. But I wasn't going to walk away from my child. I wanted to do right by her." Colter covered his face with his hands as he remembered. "So I married Angel."

Pain shot across Willa's face. She closed her eyes briefly, then nodded. "I know."

"What she didn't tell me was that she had other children, all by different fathers, all of us athletes, all of us young. One of the men was in the middle of a child custody case. He urged me to talk to a lawyer."

"You should have called me when you realized. I would have been furious, and hurt, but I would have helped."

Colter closed his eyes. "By that time, I hadn't spoken to you in over a year. I couldn't call you. I couldn't face your disappointment in me. I couldn't face *my* disappointment in me."

She kept her hand on his back. "But now there's Sylvie." Tears appeared in the corners of her eyes, too. "You have done an incredible job raising a wonderful daughter. You need to give yourself some credit."

Colter gazed at her. "She adores you."

She smiled.

His heart beat steady and strong in his chest as he asked for the impossible. "Can you forgive me?"

"CAN YOU FORGIVE ME?"

Forgiving Colter was the easy part. It was her former self she was still mad at, spinning out for years, going nowhere as she wallowed in old hurts. She didn't trust herself. Her love for Colter had been so wild and uncontrolled. She didn't know if she could handle it again.

But wow, was he sure making her feel like she wanted to try.

"For which part?"

He blew out a breath. "Let's start with cheating."

"Sure. No, wait. Have you cheated on anyone else since then?"

He shook his head, then turned those beautiful blue eyes on her. "I haven't really dated since then. Since you."

The words flowed through her, hope pulsing like water.

But seriously?

"You haven't dated *anyone*?"

He gestured in the direction of town. "There's not a big singles scene in Pronghorn."

She laughed.

"I mean, Mrs. Moran is widowed, but I don't think she'd have me."

Willa laughed harder, joy bubbling up inside of

her. "Okay, cheating is atoned for. Much worse, not telling me what had happened. I worried about you. I was hurt and worried at the same time, which is *so frustrating.*"

He took her hand, his rough fingers playing against her palm. "Can you forgive a frightened kid for not doing the right thing, knowing that kid has regretted it every day for the last fourteen years?"

Her breath caught as he wove his fingers into hers.

"I mean it, Willa. I'm so sorry. By the time I was old enough to know better, I figured you wouldn't want to hear from me."

Was there truth in his statement? Ten years ago, she would not have been open to a conversation. She was self-righteously attached to her anger and suffering. If you can blame someone else for your life stalling out, you don't have to blame yourself, or do the hard work to make changes. Colter Wayne was her excuse for a lot of unproductive behavior. Would she have allowed him to take that from her?

"Okay." She nodded, the lightness of forgiving filling her. "Okay. I'm done. I forgive you."

A huge grin lit his face, and he angled his head to the right, eyes slipping shut as he leaned toward her.

He was going to kiss her.

It was a completely Colter move. Here they were, friends again, still attracted to each other. The air was clear. His impulse was to kiss her, so that was what he was gonna do.

Unless she stopped him.

Willa placed a hand on his chest.

"There's one more thing."

His eyes opened and he looked baffled for a split second, then regained himself. "Okay. Of course. Anything."

"Do you admit that using Loretta Lazarus as a real estate agent was a bad idea?"

He laughed, long and free, his head thrown back like he used to. It felt so good to see him relaxed and laughing. It felt so good to make him laugh.

"What's funny?"

They both jumped at the sound of Sylvie's voice, Colter actually leaping to his feet like he used to when Holden came across the two of them hanging out. That only made Willa laugh harder.

"Your dad," Willa said. "That's what's funny." She stood and took a few steps toward the kitchen.

"He tries," Sylvie admitted.

Mateo stuck his head out the door. "It's time for lawn games. Humanities against STEM. My team calls Sylvie."

Colter gazed down at Willa. "I guess that means you're stuck with me."

Warmth radiated through her. Stuck with Colter sounded like pretty much the best place to be.

The others came jostling out of the house, loudly boasting about their prowess in croquet and cornhole as Sylvie led them to an irrigated pasture set up for games. Twinkle lights along the split rail fence began to glow brighter as the sun sank another notch.

Willa gazed up at Colter, letting the lightness he inspired in her take hold. His grin was brighter than any sparkle lights. She knew that look. He was still in love with her.

And she was pretty sure this spinning, joyful, powerful feeling meant she was falling for a second time.

Was this really happening?

"Marshall!" Tate called. "Let's go!"

Willa took a few steps toward the back pasture, but Colter caught her hand and tugged her back. He spun her toward him and captured her other hand.

From the pasture they heard Sylvie calling, "Daaaaad!"

With the swift grace of a dragonfly, Colter leaned down and kissed Willa's cheek.

Oh yeah. This was happening.

CHAPTER THIRTEEN

IF COLTER WAS cleaning his kitchen a touch deeper than usual, it had nothing to do with a beautiful teacher living within five miles of his home. Nothing at all.

But he may as well put out clean dish towels all the same.

He checked the clock. 7:30 a.m.

Since when was driving his daughter to school such a source of anticipation?

Saturday had gone brilliantly. Once Colter finally managed to stammer out an apology, and Willa accepted it, it was as though no time had passed at all. She was still Willa; he was still madly in love with her. Still willing to pull out all the stops to get her attention.

But they were in a better place now. Older, smarter. In Willa's case, even prettier.

"Dad?"

"Ready to go," he called back. Colter grabbed his hat and his truck keys before he remembered his daughter hadn't had breakfast yet. He set them down on the island, then looked up at his girl to offer breakfast.

She was not dressed for school.

Colter's heart seemed to land on the counter next to his keys. He tried to stave off the inevitable by asking, "What can I make you for breakfast?"

She ran a hand across her stomach. "I'm not hungry."

Colter closed his eyes for patience. "You need to eat something before school."

"My stomach hurts."

It was the fourth stomachache in the last two weeks. She wasn't sick, she hadn't eaten anything out of the ordinary, and she would have said something if it was just her cycle.

"Can I stay home?"

He sighed, which was *not* the reaction he wanted to have. Sylvie looked apologetic, but in no way willing to buck up and go to school.

"Is something going on at school?"

"No."

"Are you sure, because you were so excited—"

"My stomach hurts."

Colter nodded. He didn't doubt her stomach hurt. What he couldn't understand was why she didn't have the drive to push through. "I'm worried about you missing so much school right at the beginning like this."

"I'll make up the work."

"But that's extra work for your teachers, right?

To explain everything to the class, then have to go back and explain it again?"

Her expression fell. She loved those teachers.

Something had to be going on at school. A little voice at the back of his head wondered why Willa hadn't said anything. Was it possible she hadn't noticed?

"If you're sick, you need to get back in bed," he said, knowing he was not going to enforce that rule. This was how it had gone the last three times. She didn't feel well enough to go to school, and the minute he caved in and let her stay home, she recovered pretty quickly.

But she wasn't lying. Sylvie was in pain, he could tell by the look on her face.

Sylvie turned around and trudged back toward the bedroom. Colter glanced over at his hat and keys. Guess he wouldn't be chatting with a certain teacher before school, and possibly inviting her out so he could cook her dinner while she got ready for Community Day.

He heard Sylvie's bedroom door shut and immediately felt guilty. She was his first priority. Any feelings he hoped to explore with Willa could wait.

Colter put the kettle on the stove. He'd make his daughter some tea and toast, and at least remind her that he cared. As the water heated he pulled out his laptop.

A quick Google search for stomachaches in teenage girls brought up hundreds of sites. He was not the only parent dealing with someone suffering from mystery stomach pain. Stress and anxiety were factors, along with a host of other possible causes. That made sense, given her pattern of feeling legitimately sick until he agreed she could stay home.

Colter flipped his computer shut and paced to the window. He wanted his daughter at school. He wanted to see Willa. But if stress was the issue, pushing Sylvie to buck up wasn't going to get them anywhere.

For the last six months, Colter had been on fire to get a school up and rolling, thinking that this institution was what his daughter needed. She'd been wilting during online school, her motivation and creativity diminishing in the glow of the screen. But now she was avoiding the very institution he'd help build for her.

Maybe the stress of keeping the school alive was getting to her, too?

WILLA JUST HAD to hope no one noticed she was floating on air as she taught her lessons. If they did, they were kind enough not to mention it. Memories from the day at the ranch buzzed through her mind, and she could hardly stop smiling. She'd been wildly in love with the younger, more impulsive Colter. But the older, smarter, even more attractive Colter? She wasn't falling this time, she seemed to be levitating in love.

"I'm going to be picky about your punctuation in these essays because punctuation can literally save your life," she finished up her lesson with a flourish as she amended the phrase "Let's eat Grandma!" with the comma the sentence so desperately needed.

The class chuckled, but Mav's hand shot up, as though it was programmed to signal a contradiction at the end of any lesson.

"Couldn't you say the same about spelling?"

Willa tilted her head, questioning him. "How do you mean?"

"When you serve a meal, there's probably a big difference between handing someone a plate and saying, 'Your dinner,' as opposed to—" he pointed and emphasized his words "—'*You're* dinner.'"

Willa laughed out loud at the unexpected joke. The class joined in and Mav was awarded attention for being clever, rather than contrary. "I think you've got it, Mav. On that note, you're all dismissed. Go have a nice break."

The five students in Intermediate English stood and headed to the hallway. Willa followed them to the door with the intention of waving at Sylvie as she moved from Vander's class to Luci's. At some point she needed to check in and see how everything was going. Sylvie hadn't seemed at all upset by the revelation that Willa and Colter had been friends previously. It was likely Colter had talked to her since then. But still, Willa wanted Sylvie to know she was here to answer any questions.

The memory of Colter's kiss inspired another

smile. There were a lot of questions coming up, and not just for Sylvie.

Willa greeted kids as they crossed the hall, heading to their respective classes. The last student filed out of Vander's room…but no Sylvie.

Was she sick again?

She'd missed a lot of school already.

The first couple of times Sylvie missed class Willa had expected Colter to say something, to excuse the absence. So far there'd been nothing. Sylvie just stayed home, no word as to why.

Was Colter unhappy with the way things were going at school?

No. He'd have said something.

Then again, he hadn't told her about the board's concerns. Or even about Sylvie all those years ago.

Willa shook her head, dislodging the unproductive thoughts. A man didn't drive all over the county making home visits, then barbecue for teachers because he was unhappy with their performance. He was all in for this school.

But was Sylvie unhappy?

"Ms. Marshall!" Antithesis veered toward her on her way to Global Geography and got right up in Willa's space. "Is that lady going to shut the school down?"

"No." Willa gave her most confident smile. "So you're still going to have to write that essay."

Antithesis swung her long hair over one shoulder. "I *like* writing essays."

"I'm glad to hear it." Willa kept her smile in place

to mask her discomfort. Was *"that lady"* going to shut down the school? Surely not. What would Loretta do all day if she didn't have school drama to keep her busy? Plus, a functioning school had to be good for whatever little real estate market there was out here.

"And remember you promised that after the essay, our class gets to read the grasshopper death poem, right?" Antithesis said, pointing at Willa like there was a chance she might try to slip out of teaching them Mav's new favorite poem.

"I promise we will study *The Summer Day.*"

"Yo, A.T." Luci called from the door of her classroom. "Global Geography, let's go!"

Antithesis skipped off to Luci's class, while her initial sentence continued to sit like a lump in Willa's chest.

"Is that lady going to close down the school?"

That lady was going to be here in about fifteen minutes to discuss Community Day. Would Colter join them? Presumably not, since Sylvie was sick.

If she *was* sick. Maybe she was staying home because she didn't like the idea of Willa and her dad being…whatever they were.

The last of the students milling about in the hallway filed into classrooms, doors closing behind them. Willa tried to shake off her unease. She wished she had a message from Colter about Sylvie, but without the internet working she'd never know.

Okay. Time to get it together. One student was

home sick. It wasn't a crisis, and Willa had work to do.

Maybe Tate needed help planning for his part in Community Day?

Willa stopped herself. Tate could take care of Tate. Colter could raise his own daughter. She didn't need to get back in the habit of distracting herself by trying to solve other people's problems.

Presently, Loretta's visit was her problem to solve. Not Tate's plans for Community Day. Not Sylvie missing school.

She headed toward the front hall, intent on meeting Loretta in the main office. The pattern of light washing in from the front windows seemed different somehow. A breeze drifted down the hall. Funny how love messed with her sense of perception. The light had always seemed dimmer, the air more still.

Willa heard a familiar shuffling sound.

Oh no.

She raced down the hallway. Love wasn't altering her perception, an open front door was the culprit. Sunshine and fresh air streamed in through the front door, along with five curious antelope.

"Vander!" she called over her shoulder.

The pronghorn wandered into the main hall, taking occasional nibbles at the decor, confused as to why the food selections weren't better. Connie padded into the building after them. She raised her fur dramatically, looking like a threatening seven pounds rather than the five she normally appeared to be, and hissed at the intruders for all she was worth.

"Vander! Anyone?"

Willa kept her eyes on the animals but could hear classroom doors opening, the excited chatter of kids drifting from the hall.

"Pronghorn!" Vander shouted.

Kids jostled into the entrance hall. The animals, as domesticated as they were, clattered nervously at the energy of so many teenagers. Vander straightened his back and raised his arms, but like the last time, he was a little too happy about the animals to get them moving out the door.

"Kids, please stand back," Willa instructed. Mrs. Moran came out of her office and gently shepherded the students as Vander took on the antelope. Luci, who had no idea what she was doing, raised her arms and stood next to him. If the rodeo ever had an event for rerouting quadrupeds while wearing penny loafers and argyle, she'd take top honors.

Together they got the animals headed back toward the door as the kids chattered and cheered on their teachers. Just as the first pronghorn was about to step over the threshold, an angry woman in a yellow pantsuit blocked their way

"What is that thing doing in here?"

"We've got it under control," Vander said, moving around the animals as they clattered back into the hall.

"This doesn't look controlled to me," Loretta said.

"Loretta, we've got it," Willa snapped.

The volunteer principal pulled her head back in surprise. Okay, maybe there was a little more impatience in Willa's voice than was absolutely called for.

Vander got the animals moving toward the main door again, but they took one look at Loretta and balked.

"Can you please move out of the way?" Willa said, because why would you block a door that someone was trying to herd antelope out of?

Loretta's voice dropped. "That's no way to speak to the principal."

"You're *not* the principal." Willa turned on Loretta, exhausted by her posturing. "You don't work here, you don't have an administrative license, and you're not doing anything remotely like running this school."

All of the hubbub in the main hall ceased. Even the pronghorn picked up their heads to listen.

Willa immediately registered her mistake. She'd publicly undressed a woman who held the fate of the school in her hands. Loretta might be an enigma, but one thing was clear: she valued being a prominent member of this community above everything. The emperor's new, bright yellow clothes were strewn all around her.

"I'm sorry," Willa said. "That was uncalled for." She flailed for an excuse. "These pronghorn are getting on my last nerve."

Loretta gave her a saccharine smile. "It's okay.

You're a new teacher, and clearly don't know how a school is run."

Twenty-nine students, five teachers and one cat exchanged glances at this bizarre declaration.

"Let's let Vander handle the pronghorn," Willa said. "Students, please head back to class."

That the students were willing to walk away from a hall full of antelope and their lead teacher calling out the "principal" was a credit to them all. Loretta stepped inside, and Vander, sensing the pronghorn mistrusted the lady in yellow, gestured for Loretta to stand next to him as he herded the animals out the door.

Their hooves were loud on the steps as they exited, then they picked up the pace as they bounded across the field and out of town. An odd stillness swept through the front hall.

Vander looked questioningly at Willa, as though asking if he should stay. She shook her head. He gave Loretta one last look, then headed back to his classroom.

Willa gave Loretta an apologetic smile and gestured to the main office. "Let's head in and I'll give you an update."

Loretta remained perfectly still. Not a good sign.

"We have some fun ideas for Community Day. Tate arranged with Angie to get some ice cream, so at the end of the day we'll have an ice cream social and be available for more informal questions and discussion."

Loretta marched back to the still open front door, then spun around to face Willa.

"*If* there's a Community Day." Her voice was quiet, and somehow much more powerful than when she held a bullhorn. "After this display of chaos and disrespect, I'm not sure you and the others deserve a chance to keep this school running. I'm calling a board meeting for tonight, where we'll decide if it's even worth having a Community Day. After what I've seen today, this place should be shut down until we can find teachers who know what they're doing."

CHAPTER FOURTEEN

COLTER WAITED ON the front porch, watching for the cloud of dust signifying the arrival of Willa on the ATV. The board was already assembled in the living room, and they might as well have pitchforks and torches in hand for all they talked about working together.

Yet even given the circumstances, he couldn't help but smile as Willa turned onto his property. She really did look like the most adorable leader of a biker gang on the ATV. Maybe she'd be interested in staying late after the meeting? There had to be some school policy the two of them could go over.

She parked and pulled off her helmet. Colter trotted down the front steps.

"Everyone already here?" she asked.

He nodded.

"Okay, then. Let's go get it done."

Colter glanced at the house, then back at Willa. He leaned down, keeping his lips close to her ear. "You've got this."

She smiled back at him. "With you on my side? Absolutely."

He offered a hand to help her off the ATV. She took it, letting her fingers curl briefly around his.

Yeah, this teacher was definitely getting held back after class today.

"How's Sylvie?" she asked.

"Feeling better. She's out on a ride right now."

Willa drew her head back. "She's out on a ride?"

"Yeah, I thought it was best to have her out of the house during the meeting."

"But she stayed home sick today."

Colter frowned. He felt tense, like Willa was standing with an arm outstretched, pointing in accusation. It was ridiculous. She was just asking after a student. Colter shook off the tension.

"I'll explain later." He placed a hand on the small of her back, directing her toward the porch. "Let's get 'er done."

The scene in the living room reminded him of a bad play. Four characters, hands folded in their laps, staring at them like old-time judges.

"Hello," Willa said, as though there'd never been a moment of stress with the board. "How's everyone this evening?"

They stared back.

"How are we?" Pete asked, face reddening. "How *are* we?"

"I'm not sure a display of anger will help this grave situation," Today's Moment said.

"So you're gonna spew condescending nonsense instead?" Pete muttered.

"We're just…disappointed," Raquel said, finally

making Willa flinch. "We all had such high hopes for this school."

"We're three weeks in," Colter said. "It doesn't make a lick of sense, you being so hard on the teachers three weeks in."

"They are laying the patterns for months and years to come," Today's Moment said. "For example, we asked that our emerging adults not be subject to watching others consume living beings at lunch. And yet we hear they are sitting, shoulder to shoulder, with young people committing slaughter."

"I don't think eating a ham sandwich is a capital offense," Pete said.

"I'm sick of this," Raquel snapped. "There are real issues at the school, and you two keep airing your personal beef."

Today's Moment gave a grand shudder at the mention of beef.

Willa stretched her hands out before her. "You know we have your list of suggestions."

"Those aren't suggestions," Loretta reminded her.

"And we've been doing our best to implement the workable ones by Friday, for Community Day. What is this meeting even about?"

Raquel, Pete, Today's Moment and Loretta all looked at one another. No one had an answer.

Willa took in a deep breath. "Okay, I'm going to go out on a limb here and guess. You're worried. This school matters so much to you. The community's kids and their education matter. And I get it, these are confusing times. Raising kids has never been easy and technology brings on a host of new challenges. But let me assure you, the kids in Pronghorn? They're amazing. Every one of us in this room wants the best for them, and we've all made sacrifices. I think Loretta called this meeting, and you all showed up because you want to demonstrate to each other, and to me, how much this matters."

The room was silent in the wake of her speech. She'd hit the core of the problem: this mattered, and none of them had the slightest idea of what to do.

"Sometimes, when we don't know how to handle a situation, it's easier to find someone to blame. When we get angry, or reprimand someone, we feel like we're doing something. Raising kids is complex, expressing anger is easy."

"She's right," Colter said. "When we fight, we feel like we're standing up for our beliefs. But in this case, it's not doing us any good."

Raquel looked at him, then nodded. Today's Moment considered the statement. Even Pete seemed to get the point.

It was Loretta who shook her head. "We're here because she's letting antelope into the school and letting everyone run wild."

And the room erupted again, any real understanding lost in the fight for personal agendas.

"You promised there would be a sports program," Pete said. "I even agreed to run the bus route twice so kids could stay after school."

"Tate sent out a Google survey last week to find out what sports kids are interested in," Willa told him. "We'll move forward once we hear back from everyone."

"It's the fall. Football, soccer and volleyball."

Willa leaned toward him, eyes wide, and said, "We have thirty students."

"They can play seven on seven."

She blew out a breath and looked up at Colter. "I'm going to reiterate, we are trying to bring back sports. It's important to us, too. We've already seen the increase in connections from playing card games—"

Pete stood, face red as he yelled, "Pinochle is not a sport!"

Colter turned away abruptly so the older man wouldn't see him laugh.

"Again, we're trying to assess the interests of the students before we commit our limited resources and time to a new activity."

"Why can't you have the kids raise their hands in class?" Raquel asked. "That's how I *'assessed interest'* when I taught."

"Because today's teens are not always comfortable expressing themselves in front of their peers," Willa said, frustrated now. "These kids were deeply impacted by their years of isolation in online school. They're still learning how to be around each other."

"Can you ask them individually tomorrow?" Loretta asked. "We want to know what activities you're offering after school. Just take a head count of who wants to do what."

Colter was pretty sure Willa's long intake of breath indicated some type of meditative exercise. The teachers were still making sure everyone was placed in the right classes. Getting activities going after school would take time, and as far as he could tell, the biggest draw was a pinochle club.

"Not all the kids are in school every day. We've had some serious absenteeism." Willa's gaze flickered to him for a millisecond.

Colter could feel the censure like she'd been glaring at him.

He stood and paced a few feet away from the sofa. Willa *wasn't* glaring at him. He was overreacting. She was talking about other kids, like Neveah. Missing four days in a two-week period wasn't "serious absenteeism."

Or was it?

The board continued to argue, talking in circles, proving Willa's point about getting angry rather than productive. The only thing clear to Colter was that he needed to get out of the room before he did something stupid and asked Willa what she meant by her comment about absenteeism. He stalked into the kitchen, pressing his palms onto the cool countertop, trying to get a hold of himself. Sylvie had stomachaches. He'd done his best to get her to go to school, and driving a hundred miles to an emergency room didn't seem practical.

He'd done the right thing. You can't force a kid

with a stomachache to go to school. Having her stay inside once the stomachache cleared up didn't make sense. He'd have time to explain it all to Willa once everyone left. She'd understand. She was the one who told him he was a good dad in the first place.

Willa's speech had hit a chord with him. These were confusing times, and getting angry was a way he could feel like he'd accomplished something as a parent, even if it was counterproductive. One thing for sure, getting upset at Willa for rightfully wondering why his daughter wasn't in school wouldn't help anything.

Voices rose from the living room. Leaving Willa alone with the board wasn't a smart move, either. Colter straightened and walked back into the fray.

There he found Willa on her feet, arms outstretched as she said, "We're trying. Why can't you see how hard we're trying?"

"There is no trying." Pete stood and gestured to Colter. "Just ask the rodeo cowboy. You either hang on or you don't."

With that Pete grabbed his hat and headed for the door.

COLTER'S HOUSE WAS eerily still after the board filed out. Willa dropped back onto the sofa and buried her face in her hands.

"That's not even true," she said.

Colter's palm, strong and solid, came to rest on her back as he sat down next to her.

"I know. I'm sure there are a lot of people who consider pinochle a sport."

She gave a dry laugh. "I mean about trying. I get that Yoda had a point to make about Luke Skywalker not giving up, but trying *does* matter. In some cases, I would say trying is even more important than succeeding."

His hands crept up to her shoulders and he rubbed the tense muscles. "There was definitely a lot of trying in the rodeo. And a lot of getting thrown off a horse."

"I remember."

His gaze connected with hers. This might be a nice time for the kiss he'd tried for on Saturday. A slow smile spread across his face, and despite everything, she felt an answering one of her own. She was upset about the board, and pretty sure her chances of keeping this job had dropped below fifty percent, but somehow a Colter kiss seemed a lot more important than anything else.

Movement outside the window caught her eye. It would not do to be kissing the board president if one of the other members came back for round two of arguments.

She glanced outside. It was Sylvie, cantering into the yard. She sat tall in the saddle, a calm happiness spread across her face, like when she was reading a good book in class.

She didn't look sick.

"Was she feeling okay this morning?" Willa asked. Colter seemed to flinch with the question.

"She'll be okay."

Willa got the sense Colter was trying to solve a complex problem on his own. He could have come to her family for help, all those years ago, and he didn't. Maybe he needed help now. And helping him solve this problem with Sylvie seemed a lot more doable than keeping a school open.

"She's missed a lot of class."

Colter stood and paced to the window, watching Sylvie dismount and lead the animal into the stables. He seemed to wrestle with what to say, then finally turned back to Willa with a tight smile. "It's complicated."

Something about his posture was so familiar. He was angry and tense. It was the way he stood when he felt an injustice had been done. Ten minutes ago he'd been protecting her against the others, but she knew when Colter Wayne was mad.

A question pushed at her heart. As much as she didn't want to hear the answer, she felt compelled to ask it all the same.

"Are *you* unhappy with the school?"

"No." He scoffed. "Not at all. You guys are doing great. Sylvie loves it."

Willa pressed further. "Then why isn't she coming regularly?"

He reacted as though she'd lobbed a handful of molten rock at his chest. His expression was hurt, then folded in like a box top, presenting only anger.

Panic unraveled in her chest. She wanted to help, to not let an important issue drop. But she knew

Colter didn't react well when he was angry, which he clearly was right now. And Sylvie was at the barn, presumably brushing down her horse. She'd be coming up the front steps in minutes.

Willa stood and crossed her arms. She glanced out the window, then back at Colter. "Why are you upset right now?"

"I'm not upset."

She raised her brows in the same manner one did when finding another student copying homework.

"I'm not," he lied. "Look, sometimes Sylvie has these stomachaches—"

"Why didn't you say so?" She cut him off. "A pediatric nurse from Seattle talked to our education program once about girls and stomachaches. There's a lot of circumstantial evidence but no real answers—"

Colter stalked into the kitchen before she could finish the sentence. "Yeah. I know. I've done my research."

He was cutting her out. Just as every beautiful feeling had come rushing back, he was shutting down, *again*. She'd allowed herself to believe Colter hadn't dated over the last thirteen years because he still loved her. A much more likely reason was that he wasn't able to let anyone else in, either. There was probably a host of women he made feel like the center of the universe, then he walked away, just as they fell in love.

Hadn't she told herself not to trust him?

She gathered up her bag, keeping her face away from him. "Must be nice to have working internet."

He finally looked at her. "Willa, I'm sorry."

She held a hand up. "It's been a tense evening. Let's drop it."

A gamut of emotions ran across his face. "I *want* Sylvie to be in school."

"Great. Me, too." She headed for the door. "Let me know if I can help."

He reached out and took her arm, his fingers gentle, almost questioning as he touched her. She didn't wrench her arm away.

He couldn't seem to say anything, but he was doing a great job of holding her arm.

Finally, he managed with "I'm a good dad."

There was no inflection in his voice, but she could clearly understand this was a question.

"Of course you are. I'm not questioning your parenting, Colter. Sylvie is wonderful and I want to help you do what's best for her."

Colter swallowed hard, readjusting his fingers on her arm, his thumb running across her elbow. His gaze followed the stroke of his thumb.

How could she let him know his concerns mattered? She wanted to help, like he'd helped the teachers through this difficult time.

"Have you taken her to a doctor?"

Colter's head jerked up. "The nearest doctor is over a hundred miles away."

"Right, but if you can rule out a physical cause—"

"It's not a physical cause. She's feeling anxious about school."

The words stacked up between them, creating a wall she felt too exhausted to battle through.

Colter continued, "I think there's something going on at school that's causing her stress."

Willa stared at him. He was serious. He honestly thought Sylvie was being mistreated, or left out, or bullied. After all she and the other teachers had done to help the kids create social connections. Blood pounded through her veins, coursing through her ears.

He thought his daughter was being bullied at school, and Willa had somehow overlooked it, or wasn't doing anything about it. That was his opinion of her.

The sound of boots on the front porch signaled the end of the conversation. Sylvie was back.

"You do what you want to, Colter." Willa wrenched her arm away and reached for the door. "You always have."

Willa managed to fake a smile as she opened the door to find a beautiful, cheerful thirteen-year-old on the other side. A girl who showed no signs of illness.

"Hi, Ms. Marshall!"

Willa's breath was whisked out of her lungs as Sylvie opened her arms and wrapped them around her. She blinked, hugging the girl back.

This was so unfair. So Colter Wayne. It was one

thing to break her heart over and over, but to have such an incredible daughter, too?

"Why are you leaving?" Sylvie asked.

"I have lots to do tonight," she said, scanning the landscape. Low dark clouds had gathered, and an evening breeze stirred dust in the yard.

"Did I miss anything in class?"

"Please rephrase that question."

"Sorry. How can I make up for the class I missed?"

At this point Colter physically inserted himself between them. "Sylvie, let's let Ms. Marshall get back to the hotel. They've got Community Day coming up Friday, and I want you to get a good sleep tonight so you're up for school tomorrow."

He glanced at Willa as though to say, *"See? I want her to go to school."*

Willa attempted to communicate something along the lines of *"That's not what we're arguing about and you know it."*

Sylvie looked from her to Colter, then back again, like she had questions. Fine. If Colter was so determined to do this on his own, she wasn't going to stick around to help with the answers.

"I'll see you in class tomorrow." Willa gave Sylvie a bright smile, determined not to look at Colter.

"Bye!" Sylvie called as Colter ushered her into the house.

Willa walked across the yard to the ATV, barely keeping it together. How had she let herself get sucked back in? It took him, what, three weeks to worm his way straight back in her heart? And here she was, baffled and broken, again.

No, not broken. She was angry. Willa was not going to spend one more minute of her life nursing a heartache. If she managed to salvage this school, great. If not, she could find work elsewhere.

The ATV seat was hot after baking in the evening sun. Willa turned the key in the ignition, ready to tear out of there.

Nothing.

Willa screwed her eyes shut in frustration and tried again. What was she forgetting on this stupid machine? She turned the key again and the engine came back at her with some kind of weak protest.

She didn't care if she had to walk back into town at this point, there was no way she was asking Colter for help.

Of course, it would be nice if he offered.

But no. That was off the table. She stared at the machine, refusing to let tears gather in her eyes. "Turn on!" she commanded over the ache in her throat.

The screen door clapped shut. Willa glanced up to see Colter jogging toward her.

Because he just had to contradict everything.

Colter stopped a few feet from the ATV. He folded his arms, looked over his shoulder at the house, then back at her.

"You never reached out."

"What?"

"You never reached out. When I disappeared."

Were these words honestly coming from his mouth right now?

"Colter, I was heartbroken." She placed a hand over her chest, as though a vise was needed to keep the remaining pieces intact.

"Yeah. We've established that. I was a jerk, loud and clear, and regretted it for the last fourteen years. But you never tried to contact me."

She shook her head. This was too much. "That seems a lot to ask of a nineteen-year-old."

"It's a lot to ask of a twenty-one-year-old to raise a daughter on his own. It's a lot to ask of Pete to drive for hours every day to pick up kids whose parents can't or won't take them to school. It's a lot to ask of Today's Moment to trust society to educate her kids. I'm not saying you should have called. I'm saying I was hurt that you didn't."

The words washed through her. She'd been in so much pain it had never occurred to her he was hurting, too.

"Holden called."

That shocked her. "My brother called you?"

"He was my best friend. I couldn't face him because, as we're all completely clear on, I was in the wrong. But he left a lot of messages, wanting to know if I was okay. Your mom called. I wasn't smart enough at the time to respond to their offers of help, but it meant the world to me that they cared enough to worry. I didn't get so much as a text from you." He studied the ground, clearly trying not to cry. "I loved you more than anything in the world.

I can take full responsibility for destroying our re-lationship. But when I disappeared, you didn't care enough to even wonder if I lived or died."

It felt like she'd gripped an electric fence with both hands, the accusation pulsing through her. She hated arguing. She'd never known how to fight, and as much as she would have preferred flight, at present the ATV wasn't cooperating.

"I don't even understand why we're fighting. Is this about Sylvie or me?"

"It's about all of us." He was reacting now, not thinking anything through. "We're not fighting. I'm *telling* you, you weren't the only one who was heartbroken."

She gestured toward the house. "I'm trying to reach out now, to help fix things."

"Sylvie and I don't need to be fixed."

"You know that's not what I meant." He refused to meet her gaze, but she kept talking. "Your girl is avoiding school and I'm concerned."

"I don't want your pity. I want to believe I haven't spent the last fourteen years in love with someone who sees me as some kind of a project."

"You're not a project. I'm trying to help you."

"Can you hear yourself right now?"

"Can you hear *yourself?* What am I supposed to do? Reach out? Not reach out? Have some kind of sixth sense as to when it's okay to care about you?"

Colter folded his arms, his voice hoarse as he struggled with his words. "But did you? Be hon-est, did you ever?"

"Did I what? Care? Of course I care."

"What was it you said in the truck the other day?" Colter mimed thoughtfulness. "We were just two kids with unrealistic dreams?"

Wind pushed a lock of Willa's hair in front of her face. She batted it away. "Given what happened, I think that's a pretty fair assessment."

Colter stepped back, like her words were a kick to the chest as he teetered on a canyon's rim. The silence grew between them as he fell away.

Finally, he shook his head, as though trying to place where he was. He raised his gaze to meet hers. "I can parent my own daughter."

Colter reached in front of her, gripping the throttle of the ATV with one hand and the keys with the other. The vehicle roared to life. Colter turned away and stalked back into the house.

CHAPTER FIFTEEN

COLTER KEPT BOTH hands on the porch railing to steady himself. The sun seemed to pause at the edge of the horizon, a last hurrah of color before darkness fell. Intuitively, he'd built this porch facing west, giving himself an unobstructed view of one glorious sunset after the next. He was going to stand here in the face of this miraculous beauty, alone, even if he irrevocably broke his own heart in the process.

Twenty-four hours ago, Colter had aired every insecurity he had to Willa. His fear of being an inadequate father. His fear that he really didn't know what he was doing with his kid. His fear the mothers of Pronghorn were right about him.

But here was something a whole level deeper: his fear that Willa never loved him, that he'd spent the greater part of his life in love with someone who'd never cared much to begin with. Someone who didn't think he was capable of raising his own daughter.

Yeah, it was a lot.

And par for the course, he hadn't heard a word from Willa since then. Vander had texted with a couple of questions, and Tate called to run an idea past him for Community Day, but Willa? Nothing. Just like the last time.

Colter glanced into the house, ready to berate his parenting. There had to have been something else he messed up recently.

Sylvie was curled up with a book in the living room.

Huh.

If he were a truly terrible dad, his thirteen-year-old probably wouldn't be at home, reading. Come to think about it, his daughter liked books, was good with horses, and could fix squeaky hinges in lockers all on her own. Everyone who got to know her inevitably said something about what a great kid she was.

Heck, even Angie liked her.

His daughter was a good human being. And like a lot of only children, she was more comfortable around adults than she was around people her own age. But she was only thirteen; his parenting years were far from over. As a parent, his job was not to stop and wonder if he was a failure, but to help her through this difficult time.

Colter pushed away from the porch railing and stalked into the house.

He sat down on the sofa facing Sylvie. "Okay kiddo. You've got two choices."

She looked up from the book, baffled.

"You tell me what's going on at school, or you talk to one of your teachers about it."

She refocused on the book. "Nothing's going on."

"Strange as it may seem, after seeing you every day of your life, I can tell when something's up."

She widened her eyes at the book, as though more room to see the words would help her escape from his insight.

He waited.

"I have stomachaches."

"And I think those stomachaches are caused by stress. I think you're anxious about something, and there's nothing wrong with that."

She finally set the book down and gave him something like a glare. Colter held strong.

"What's giving you stomachaches?"

Sylvie huffed out a breath, lolling her head back. "It's like… It's a lot."

"School?"

"Yeah."

"Are the classes too hard?"

"No." She scoffed.

Because heaven forbid a class be difficult for his kid.

"But like, we get there, and Coach Tate has us play these games, and it's fun and all. But then I have Mr. V's class, where we always discuss things. And in Ms. Walker's class a lot of times it's a simulation, or group work, or something."

Colter was really struggling to figure out how all this was causing stomachaches. He nodded, as though she was making perfect sense.

"I've just been talking to a lot of people."

The situation became clearer.

"And then lunch is like, I don't know where to sit. And you have to sit at one of the crowded tables, you're not allowed to sit by yourself."

"Because the teachers want you to be social, right?"

"But I haven't had lunch with anyone but you in three years. It's exhausting. I'm really tired and then—" Sylvie faltered. She looked down at the book in her hands and turned the pages without reading them. In a quiet voice she said, "Then people pick pinochle teams and it's stressful."

Colter stared at his brilliant, wonderful daughter. She'd never had to negotiate a crowd of teenagers before. She was barely a teenager herself.

"So you're interacting with classmates all morning, then it's lunchtime and things get more social. You must be pretty tired by the afternoon."

She nodded. "The school is so small. There's no place to get away, or take a break."

Colter pulled in a deep breath. He could raise his daughter on his own. He'd done a great job.

But he didn't have to do it alone.

"You know who can help with this? Your teachers."

She opened her book back up. "They're too busy."

"Not for you, they aren't. Not by a long shot." He stood up. "Let's go."

"Now?"

"I'd have you call, but I doubt the internet is working."

Sylvie hesitated. She didn't want to admit he was right, but he'd bet anything she wanted to go into town and visit the teachers.

"We should take them cookies," she said.

He nodded, trying to keep a straight face. "Of course."

Sylvie took a few steps toward the kitchen, then stopped. She turned to Colter with a look of cool appraisal.

"What's at the bottom of the box?"

He froze, all parent glory washing out of him.

"What box?"

She rolled her eyes.

Colter didn't know how to respond. It was a direct question, and he'd always been honest with his daughter.

"What is it?" she asked. "Is it bad?"

Bad? No. Foolish hope on his part? Probably.

"It has to do with Ms. Marshall, doesn't it?"

Colter nodded. Sylvie was prying open a whole big can of worms here, but he wasn't going to lie. He had no idea what to tell her, but lying was off the table.

"Is it Kermit the Frog? Do you actually have Kermit in the box?"

Colter sputtered out a laugh. "No. It's not that bad."

"Then what is it?

"It's just a few things, from when I knew her before."

"And you kept these things in the bottom of a box you don't open?"

Colter kept his back straight as he faced his daughter's insight.

"Sometimes I open the box."

"You like her," Sylvie stated.

"I do."

"Me, too." She crossed her arms and widened her stance in a posture anyone would recognize as exactly like his. "You can tell me about it, or you can talk to one specific teacher, but you can't keep stuffing whatever it is in the bottom of an old box."

"Willa's pretty busy right now. I'm going to give it some time—"

Sylvie stopped his words with a shake of her head, accompanied by a slow smile. "Ms. Marshall's not too busy. Not for you," she quoted. "Not by a long shot."

"I'M SO HUNGRY," Vander said.

"Stay with me," Willa encouraged. "We're close."

"Let's just crack open a can of soup." Luci rested a hand on the sleeping hedgehogs in the box next to her. "That way we can get to bed earlier."

Willa looked up from her list, shocked. "It's Thursday. We always eat at The Restaurant on Thursday nights, at your bequest. Self-care and all that."

Tate ran his fingers through his hair so it was sticking straight up. "How did Thursday nights at The Restaurant become self-care?"

"I dunno, but I can't eat any more canned soup," Mateo said. "It was okay until we went out to Colter's ranch. That meal reminded me how much I like actual home cooked food."

"Everyone, focus," Willa snapped. They still had a good hour of work left, and that was *if* everyone stopped complaining. "I know it's late, but we've got to finish the plan for Community Day or we'll be looking for jobs come Monday."

A faint scratching sounded at the edge of the table.

"The friends are already waking up." Luci gestured to the cuddly, spiny creatures. "It's late. And it's *Thursday.*" She closed her eyes, as though somehow it being Thursday was just too much to deal with.

Willa pressed her lips together. This was a disaster.

And yes, without a doubt she was fixating on Community Day because it was better than thinking about how she'd hurt Colter and once again been too attached to her own suffering to think about how her actions affected him.

He'd overreacted when she offered to help with Sylvie, but she'd known that was a sore point from the start. She could still see the frustration on his face when Raquel had told him sometimes a girl just needed a mom, then offered to take her shopping at some place called N'Style. As though any establishment with an unnecessary and misused contraction could possibly be *in style*.

Yet despite this, she'd buried her frustration with the board under the guise of trying to help Colter with a problem he clearly wanted to deal with on his own. Then, when he'd gotten upset, she'd thrown up her defenses and curled into her own hurt, like the hedgehogs when they sensed danger. Spikes out, communication shut down.

Even now she could feel herself avoiding pain by trying to wrangle others into her plans for Community Day.

But they really did have to knock it out of the park tomorrow.

"Tate, what do you think about an organized soccer game, kids against community members?"

"Why does it have to be soccer?"

"Because most people know how to play soccer. Plus, until the board grants us more money, the only PE equipment we have are soccer balls, right?"

Tate straightened. "We also have a jump rope."

Willa let out a deep breath. "What do you have against soccer?"

"I don't like it."

"Everyone likes soccer. It's literally the most popular sport in the world."

Luci stood and picked up the box of hedgehogs. "What did you have in mind, Tate?"

Tate leaned back and crossed one ankle over his knee. "I have a lot of interactive movement games I think people would enjoy learning."

Willa tried to keep calm. The pressure for sports came from Pete, and if she'd learned anything about the old rancher it was that "newfangled" and "loosey-goosey" were swear words. If they couldn't give him an exact replica of a 1950s education, a close approximation would have to do. Interactive movement games were the sort of thing she absolutely supported on a philosophical level, but on a practical level, they needed to give the board what they asked for. Soccer wasn't American football, but it was the next best thing.

Luci set the container of now wiggling hedgehogs next to the boxwood shrubs. A critter placed its paws on the edge of the box and glanced around, then waddled over the edge, into the hedge.

"Do you think that satisfies demands number fourteen, twenty-one and thirty?" Willa asked.

"No, but nothing's going to," Tate said.

"We have to show the board we're taking their requests seriously."

"I'm not taking them seriously," Vander said. "I'm happy to be respectful of the belief systems in this area and allow kids to opt out of certain lessons, but I'm *not* running an after-school music program."

"And I'm not writing up ten-page lesson plans for every class I teach, because there's no way anyone is going to read forty pages of theory, application and state standards every day for the whole school year," Luci said. "They can look at the class calendar and ask questions like the kids do."

Willa closed her eyes. How was she going to get everyone on track?

A rustling sound drifted over from the opening to the street. Willa whipped around, not in the mood to entertain another group of pronghorn.

"Hey!" Angie barked at them. "It's Thursday."

The teachers stared, slowly comprehending the situation. Angie had left her natural habitat at The Restaurant and was standing in the courtyard with an assortment of mismatched paper sacks.

"I don't do takeout." She marched across the courtyard and dropped the sacks unceremoniously on the wrought iron table. "So don't get used to it."

Willa gazed at the bags, then up at Angie. Tears pressed at the back of her eyes. "You brought us food?"

Angie gave her a dry look. "What else would I bring?"

"Th-thank you," Luci managed to croak, before she actually started crying.

Tate peeked into a bag, then stood abruptly and took long strides around the table, folding Angie into a hug.

She must have brought beer.

"Enough of that," she commanded, landing awkward pats on Tate's back.

He let go and trotted back to the table, wiping tears from his eyes. Then he opened a bag and dug into the first dish he came across. Creamed corn? It looked similar to something that could be labeled creamed corn.

Angie put her hands on her hips and nodded

firmly. "You kids are gonna do fine tomorrow. I'm refusing service to anyone who says otherwise."

And while that might not be much of a threat, it was a generous vote of confidence on her part. Angie held up a hand to silence their gratitude. "I haven't got all night to stand around chatting. Eat your meal." With that she spun on her heel and tromped back out onto the street.

Willa's coworkers got busy opening up Tupperware containers, exclaiming over what had never been more than mediocre food at best, and passing around cans of PBR and Coke. They *were* going to do fine. Better than fine, if she could get out of everyone's way. She didn't need to replan and overplan Community Day in an effort to distract herself from her own problems.

She needed to focus.

Willa placed her fingertips on the table and closed her eyes. What did she want?

She *wanted* to work at Pronghorn Public Day School. She'd come to love her coworkers, and the kids. She loved the landscape and even this quirky, cantankerous town.

She was still in love with Colter Wayne. Learning to trust herself enough to move forward in a relationship with him was scary. And yeah, he'd overreacted a few days ago. He'd always been impulsive. He was always going to be impulsive and this wasn't going to be their last fight about it.

Willa focused on the pressure of her fingertips against the table as she smiled. They were going to have more fights. Because he was worth fighting for, and with.

The rustling came from the opening again and this time Willa distinctly heard the sound of hooves.

"These pronghorn!" Willa stood up. "Git! Get out. The hedgehogs are having their ramble and you need to—"

She stopped abruptly, because she was staring not at wily antelope, but at Colter, Sylvie and the horses they'd ridden in on.

"You mind if we just stay a minute?" Colter asked.

Sylvie pulled a tin of cookies out of her backpack and held them out, as though cookies could secure their welcome. Which, while unnecessary, was definitely appreciated.

Willa recovered. "Sorry. Right. Stay as long as you like."

Stay all evening. Move in if you want to.

"I need some help." His chest rose and fell with a breath. "Sylvie's got a situation going on, and we thought you might be a good person to talk to about it."

Willa smiled at Sylvie, who seemed nervous but determined. Then she glanced back at the table of teachers who still had Community Day to plan. They'd asked her to be their leader, not their dictator. Right now, the best leadership she could bring was to get out of their way and let this happen.

Her gaze connected with Colter's. Could she get out of her own way, and let *this* happen?

That man had been in love with her since she was

sixteen. His love had always felt wild and dangerous, and in all likelihood it would still feel dangerous when she was seventy. It was scary to think
about letting herself fall again.

So maybe the trick here was not to overthink it?

"Yes. I'd love to chat with you, Sylvie. Have you
seen the hedgehogs?"

"I've seen the ones Ms. Walker takes to class.
They're so cute when they're sleeping."

"They're awake now, and even more adorable.
Let's go check them out." Willa glanced over her
shoulder as she led Sylvie to the boxwood. "You
guys, your plans are great. I was being weird about
the cohesion stuff."

"Really?" Vander asked.

"I'm just tense," she admitted. "I get bossy when
I'm tense."

Colter chuckled. She gave him a quick glare, but
smiled as she turned back around. He was going to
have to get used to her quirks, too.

Colter joined the teachers at the table, but Willa
could feel his gaze on her as she and Sylvie played
with the hedgehogs. The little creatures waddled
and rolled around like the balls of spiny adorable-
ness they were.

As Sylvie relaxed, she started to talk. Her words
sounded rehearsed, and Willa had a pretty good
idea of who she'd rehearsed them with. Over time,
and in between exclamations about the cuteness of
hedgehogs, Willa managed to get a handle on Sylvie's concerns.

Sylvie picked up a hedgehog and it curled its body around its arms and legs. Willa took the opportunity to clarify what she was hearing. "Sounds like school is a little overwhelming sometimes?"

Sylvie nodded.

"There's no downtime." Willa surprised herself as the words came out of her mouth. They'd all been trying so hard to help the kids socialize that they hadn't thought about the need for quiet reflection, too. "It must be pretty hard going from being at home with just your dad and the horses, to being around other kids all day."

"I like school," Sylvie said, almost like an apology.

"Of course, but that doesn't mean it can't feel intense."

The girl met Willa's gaze, a frank appreciation of being understood shining in her eyes. It was hard for Willa to admit that they were putting too much pressure on the kids to be social, but it wasn't the first mistake they'd made, and it wouldn't be the last. They were new at all this, and Pronghorn had different needs than most schools.

"I have an idea," Willa said. "What if we put a reading nook in the main hall? That way you, and other students who want to have some quiet time, would be close to the others, but still on your own."

Sylvie nodded. "Like a reading club."

"Great idea. We could have some comfy chairs and lamps, like a little living room. The rules would be it's for reading only, but during break, and lunch and free time, anyone can go and hang out. It could give you a break, but you'd still be around everyone else."

Sylvie nodded, then she gave Willa a sly smile, a spot-on replica of Colter's as she said, "My dad can help you build it."

CHAPTER SIXTEEN

IT WAS THE first time there'd ever been a traffic jam in Pronghorn. Trucks, Lyfcycles, old hatchbacks and, of course, ATVs came from all directions, filling up the empty field next to the school.

Colter had to park a good quarter mile past the school. He'd thought he was early, but it was hard to get anywhere early in this community. His plan was to catch Willa before the day started but it looked like the event was already underway. He'd have to wait to talk to her.

He'd never been good at waiting.

Community members flowed toward the building. There was an air of carnival excitement. And these weren't just families with kids in the school. Ranchers who hadn't stepped foot near the school since they graduated two or three decades ago were bustling up the steps, anxious to get a look at the teachers who had caused such a stir.

Colter glanced back in the direction of the highway. Connie sat in the middle of the road like she owned it. In the distance a herd of pronghorn watched with interest, wondering about the sudden infestation of people in their town.

Sylvie picked up her pace, moving resolutely toward the school. Like the other students, she had a job to do. Colter followed, intensely aware he was about to be in the same building as Willa.

Last night she'd been brilliant with Sylvie. But given that they were surrounded by her coworkers, his daughter and a family of hedgehogs they didn't have a lot of privacy. He needed privacy for what he intended to say to Willa.

I'm sorry.

I want you to interfere with my parenting.

We need to figure out how to disagree without hurting each other, because there's no one I'd rather argue with for the rest of my life.

The front door to the school was propped open; cheerful, excited chatter flowed out into the cool morning.

This time, the teachers were ready.

"You're in the blue group," Luci informed him, placing a blue sticker on his lapel. She lowered her voice and gave him a sly grin. "A completely random assignment on our part."

Colter glanced at the groups assembling in the hall. The *completely random* groups split up families and friends, ranchers, commune members and everyone else. People would need to get along with folks they weren't always comfortable with, and no group was likely to get too rowdy about one topic or another.

"A highly strategic, random assignment," he muttered back.

"Group dynamics is an important part of social studies."

Tate handed him a slip of paper, also blue. "Here's your schedule for the day. These two will be your leaders." Tate gestured to Antithesis and Mason, who both wore blue shirts. Mason had a standard blue T-shirt. Antithesis was swimming in what looked like a men's blue button-down from the 1980s, and orange pants.

"Hey," Brad Johnson, a local rancher and father of two girls, stopped Colter. He held up his phone. "I can't get a signal. Do you know how to connect to the internet around here?"

"I...um..."

"Internet's not working today," Mateo told him with an easy smile. "Sorry."

"Has anyone seen my bullhorn?" Loretta came bustling down the hall. Without the bullhorn, she wasn't quite imposing enough to get people to stop what they were doing and look for it. She cupped her hands around her mouth. "Everyone, I can't find my bullhorn. And If I don't have a bullhorn, you can't hear me," she warned.

Colter noticed movement out of the corner of his eye, then heard the soft click of Mrs. Moran's office door closing.

But he didn't have time to find Mrs. Moran and give her a high five for hiding a bullhorn, because at that moment the crowds seemed to part. Willa appeared at the other side of the hall, floating toward him like an angel.

No, it was more like she was barreling toward him at full speed, like Willa. Which was way better than an angel.

Unfortunately, the moment she saw him she corrected course, veering to the right. Years on the circuit kicked in and he jumped in her path to cut her off.

"Willa."

Her face flashed concern, then annoyance, then finally flushed with a touch of humor. She gestured to the organized chaos around her. "You need something?"

"Can I talk to you?" he asked.

She paused for a nanosecond. "Kinda a big day around here."

The hall was now teeming with people. Everyone had a sticker on and seemed to know where to go. Colter had a feeling Willa was probably supposed to be on the receiving end of some of these people in minutes if not seconds. He reached out to touch her arm anyway.

"Willa, I'm sorry—"

She cut him off. "What did I say about using that word?"

"I apologize?"

She harrumphed and crossed her arms, but Colter could tell she was trying not to laugh.

"I have remorse."

Her lips twisted as she glanced up at Loretta's

excessive and looming signage. Choose Joy was firmly in its place this time.

"You were trying to help with Sylvie, and I got—"

"No." She reached her hand out to his arm, and his arm was sorely disappointed when she stopped herself from placing it on his bicep. "I was trying to solve your problems for you." She looked down and shook her head. "I felt scared, and nervous about this school. So I stuck my nose in your business."

"I could use your nose in my business."

She laughed. "Colter, this is my pattern of avoidance. I try to solve everyone else's problems because it's easier than dealing with my own. So *I'm* sorry. You are amazing with Sylvie. She's an incredible kid and of course you had it all handled. I never should have said anything."

Her words washed through him. Colter glanced over to where Sylvie and Oliver were leading a group with red stickers down the hall. She walked backwards and talked to them, pointing to a classroom.

"I do the best I can," he told Willa.

"Your best is incredible."

Colter felt a lump mushroom in the back of his throat. He was here to apologize to Willa, but if he opened his mouth right now the entire community was going to see a former rodeo champ bawling, and that wasn't a great kickoff to Community Day.

She seemed to sense this, and kept talking. "I have a very bad habit of jumping in and solving other people's problems when I don't know how to deal with my own. It's a lot easier to point out other people's mistakes and solve them than it is to face mine."

He gazed at Willa. Her face was calm, but he knew that look, masking a wash of emotion beneath. This really, really was not the time for a heart-to-heart, or a kiss.

But dang, did both seem like great ideas.

"We can talk later," Willa said quietly. "I'm sorry I interfered—"

"I want you to interfere! All the time. Get in my business. Help me with my daughter."

"Shh." She stepped closer, which was not a good strategy if her goal was to keep him from talking. Or kissing her. "I've got a big day here."

"Tell me your problems." He brushed his hand against her wrist. "Let me help you solve them, or at least rub your shoulders as you vent."

She glanced down to where his fingers rested on her wrist. It would take the smallest movement to be holding her hand. "I don't know how to let this happen again," she whispered. "I'm scared. I loved you with everything I had, and I'm scared of feeling so much again."

His pulse picked up, pounding through his body. This *was* happening again. It was going to be tough. There would be growing pains. But if there was one thing Colter could say about himself, he knew how to get things done. He grinned. She read his mind and shook her head, but he held eye contact with her. "Let me help you with that."

She tried to tamp down a smile, but it wasn't working.

"Willa?" Luci called over. "Can you explain the schedule here?" Luci gestured to Pete, who looked steaming mad. Next to him Today's Moment was saying, "I don't need a sticker."

Colter gestured to the other board members with his thumb. "I'm gonna go solve that problem for you right now."

A real smile broke out. "Thank you."

"First class starts in five minutes!" Tate called out. "Please make your way with your group to the appointed classroom. Yellow group can follow me outside."

Colter turned from the announcement back to Willa, ready to get in a quick proposal of marriage before the day started, but she was already gone, heading down the hall toward the library.

He successfully wrangled the other board members, and even Loretta, into their approved groups. But he felt too light, too excited to stay in one place. Colter ambled along the hall. In Luci's classroom she had her group doing a simulation of Indian Ocean trade. Next door, Vander's community members and students were in groups of three, dissecting owl pellets. Pete was pulling a mouse skull out of his, talking animatedly about the owls on his property. Mateo's warm laugh flowed from his classroom, where people sat around tables in the lamplight as students explained the math concepts they were working on, and how it was all interconnected. Colter peeked out the open back door. Tate's group was involved in a game, and it was fun to see Today's Moment laugh as she picked up her flowing orange robes to run from one place to the next. The young sheriff, Aida Weston, had even come out of her office to watch. And sure, she was watching from the sidelines, arms crossed and glaring at Tate the whole time, but she wasn't giving anyone a ticket, so that was good. Her police dog sat alert at her heels, and Colter guessed if Greg had his druthers he'd be in the thick of the game.

Colter reentered the school and finally allowed himself to go to the library. Willa stood at the center of the tables. She wore a pale blue sleeveless dress, her bangs brushing against her forehead, eyes bright as she explained the individual reading challenge the kids were participating in. Then a student at each table executed their part in the presentation. Willa crossed her arms and listened to the kids with her full attention.

She was so confident in a classroom, like she was born to help young people navigate the drama and chaos of these years. She knew which book to place in the hands of each kid to help them make sense of the world.

What could Pronghorn become, with someone like Willa teaching here? What could he become?

Colter felt a soft pat on his arm. He looked down to see Mrs. Moran. "Can you come help in the kitchen for a moment? It seems we have too many chefs this morning and I need to borrow your herding skills to direct traffic."

Colter took one last look at Willa, then followed Mrs. Moran down the hallway. From the kitchen he could hear animated voices as parents were eager to get involved.

Then he heard Angie bark out orders. Colter stopped at the threshold to the kitchen. Mrs. Moran patted his arm. "A good job for the rodeo cowboy, getting everyone in their place and on the right track."

Colter laughed. "I'm happy to help. I want to do *something* around here."

She looked at him sharply. "You've done so much already. You got the idea rolling, you donated more money than anyone, you got the hotel fixed up for the teachers." She put her hands on her hips, exasperated. "You're not allowed to sell yourself short here, Mr. Wayne. Imagine what would have happened with the school board if you weren't the president?"

He chuckled. She pointed a small, wrinkled finger in his face. "I'm serious now. You've done as much for this school as any one of those young teachers and we all appreciate it."

They heard Angie bark at someone, followed by a tray clattering on the ground.

"And presently, you're needed in the kitchen."

A NOW FAMILIAR feeling of exhaustion and elation buzzed through Willa. Unfortunately, it was only one o'clock. She still had to get through lunch and the ice cream social. Then there would doubtless be some long, contentious board meeting.

And after that there was always, you know, facing her fears and choosing to let herself love again.

Willa emerged from the library. Most of the community members would be through the lunch line by now, ready for ice cream, ready for her attention.

And Colter? What was he ready for?

Slowly, she made her way down the back hall. Snippets of conversation caught her attention.

"…my favorite teacher was Mrs. Moran. Of course, she was the 'young teacher' back in my day," an older woman was saying to Sheriff Weston.

"…seemed like I had lunch detention every other week." A woman in a denim jacket dropped her hand on Greta's shoulder. "Apple doesn't fall far from the tree, does it?"

"…right here. That's where I asked your mother to prom," a rancher in his seventies was telling a woman in a flowing orange skirt.

Neveah glanced nervously at her aunt, who was dressed in jeans and the same ball cap she'd had on with her nightgown. "This place isn't as bad as it was in my day," the aunt admitted. "I mean, it's all smoke and mirrors, right? But I think these teachers actually care."

Willa hoped her small vote of confidence would manifest in more support for Neveah to come to school. Only time would tell.

She passed Pete as he pointed out a black-and-white photograph to a group of kids. It was one of fifty framed images lining the hallway outside of the gym. "That's the year we made it to state. You can't imagine what it was like for our little team from Pronghorn to head to Portland for the final game. Made me feel like we could accomplish anything if we worked together. I'll never forget that crew."

Willa caught his eye. He gave her a small nod. *That's progress.*

Willa walked into the cafeteria. Many community members were already finished with lunch and milling about outside the open doors. Rather than waiting to pounce on her, parents and community members chatted easily. A few students were even teaching a group of parents to play pinochle.

She turned to the lunch line. The sandwich bar they'd planned for the day was augmented with a green salad, fruit salad and several bags of chips. Behind the counter Angie gave a man a hard time about coming back for thirds but served him anyway.

Willa smiled. This was why everyone in Pronghorn helped ensure The Restaurant stayed in business.

Then the man, Angie and everyone else in the room seemed to disappear as a gorgeous rancher came jogging over to her.

"How'd it go?" he asked, offering her a plate with a massive sandwich.

Willa couldn't exactly fill her lungs with air to answer. She just stared into a pair of bright blue eyes. She lifted her hands to take the plate from Colter and her fingers brushed his. They held the plate together, fingertips barely touching, staring at each other in the middle of the largest crowd Pronghorn had seen in two decades.

She was really hungry, but not at all interested in looking away from Colter.

Could she lean down and take a bite of the sandwich while still gazing at him?

"There's a light coat of mustard on both sides, ham, Swiss cheese, sweet pickles and extra lettuce. Did I remember it correctly?"

Okay, now she was seriously hungry. But again, if she made a move their fingers would no longer be touching.

"Everything okay?"

Willa grinned. "I think so. I mean, they might still shut down the school—"

"—if they want to start a riot," Colter finished. "You guys nailed it today."

She laughed. "Yeah, I think this went okay."

"It was incredible," he said.

She could do this. Rekindling her relationship with Colter was frightening, but she was a different woman than she'd been at nineteen. She was strong and flexible now.

"Colter." She shifted her hands under the plate, so their fingers interlaced. A smile spread across his face and he reddened.

"Willa?" he asked, settling his fingers more firmly against hers.

She drew in a breath. She was in control. There would be no more drifting and reacting to circumstances. She would shape the life she wanted.

"Colter, I was wondering if you'd like to go out to dinner with me?" His smile grew even brighter. If he got any closer he was going to smush her sandwich. "I could pick you up on the ATV, and we could go to this place in town with a limited menu and terrible service—"

Colter leaned across the plate, his eyes shining like they did when he was about to kiss her.

"I have found my bullhorn!" Loretta's voice reverberated throughout the cafeteria. "I have found my bullhorn and I have an announcement to make."

Colter slowly closed his eyes and groaned.

"Everyone, please join me outside," Loretta commanded.

"We don't have to be present for this, do we?" Colter asked.

Did they? The announcement was probably about her job, and the school Colter had worked tirelessly to ensure for his daughter. But did they have to go outside and listen?

"We gotta go," she said.

"I don't know that we 'gotta.'"

"I think we do gotta."

"I need all board members to assemble," Loretta called out.

Colter rolled his eyes and removed his hands from

the plate they were holding, leaving her fingertips sad and alone.

It did, however, free up a hand to grab her sandwich so she could take an enormous bite.

He grinned at her, then trotted ahead to stand with the board, which had apparently made its verdict without consulting its president.

Willa took a second bite of her sandwich and followed the stream of people outside.

A warm breeze set the prairie grass waving. On the outskirts of town, a herd of pronghorn grazed placidly. Hart Mountain rose in the distance, blue and smoky in the fall sunshine.

Colter stood with his hands behind his back but gave Sylvie a wink. Her anxious expression relaxed a bit.

Luci pressed against one side of Willa, and Vander scooched in on the other. Tate stood behind her, and Mateo crossed his arms and moved in front of the group, as though his good nature could protect them from getting fired. The formation made her feel like they were a team of powerful, if exhausted, superheroes.

"Well, I just want to say—" Loretta paused, looked around dramatically, then threw back her head and angled the bullhorn to her mouth, "Hellllloooo Pronghorn!"

The teachers groaned.

"Can she just get it over with?" Tate asked.

"No," Luci shook her head. "She can't. It is not possible for Loretta to do anything efficiently."

Loretta continued on the bullhorn, a combination of bad jokes, mixed metaphors and properties that might be hitting the market in the near future.

Finally, she said, "Now, as you all know, we've had a few problems with our little school."

The crowd quieted.

Loretta gestured to the teachers. "Not everyone was on the same page."

"Or even reading the same book," Mateo muttered.

"Two weeks ago, the board delivered a list of requests to the teachers and asked them to implement them by today."

Willa's heart sank. They'd done so much, but they certainly hadn't fulfilled the board's demands, or even come close. She scanned the board members, her eyes resting on Colter. His gaze was steady, and reassuring. *This isn't over*, he seemed to say.

But her eye contact with Colter was cut off when Today's Moment marched in front of him and grabbed the bullhorn.

"Oh, for fire's sake, Loretta!" Today's Moment could be heard over the crowd. "Enough already."

Pete moved to stand next to Today's Moment. "You want to do this?" he asked.

She inclined her head and smiled—*at Pete!* "You seem poised to voice the truth. Please." She handed him the bullhorn.

"I had a real good time as a student at Pronghorn High," Pete's voice reverberated through the crowd.

"I had good friends, I was involved in sports, I met my beautiful wife in this building. I wasn't a model student, but I learned a lot. What I've come to understand is that I took my education for granted. I didn't have the slightest idea how hard my teachers were working, or what went into running a school." He paused, the bullhorn gently echoing over the prairie grass. "We all want what's best for our kids here in Pronghorn. Sometimes it's hard to know what the best is. We might disagree, and because this matters, we might disagree pretty loudly. Two weeks ago, we did give those teachers a list of demands. We all had a lot of feelings and fears about this school. We all wanted school to suit our worldview. But what we didn't think about was that part of the point of school is to experience the worldview of others."

Willa pulled her coworkers even closer. She was not the only one getting choked up at this speech.

Pete handed the bullhorn to Today's Moment. "Our teaching staff was unable to meet all our demands because our demands weren't reasonable for this situation. Every one of us has a different idea of what school should look like. But I think we can all agree having in-person school, led by a group of hardworking teachers, is good for everyone."

Willa felt like she might cry, and when she went to press her fingers against her tear ducts, she was surprised to find she already was crying. She also became aware that she was being hugged, and hugging her fellow teachers. Tate was whooping,

Vander and Mateo were exchanging high fives and Luci clung to Willa, eyes shut tight against her own tears.

"Hold up!" Colter's voice came reverberating through the bullhorn. "We're not quite done here."

Willa looked up, surprised. Then she saw the reckless smile on Colter's face.

Uh-oh.

"When I was eighteen, I was reckless, impulsive, and in love with the smartest, most beautiful girl."

Willa untangled herself from her coworkers, intent on grabbing the bullhorn. Impulsive wasn't a self-descriptor Colter could use in the past tense.

"But I made some big mistakes. Then I tried to get out of those mistakes by making more until I hit rock bottom. Which is in Reno, by the way."

The crowd chuckled. Willa took a step toward Colter but Luci held her back, grinning as she said, "I wanna see how this plays out."

"Slowly, I put my life together, piece by piece, in Pronghorn. I raised a smart, creative kid who you can thank for all the working lockers in the building over there."

A cheer for Sylvie went up through the crowd, led by her teachers.

"Like a lot of us around here, I didn't enjoy watching my child suffer through distance learning. When I got it in my head to raise money to hire teachers for in-person school, I had no idea what we were in for. Then this crew showed up." He gestured to the teachers. "And Loretta, you were right, you did good when you hired them."

Loretta preened, like she hadn't been trying to fire them for the last two weeks.

"What I didn't expect was that one of those teachers would be Willa Marshall, the girl I'd been in love with all those years ago."

A hushed "Awwwww!" rippled through the crowd. Willa wanted to bury her face in her hands, but that would mean breaking eye contact with Colter, and that didn't feel super possible.

"Willa, I missed you so much. I missed us." The crowd let out cheers of encouragement, firmly on Colter's side here. "And as a wise frog once said—" Colter moved into Kermit voice "—maybe you don't need the whole world to love you. Maybe you just need one person." He grinned at her. "Willa Marshall, would you let me be that person?"

Luci let go of Willa's arm and Tate gave her a gentle nudge. Willa walked toward Colter. He lowered the bullhorn, grinning at her.

"Willa, I'm in love with you. Have been so for a long, long time and I don't see that stopping anytime soon. I don't have the right to ask anything from you. So I'm gonna beg, would you please give me a second chance?"

"I'm giving *us* a second chance." She gazed into his gorgeous blue eyes. "I love you, too, Colter."

Colter gave a whoop of joy, like he'd just broken eight seconds on a bronco.

"She loves me!" he hollered into the bullhorn.

Willa reached up and snatched it from him, whispering, "What happened to not drawing too much attention to yourself?"

He grinned at her. "I'm drawing attention to you."

"So it's not enough I get the spotlight for teaching, now the whole town knows I snagged the most eligible bachelor in a two-hundred-mile radius?"

"They're all going to find out eventually." He glanced at her lips, then into her eyes.

They were all going to find out *right now*. Willa wrapped her arms around his neck and rose up on her toes.

Her lips brushed his, tentative for only a moment. Colter's arms wrapped around her waist, pulling her close. He deepened the kiss, until the school, the board and all of Pronghorn disappeared, leaving nothing but the shelter of Colter Wayne.

Until a young woman's voice yelled, "Yeaaaaaaaaah! Yes! Go Dad!"

Willa, and all of Pronghorn, turned to see Sylvie jumping up and down, fist-bumping the air and yelling.

Suddenly aware of what she was doing, Sylvie clamped both hands over her mouth, eyes wide with embarrassment. But also joy. Willa reached out an arm to the girl and Sylvie rushed to them, joining in the hug. Willa tightened her arms around both of them. Colter's hand cupped her cheek and tears gathered on his lower lids as he gazed at her. "Welcome home, Willa."

Somehow Loretta had gotten a hold of the bull-horn again. After reminding the crowd she had experience as a wedding coordinator, she said something about hosting exchange students.

Colter had apparently decided they didn't need to stick around any longer. He wrapped one arm around Willa, the other around Sylvie and the three of them moved away from the crowd.

"My dad has a box he needs to talk to you about," Sylvie said.

"Hold your horses." Colter ruffled his daughter's hair.

"You're not a great example of horse holding," Willa reminded him.

Sylvie laughed. Colter readjusted his arm around Willa's waist. "Maybe you can help me refine my patience?"

"Maybe," she conceded. "But not today. What's in the box?"

EPILOGUE

THEY WERE FINALLY, BLISSFULLY, alone in Colter's living room. A week had passed since Community Day, and school was now in full swing. This board meeting had been productive, but it stretched out a little long in a heartfelt string of cleared-up misconceptions, apologies and plans for the future. Then it finished with a bizarre thirty-second quip from Loretta they probably should have taken an hour to discuss.

"That can't be true," Willa said, carrying coffee cups back into the kitchen. "We don't actually have fifteen international students arriving on Monday morning."

"I've learned not to use definitive statements when it comes to Loretta." Colter caught her hand and tugged her toward the front door.

"Placing international students takes like a year of planning, they have to vet host families, make sure the school is a good fit."

Colter grinned. "Maybe she meant next year."

"I mean, the only way she could have gotten exchange students this late was if they were unhappy in their original placements and there was something major, like they broke rules, or families refused to keep them—"

Colter's smile faltered as this possibility took shape in their minds.

Willa shook her head. "You know what? I'm not going to think about it."

"Good plan." His smile returned. "I've got something else for you to think about."

But Willa was already thinking about something else.

Over a month ago, she'd uprooted her life, started her career, made the closest friends she'd ever had, saved a school and fallen in love again.

Might as well make another positive change while she was at it.

"Sounds good. There's something I've been wanting to ask you," she said.

Colter, his fingers still woven though hers, reached over and pulled a wrapped gift from the kitchen counter, and continued toward the front door.

"Is it about the box? Because we're finally talking about it today." He held up the rectangular gift, wrapped in simple brown paper and tied with string. Pressed wildflowers adorned the top. "Sylvie wrapped it," he explained.

Willa laughed. "Okay, that makes more sense."

She followed Colter onto the front porch. The breeze was still warm, but a hint of fall was in the air. Across the yard, Sylvie was riding in the arena.

When she saw them emerge from the house she waved, then yelled to her dad, "Let's get 'er done!"

Colter held up the gift, then placed a hand on Willa's back, guiding her toward the firepit, where several bouquets of wildflowers adorned the area, and a bottle of champagne was chilling in a bucket of ice.

Like a literal bucket that someone might use to offer hay to a horse.

She furrowed her brow. "Are we celebrating?"

"The end of that meeting? Absolutely." He pulled her toward him, catching both of her hands in his.

Willa gazed into his eyes, and the promise of love and adventure she'd always seen there set her heart racing. Little did Colter know they'd be celebrating a lot more with that champagne.

If he says yes.

Who was she kidding? Colter was the one person on earth who would say yes to a marriage proposal/plan a few weeks in.

She took a steadying breath. "I have a question for you."

"Can I give you your present first?"

Willa nodded. She was so nervous. But that was a lesson she'd learned. She had to get out there, be nervous, get scared and create the life she wanted. Colter was as wild and precious as this one life she'd been granted, and she wanted it share with him.

But she also wanted to know what was in *the box* Sylvie kept pestering her dad about.

Colter sat down on the bench and handed her the gift. Her hands shook as she fumbled with the wrapping paper. She was surprised to see Colter's hands shaking as well.

Under the paper was a handcrafted cedar pencil box.

"I love it!"

A relieved smile spread across his face.

"It's beautiful. I can keep it on my desk." She turned the box in her hands, examining it as a realization hit her. "Did you make this?"

Colter swallowed and nodded. "I made it fourteen years ago, the week before the National Championships."

Willa stared at the box, letting all the good memories of their young relationship filter in. "You kept it all these years?"

"Open it."

Willa lifted the lid: old sticky notes with her handwriting, a three-by-five of her senior picture, a hair tie.

Colter reached into the box and pulled out a small velvet bag.

Wait, was he preempting her marriage proposal?

Colter got down on one knee. "Willa, I love you. I wanted to kiss you the first day we met. I wanted to marry you the second day. We were just kids, but our love was real, and our dreams were valid."

His finger shook as he opened the drawstrings on the bag.

He was totally proposing before she had the

chance to propose. Which was what happened when you even blinked around Colter Wayne.

But there were worse things than the love of your life holding out a ring.

"Marry me, Willa?"

"Yes!" She placed her hands along the side of his face and leaned her forehead toward his. "Yes. Absolutely. Will you marry me?"

His brilliant smile broke out, his blue eyes shining as he nodded slowly. "Oh yeah."

Colter leaned back and slipped the ring on her hand. Her finger immediately dipped with the weight. Willa took her first good look at the ring.

It was very, very tall. And wide.

"It's horrible, I know. I'm sorry." He gestured to the massive conglomeration of diamonds and gold. "I bought it when I was twenty-one."

Willa laughed. "It's…enthusiastic."

"It's garish. But it *is* real. This is what happens when a hotheaded young man is madly in love and has a pocket full of prize money from the Greeley Stampede."

He'd held on to the ring for years, somehow knowing this relationship was right. They'd grown apart from one another, strengthened and changed over the years, but their hearts were still a perfect fit.

"I'm planning to get you a new ring."

"Oh no. No way." Willa held up her hand to examine the ring. "I love it." She swallowed against the emotion rising in her chest. "I love you, Colter."

"I love you so much, Willa. I always have."

She glanced toward the arena, where Sylvie had given up the pretense of riding and was watching the proposal with a big grin on her face. "Sylvie's on board?"

"Are you kidding? She's all the way on board. She built the ship."

Willa laughed. "I'm so happy, Colter. The adventure of my life keeps unfolding and now that I have you and Sylvie, I can't wait to find out what happens next!"

Colter leaned toward her, head tilted, eyes bright. "Oh, I can tell you what happens next."

His lips met hers in a kiss that promised adventure, and felt like home. This was the life they would create together.

* * * * *

Don't miss the next book in Anna Grace's
The Teacher Project miniseries,
coming September 2024 from
Harlequin Heartwarming